he name aloud. Even the sound of it conjured up the vision of a barren, hostile land. He shrugged. Let her live out her miserable existence at Rannoch. Let her believe her son was dead, she would never profitably farm such land and the effort would slowly erode the money she had obtained for "Kircaldy", money she had stolen from him. There was no free negro labour in Scotland, within a decade she would be reduced to poverty and misery. He turned to face Arnold Mathews.

"I'm glad I'm back, Arnold, and I'm glad I came to you."

The guarded expression left the older man's face and he smiled. "Do you wish me to write to Alizon and let her know the child is alive?"

"No! I never want to hear her name again and when Alasdair is old enough to understand, he will be told that his mother is dead! Do you understand me, Arnold? She has forfeited any right to him!"

"You took him from her, Darnley. You share the blame." Arnold Mathews reminded him quietly, but Darnley did not hear him. The words did not penetrate the hatred in his mind . . .

Also by Lyn Vanner

JENNET
JESSIE
RANNOCH CHASE

and published by Corgi Books

Guardian of Rannoch

Lyn Vanner

CORGI BOOKS

A DIVISION OF TRANSWORLD PUBLISHERS LTD

GUARDIAN OF RANNOCH

A CORGI BOOK 0 552 11985 7

First publication in Great Britain

PRINTING HISTORY
Corgi edition published 1982

This book is set in Highland 10 on 11 pt.

Corgi Books are published by Transworld Publishers Ltd.,
Century House, 61–63 Uxbridge Road, Ealing, London, W5 5SA

Reproduced, printed and bound in Great Britain by
Hazell Watson & Viney Ltd, Aylesbury, Bucks

Chapter 1

It was the sound of a weak, frightened voice, resembling the distressed mewing of a small kitten, that at last penetrated his hazy, half-conscious state. There was no recollection of time, place or bodily sensations, only a grey fog that clogged his mind and the faint but insistent crying.

With an effort Darnley Kirkbride reached out slowly, tentatively exploring the darkness for some object of stability. His fingers, stiff, cold and numb though they were, closed around a small rock no larger than a big pebble then sank into the soft shifting sand. The crying was louder now and he could hear the dull thudding of waves breaking on the shore. He groaned as he struggled to sit upright, coughing, retching and choking the salt water up from his lungs and stomach. After the bout had passed he stared around him, then as comprehension dawned he passed a shaking hand over his eyes and muttered a heartfelt prayer. Now he remembered it all.

The weather had been bad when the *Randolph* had left Annapolis, but it had not concerned him unduly for he had been born and brought up in Charleston and though he respected the elements they held little fear for him. The storm had gained in force once they had left the bay, but it was not until he had heard the rending, splintering sound followed by the deafening crash as the main mast snapped and fell, the shouts of the crew and the screams of terrified, hysterical women that he realised that the ship had struck and was foundering. He had pushed the coloured nurse, Tammy, out of the door before him, yelling at her to get up on deck, he had looked frantically around the small cabin and had wrenched a length of cord from his trunk and with difficulty had lashed the little boy to his back.

A fresh wave of coughing shook him, racking his already exhausted body, but over the harsh rasping the frightened cries could still be heard. Alasdair! His hand found the cord. It was slack but when he tugged on it the cry became one of pain. His eyes had become accustomed to the darkness and as he scooped up the child in his arms he could see the ashen face, the blue lips, and he felt the deep shudders that shook the little frame. How the child had survived he did not know, but holding the boy to him, trying to generate some warmth into the shivering little body, he again spoke a few grateful words of prayer. He could not remember what had elapsed between this first moment of relief and realisation that they had both survived and that time, so distant, so indistinct now, when he had stood on the splintered, surf-battered deck and looked down for a split second at the raging sea. Then he had jumped. He remembered the numbing, deadening shock to his body as the freezing water had sucked him down and then . . . nothing.

Still holding the child tightly to him he rose unsteadily and began to stagger up the beach towards a faint pinprick of light that stabbed the darkness. He plodded on, each step an effort, yet the light seemed to grow more distant. The sand had given way to soil and scrub and clumps of coarse grass, and in the gloom he could make out the towering black shadows of trees. He sank down, feeling the dizziness of exhaustion sweeping over him. He would rest for a few minutes. The light at last seemed nearer and larger.

"Not much further now, son. See, over there, the light. Soon we'll be warm and dry." They were the first words he had spoken to the child, and although the boy could not understand him he felt that they at least offered some comfort. Again he got to his feet and stumbled forward.

By the time he reached the small house he had not the strength to raise his arm to knock and the sound that issued from the salt-cracked lips was no more than a croak. It was the crying of the little boy that was heard by Jacob Middleton and his wife. As the door was opened Darnley, collapsing at their feet, said only two words that were comprehensible, "The *Randolph*."

The Quaker couple nursed them both back to health. In that small closely-knit community Darnley found only concern and goodness and a simple directness of purpose that was to give him much food for thought. The story of their survival had been told and the whole community had given thanks for their deliverance, but it was to Rachel Middleton that Darnley confided his reason for taking passage on the ill-fated *Randolph*. When he had finished relating the story, Rachel gazed at him with sadness and reproach in her mild grey eyes.

"Judgement and punishment for thy sins belongs to Jehova, but atonement lies with thee. He has shown thee mercy, delivered thee from the storm, look upon it as a sign. Think, my friend, upon the anguish thou hast inflicted upon the child's mother. Can there be no reconciliation between thee?"

"That I can't say, Rachel. I tried . . . I wanted to marry her, but she accused me of selfishness and greed."

"And were her accusations true?"

"In honesty I must admit that there was some truth in them, but I wanted Kircaldy for the child."

"Then thou must pray to Jehova for guidance. I cannot influence thee."

Rachel Middleton rose to see to Alasdair and left him to his deliberations. He walked down towards the beach and stood watching the surf breaking over the rock-strewn sand. He had not lied to the Quaker: he had wanted the plantation for his son, it was Alasdair's birthright, but he had also determined that the boy would be brought up as he saw fit while Alizon. . . .

He saw her again as he had first seen her when she had come as a bond servant to the plantation on Goose Creek. Thin and drawn, the cotton housedress emphasising the emaciated form, the huge dark eyes dominating the small face, the almost silver-blonde hair confined beneath a plain cap. Then the image changed and he remembered her as his father's wife, a beautiful woman in fine clothes, and he remembered with bitterness the enmity between them, the love, the passion. He could see her now as a widow standing amidst the devastation the hurricane had left in its wake and he remembered how they had planned to rebuild Kircaldy together, and by then she had been pregnant with Alasdair, his son.

He kicked viciously at a small pebble, remembering the violent quarrel in the nursery which had prompted him to take Alasdair and leave for Boston, vowing that Alizon would never see the boy again.

Dark clouds laden with rain were moving ponderously across the sky and the sea was the colour of gunmetal. The wind was cold, and watching the boiling white spray as it beat against the rocks he shuddered. He would never know how they had managed to survive that storm, but Rachel Middleton's words took on a deeper meaning to him as he watched the growing anger of the sea. "Think upon the anguish thou hast inflicted upon the child's mother." He repeated the words out loud, trying to picture Alizon's grief. "Jehova works in mysterious ways" was a favourite saying of Jacob Middleton's, he reflected soberly. Until Alizon had stepped ashore from the *Providence of Montrose* with the other drabs his life had been one of ease and comfort, without complications.

He pulled his rough coat around him and sat down on a huge piece of driftwood, half the trunk of a mangrove, washed ashore far from its native Florida. He knew little of the life Alizon had led before she had been transported to South Carolina. He knew she had suffered. Just to travel in the transports was suffering enough, to survive was almost a miracle, yet she had experienced far worse than that floating coffin, she had been one of the few who had lived through the horrible Massacre of Glencoe. She had named her child for the fierce old Highland chief who had been butchered and whom she had called 'Grandfather MacIan', and the crime that had brought her here, halfway across the world, had been her attempt to kill the man who had murdered her family.

He felt the first drop of cold rain fall on his face and he rose, quickening his steps back towards the cluster of buildings that surrounded the Meeting House. He would go back to Charleston and he would marry her. He refused to think of the accusations, the recriminations that would greet his return. He would admit his fault, beg her forgiveness, but he would not take no for an answer this time. They could put the past behind them, if for no other reason than that of the child, Alasdair. They had all suffered enough.

He attended the Meeting of the Society of Friends for the last time, the child sitting quietly on his knee, while the pastor and all his friends prayed for them both. He passed the child to Rachel when at last the prayers were finished and rose.

"My friends. . . ." He began the speech he had rehearsed, but looking around at the faces of the congregation he could not go on. "All I can say is thank you. I must leave you, but I shall never forget what you have done for me. . . ." For the first time in his life he felt humbled, and taking the little boy from Mistress Middleton he walked from the room.

He had procured a horse with the money Jacob had insisted on giving him and was surprised to find how close the Quaker settlement was to the port of Annapolis. He had expected a long and hazardous journey, for the road was no more than a trail, yet a day's ride brought him within sight of the town.

After the isolation of the small coastal community the town appeared busier and noisier than ever, and he felt his spirits rise. He found a tavern and obtained a bed for the night, and after paying one of the serving girls to tend to the little boy he went down into the tap room. Hearing from the landlord of the dangers of travelling to Charleston by land, he decided that the only course was again to risk the short sea passage. He was more than a little uneasy at the thought, but it was the quicker and the safer route and the sooner he returned to Kircaldy the sooner he could make his peace with Alizon.

Next morning he went down to the wharves and found that there was a packet leaving on the afternoon tide. He returned to the tavern, packed up what few belongings he had—all given by the Middletons—and then sold the horse to pay their passage. The fact that he had very little money did not trouble him greatly. Once he reached Charleston he had friends who would lend him transport to carry them both up Goose Creek to the plantation, and he had money in trust with the attorney.

As the small craft left the port he took the child below. In the heavy swell, the sullen sky, the freshening wind, he drew comparisons to that last nightmare voyage. It would be mid-morning, weather permitting, before the ship would sail between James' Island and Sullivan's Island and into Charleston Harbour, so he settled himself as comfortably as he could on the bunk, the little boy asleep beside him, his thumb in his mouth. His feelings for Alasdair surprised him. He had never thought that a child could mean so much to him. Being the sole surviving child of his parents, the only children Darnley had come into contact with were the offspring of some of his friends, and they were usually whisked away by their nurse or mother upon his arrival. There were the children of the Negro slaves on the plantation but he had never even given them a second glance.

He looked down at his sleeping son. The curls clustered on the forehead were the same light, sandy colour as his own, but beneath the closed lids the little boy's eyes were large and dark brown like Alizon's. "Kircaldy belongs to neither Alizon or I, it is yours, Alasdair Kirkbride, it is all yours!" he muttered before closing his eyes.

It was almost noon before the ship crept slowly past Sullivan's Island and into the harbour. Several of the wharves had been repaired after the damage of the hurricane but there were many still under construction. Threading his way between the workmen and the gangs of Negroes loading and unloading the larger merchant vessels, he made his way from the waterfront along Granville Bastion towards Meeting Street and the home of Edward Ashe. Edward would be overjoyed to see him, he thought, and Elizabeth would tend to Alasdair who was unsettled, hungry and fractious. Shifting the child onto his other arm, Darnley thought that it was a miraculous feat that he had managed to attend to the child for so long by himself without the aid of a woman. There had been some difficulties, swaddlings and diapers had been a mystery to him, but he had managed somehow.

His knock was answered by the Ashes' manservant who looked rather surprised to see him with the infant in his arms. "I'm afraid Master Ashe is away from home," he replied to Darnley's enquiry.

"Is his wife, Mistress Elizabeth, at home?"

"No, sir, they've all gone a visitin' ole' Master Ashe up on the Ashley River."

Darnley nodded and thanked him, turning away slowly. He was disappointed—he had been looking forward to seeing Edward's face when he realised that his friend had not perished after all. Alizon must have heard of the wreck of the *Randolph*, he mused as he made his way towards Church Street. His intentions were to marry her before the shock caused by his "return from the dead" and the restoration of her child, and the subsequent relief, had given way to anger.

At the home of Arnold Mathews he was much relieved to find both the master and mistress at home. As he stood in the wide hall while the servant went in search of his master, he sighed deeply. At last he felt he was home. Some measure of security and confidence were returning. Arnold would lend him a carriage and no doubt Beatrice would insist upon accompanying him to Kircaldy. In a way it would be a relief to relinquish Alasdair into Beatrice's capable hands, he thought, feeling the warm damp patch on his arm where the child rested.

"My God! Darnley! It is you! I thought Hopkins had got the wrong name!" Arnold Mathews' face was a picture of incredulity and disbelief. "You were reported dead, both of you!"

There was a short cry as Beatrice Mathews appeared in the hall. "Heaven be praised! I can't believe it! Darnley Kirkbride, is it really you?"

"It is, Beatrice! We are both safe and well, thanks to good fortune and the kindness of the Quaker Community beyond Annapolis!"

Beatrice took Alasdair from him, tears sparkling in her

eyes. "Thanks to the mercy of God! You were ever a one inclined to wildness!" she chided him. "The poor little mite is cold, wet and hungry!" she scolded as Alasdair began to cry. "I'll have Lucy take him. How you've managed to care for him for so long is beyond me!"

"I thought I managed quite well, but he'll fare better with a woman—he'll be with his mother soon enough now!"

Beatrice had started to ascend the staircase but at his words she stopped and turned. Her gaze went quickly from Darnley's face to that of her husband.

"Take the child up to Lucy. I'll take Darnley into the parlour, he looks half-frozen. Tell Hopkins to bring brandy and prepare a meal!"

Beatrice nodded and continued her ascent. Noticing his friend's downcast eyes and the sombre note in his voice, Darnley felt the first stirrings of unease.

"Arnold, what's the matter?"

Arnold drew together the double doors of the small parlour and motioned Darnley to a chair near the hearth.

"Is Alizon ill? I realise she must have suffered because of me. . . ."

"She was ill. No woman should have to endure the anguish you deliberately caused her! We thought for a time she would lose her reason, that she would die fretting! Why did you do it?"

Darnley did not miss the note of harsh anger in Mathews' voice. "Because at the time I hated her. She wanted to take everything from me. She had Kircaldy and she refused me the right to see and supervise the upbringing of my own son! I hated her for that and so I took Alasdair to hurt her and . . . and because he belonged to me!"

The glass shook for a second in Arnold Mathews' hand. "Alasdair is. . . . is *your* son? Everyone thought. . . ."

"I know what everyone thought, that he was my father's son. But Alasdair is mine! He's mine! Only Alizon and I knew and perhaps that French girl, Gabrielle. She swore she would lie, that she would take her case before the courts before she would admit it publicly! I wanted to marry her, for Alasdair's sake, but she refused. Alasdair is a bastard, my bastard! It's not a pretty tale, Arnold, is it? I'm not proud of it, but I loved her and I believed she loved me. I still want to marry her. I want my son to be legitimate, I want Kircaldy for him. It belongs to him, not to Alizon!"

The older man sat down heavily after refilling his glass, choosing his words carefully in his mind. There was no way he could soften the blow, no way he could talk around the subject. "Alizon has gone and Kircaldy no longer belongs to a Kirkbride."

Darnley stared at him hard, the colour draining from his face, then he jumped to his feet. "Gone! Where's she gone? When did she go? What do you mean about Kircaldy?"

"Darnley, you can't blame her! She thought you were both dead! She tried to find you, God knows she tried! She employed agents to search and she waited through an agonising time until the news came about the wreck of the *Randolph*, then there was no reason for her to stay here. Charleston was not her home, and she was brought here against her will. She went home to Scotland taking Gabrielle with her."

"And Kircaldy?"

"Sold. I myself arranged the sale. Joseph Elliot bought it. Everyone thought you were dead, she was within the law. She had lost her child, her husband and you, what was there left for her here?"

"August, before the autumn storms."

"When did she go? How long ago?"

Three months, he thought, then cursed himself for lingering so long with the Middletons. If he had known . . . if he had known what she had intended to do! "Will Elliot sell back Kircaldy?"

"I doubt it, besides, what will you pay him with? There is a little money that belongs to you, Alizon would not have it. . . ."

"No doubt she had enough, she could afford to be generous!" The words were spat out with venom.

"Your father was one of my closest friends, but I must say this, Darnley. You have only yourself to blame! What will you do now?" Arnold Mathews asked, abruptly changing the subject to try to stem the tirade of wrath that was rising to Darnley's lips.

"I'll follow her! I'll find her and I'll take what is mine and she can't refuse me, she won't refuse her son!"

"Let it be, Darnley! Enough harm has been done, the wounds on both sides are too deep to be healed! Stay here, seek the Governor's help, start again, there is plenty of good land! Build again for yourself and Alasdair. Leave Alizon alone, you've caused her enough heartbreak!"

Darnley turned away from him and stared unseeingly out of the window down the street. "What . . . what did she intend to do. . . ."

"Go back to Glencoe. Build a house on some bleak and isolated moor called Rannoch and try to farm."

Darnley laughed derisively. "Farm that godforsaken wilderness! And the house . . . ?" He knew that if it had a name and that name was Kircaldy, he would find her and he would kill her.

"Rannoch Chase. She told me it was named a long time ago and I remember Gabrielle asking her if she could be happy with her bitter memories in a land of harsh climate and so much bloodshed."

"Rannoch Chase." He repeated the name aloud. Even the sound of it conjured up the vision of a barren, hostile land. He shrugged. Let her live out her miserable existence at Rannoch. Let her believe her son was dead; she would never profitably farm such land and the effort would slowly erode the money she had obtained for Kircaldy, money she had stolen from him. There was no free Negro labour in Scotland, and within a decade she would be reduced to poverty and misery. He turned to face Arnold Mathews.

"What advice should I ask of the Governor? What help can I expect?"

"Explain your position. Johnson was an old friend of your father's, too."

"Johnson?"

"He's the new Governor. A good man. An old soldier, some say a Jacobite. His advice will be sound. Forget the past and look to the future, my boy. Charleston is growing fast, there is plenty of room for expansion and fortunes can still be made. You are well-known, your family is well established, borrow what you can and start again."

At last Darnley nodded.

"Stay with us until you have seen Johnson and found your feet. You can't go on caring for the child by yourself and I doubt if Beatrice would even hear of it!"

"Thank you. I'm glad I came back, Arnold, and I'm glad I came to you."

The guarded expression left the older man's face and he smiled. "Do you wish me to write to Alizon and let her know the child is alive?"

"No! I never want to hear her name again and when Alasdair is old enough to understand, he will be told that his mother is dead! Do you understand me, Arnold? She has forfeited any right to him!"

"You took him from her, Darnley. You share the blame," Arnold Mathews reminded him quietly, but Darnley did not hear him. The words didn't penetrate the hatred in his mind.

Chapter 2

The library of the Governor's house also served as his study, Darnley surmised, judging from the profusion of papers, quills, ink horn and other sundries that covered the top of the large black oak table set before the long window. Governor Johnson was no stranger to him for he was also a "Goose Creek Man," owning a plantation further up-river than Kircaldy. At the thought of Alizon's betrayal the hard gleam returned to Darnley's eyes. Johnson would help him. If there was any way of getting Elliott to sell, Johnson would know of it. His deliberations were interrupted by the appearance of the Governor himself. He was a tall man with iron-grey hair, aquiline features and an air of command that was completely natural. His dress was plain, the coat and knee-breeches of sombre brown merino, the cuffs trimmed with braid and the coat adorned with the plainest of buttons, while the waistcoat, at a time when such garments were often ostentatious almost to the point of gaudiness, was of dull gold brocade.

"Sir, it was good of you to see me at such short notice, I realise that you must have more pressing affairs. . . ."

Johnson waved aside the pressures of business. "How could I refuse? It was assumed you had drowned—my predecessor went to great pains to discover your whereabouts. Mistress Kirkbride was, I understand, prostrate with grief and worry!"

The piercing blue eyes were questioning and Darnley quailed a little before the gaze, remembering once when he had been twelve years old he had been caught in a scrape by his father and Johnson.

"Unfortunate business that! But I'm not the Lord Advocate, only the Governor. Mistress Kirkbride has returned to Scotland and now you turn up again. . . ."

"Sir, it is about that matter that I have come. I want your advice. I had my reasons for leaving for Boston but I had no idea that Alizon would sell Kircaldy. I want it back. Is there any way Elliott can be persuaded to sell?"

Johnson pressed the tips of his fingers together and studied them closely. "You mean is there any way he can be coerced into selling it back to you?"

Darnley did not reply. Johnson had an uncanny knack of probing deeper into his thoughts than he would have wished, and it unnerved him.

"What does Arnold Mathews have to say on the matter?"

"That as far as he can see the deed was drawn up correctly and the procedure of the sale was according to the letter of the law."

The Governor nodded slowly. "Then in law there is nothing that can be done. Mistress Kirkbride assumed you dead, as did everyone else. . . ."

"But there was no body as proof!"

"Your father's body was never found. Do you still think

he is alive? You know as well as I do that in a land like this, with the tempestuous elements we are subjected to, it is a common thing, a fact of life . . . or death. You were assumed dead, she was within her right. Her husband and her son both dead and you, too. The property belonged to her to keep or dispose of as she saw fit, and she chose to sell it."

Darnley bit back the words that rushed to his lips. Only Arnold knew that Alasdair was his son and not his father's and he would not have the child's bastardy discussed in every parlour and tavern in Charleston. Alasdair was his trump card, but it was a card he would never play. He would get the plantation back somehow, but not at the expense of his son's social standing. "Then if Elliott refuses to sell, and Arnold is sure he will, all I can do is start again; there has to be something for Alasdair."

"I'm glad you are being so reasonable. Now, have you anywhere in mind? Collaton County?"

"I don't have the funds at the present time . . . that . . . that was the other reason I came to you for advice."

"Or a loan, you mean?"

Again the same directness, Darnley thought as he nodded.

"I can advance you a certain sum but not enough to purchase land on the scale you wish. Most of my money is tied up in crops, that I know you will understand, and with this damned war going on with both the Spaniards and the French harrying the merchantmen and the restrictive Maritime Act, one never knows when or even if your cargo will reach England. To add to all that there is the little matter of the Church Acts."

"There has never been any trouble before between Episcopalians and other religious sects."

"That's just it! The Royal Charter states quite clearly 'As the country comes to be sufficiently planted and distributed into fit diversions, it shall belong to the Parliament to take care for the building of churches and the maintenance of divines to be employed in the exercise of religion, according to the Church of England.' And what have we? Baptists, Huguenots, Quakers and everyone building churches and employing ministers! And to cap it all, whose voice is loudest in shouting that he is independent of all authority save Christ's? None other than the Reverend Mr Marston, the rector of St Phillips!"

Seeing that Johnson was about to launch forth upon his opinions of the renegade rector and his policy of the enforcement of the Church Acts in particular, some of which he had heard the previous night from Arnold, Darnley hastily interrupted.

"I'm sorry, sir, to have bothered you at such a time. I would be most grateful for any sum you can advance me—it will be a start. I've taken up enough of your time already."

Johnson's manner became a little calmer as he crossed to the table and quickly wrote out a bond which he signed and handed to Darnley.

"Good luck to you, Kirkbride. No doubt we shall be seeing more of you, but stay clear of that infernal Marston, you heed me?"

"I have enough troubles without becoming embroiled in Mr Marston's misguided crusade. Goodbye and thank you again, sir!"

Once back in the street he looked down at the piece of parchment. Three hundred guineas. He folded it and placed it in his pocket. Hardly enough to buy more than the creek bottom land at Kircaldy. He felt resentful and dejected. Arnold was already giving him bed and board and a home for Alasdair, he couldn't ask him for more and he might as well forget Kircaldy for ever! His mood was too incensed, too rancorous to return to Arnold's house. He was grateful to both Arnold and Johnson, but the small amount he had would not solve his problems or in any way assuage his ever-increasing fury against Alizon.

His steps took him towards St Michael's church and into St Michael's Alley and the King's tavern. He needed time to think, to formulate his plans, to try and work out some basic structure for the future, but after one tankard of ale he rose, finding the company of the few merchants tedious and depressing. He walked the length of Broad Street which ran down to the wharves, where he hoped the sight of the activity on the quays would dispel his lethargic mood.

The customers of the Barque Minerva were far from quiet and some of them far from sober, but the noise and laughter lifted his spirits. He took the tankard from the landlord and settled himself in the corner by a small window from which could be seen the tall masts and rigging of the merchantmen waiting for the tide. The hubbub of noise all around him grew louder, for it was midday and the place was full of overseers, seamen and not a few doxies. The atmosphere was not conducive to serious thought, but Darnley decided that he could put off unpleasant decisions for a few hours longer.

He leaned his head against the hard wooden back of the high settle, staring aimlessly at the smoke-stained ceiling. He could go into trade, turn merchant, but then he remembered Johnson's comments upon the uncertain state of the sea lanes running between the islands of the West Indies and England. With his luck, after having sunk all his money into a profitable cargo, chances were that it would never reach its destination. Silently he cursed the Maritime Act which forbade the Colonies to trade with any country other than Britain. He cursed, too, the eternal war that had raged between France and England for as long as he could remember, at least since William of Orange had been on the throne, and now that he was dead and his sister-in-law, Anne, was Queen, still the war continued!

The noise around him was intense but from somewhere behind him he caught occasional words which dragged him from his ruminations. He heard the words "Havana", "Martinique", "good prices" and "gold to be had". He strained to hear more of the conversation, though he could not see the speakers. He wished the noise and laughter that filled the small room were not quite so raucous. "Easy cargoes" was the next information he heard.

Suddenly the pieces fitted neatly together; he realised what it all meant. Privateers! Whoever they were, they were engaged in evading the Maritime Act and selling cargoes to the French on Martinique and the Spaniards in Cuba. Everyone knew it went on, and the war made it easier for them. The runs were short and without much risk; the French and Spanish merchants asked no awkward questions, providing you knew the right ones to approach. And the cargo, once sold, brought good money.

All semblance of dejection had gone from his face now. If he could throw in his lot with a group such as these . . . he had no knowledge of seamanship but he could purchase a cargo, even a part share in a small vessel . . . but there were Arnold and Johnson to consider. How could he explain away his seeming idleness that accumulated wealth? Trade! He would purchase a small warehouse to use as a legitimate cover, he could afford to send small cargoes by the legal route to England. And when he had enough money he could buy another plantation and it wouldn't take him years to do it!

He beckoned the tavern maid and ordered another tankard, plus one each for the party of men who were sitting behind him. The girl's eyebrows rose questioningly, but he slapped her on the buttocks and told her there would be something for herself. Winking, she went off and returned bearing a large flat wooden platter laden with tankards, which she placed on the rough table before the mystified men.

"Compliments of the gent behind!" she said, jerking her head in Darnley's direction.

The group eyed the ale with suspicion and then glanced furtively at each other. At last one man nodded and another rose and peered over the top of the settle.

"You sure you ain't made a mistake? Ain't never set eyes on you before, sir?"

"No mistake." Darnley grinned.

The seaman's suspicion was apparent and there was a guarded, cunning look in his eyes. "What's your game then?"

Darnley picked up his own tankard and pretended to inspect it carefully. "It's not my game, it's yours! I believe it is called 'Fending for oneself' or perhaps 'turning a blind eye to the Queen's Regulations'."

The man's face became completely blank, devoid of any expression.

"Thankee for the ale, sir, but I can't say as I know what you mean." He lifted the ale in a gesture of gratitude and prepared to sit down.

"Then maybe it's better to speak plainly. Privateering!"

The blank expression disappeared, to be replaced by suspicion and fear, while the others exchanged uneasy glances. "Beg pardon, sir, but you a Revenue Man?"

Darnley laughed. "Good God! No! Just a gentleman of fortune, shall we say." Or lack of it, he thought bitterly. "May I join you, gentlemen?"

There was a pause during which the man on his feet eyed Darnley with uncertainty. At last he nodded, gesturing for a stool to be brought.

Once settled, Darnley drained his tankard, his eyes wandering over the faces of the group that sat before him. At last he leaned forward and addressed the man who seemed to be their spokesman, for not one of the others had uttered a syllable. "I have a little money to invest in what I will call 'merchandise'. I'll be quite honest with you, gentlemen, I have no knowledge of the sea and my last experience with ships was unfortunate, to say the least. But I would be prepared to invest in a cargo or even to buy a part share in a good fast ship, providing the price was right."

The man stared down at his weather-beaten hands. "You are aware of the Acts and the punishment for those caught?"

"Naturally, but it's an unfair law that prevents men from trading where they will. I am well-known and respected amongst Charleston's citizens, the Governor was a friend of my father's, but due to . . . circumstances I lost my plantation. I will be above suspicion. I will purchase a small warehouse which will—apparently—be my legal occupation. I can be a great asset to you, gentlemen. Think about it!"

"You sit safely at 'ome while we run the risks, not much of an asset if you ask me!"

"The profit on the cargoes, the warehouse in which to store them and through which to dispose of them, without the furtive and risky business which you are now forced to endure, would you not call that an asset?"

"Could be all talk, Jake, could be a Revenue Man spinning us a tale, baiting his trap!" another muttered.

"I can't prove that I'm not a Revenue Officer, you'll have to take my word for it, but I intend to make money one way or another. I have a reason, a very good reason! I have a son whose inheritance was sold by his mother and I intend that he shall have it back!"

The man called Jake shrugged. Money for women, ale, good food he could understand, but for a lad who having come by it easy would no doubt squander it, was to him a fool notion. He shrugged at the queer ideas the gentry held.

"Well?" Darnley's voice was harsh.

"I dunno, have to talk it over with the lads 'ere."

"That's fair enough. When will you have reached your decision?"

"Tonight, I reckon. Meet us here at ten o'clock."

Darnley nodded and rose. He had come completely into the open with them and now there was nothing he could do but wait. He was certain that they would make enquiries about him, but knew that if they asked too many questions of the wrong people they would be putting themselves at risk. As he left the tavern he smiled to himself. Governor Johnson would be horrified if he knew what his money was to be used for and Arnold . . . well, Arnold would certainly not approve. The smile vanished and his mouth set in hard, stubborn lines. He would get it all back somehow, everything that Alizon had robbed him of.

The house was strangely quiet when he returned. Arnold must be out, probably Beatrice was shopping or returning a call on a friend, Lucy would be in the nursery with Alasdair. He made his way to the top of the house and opened the nursery door. Lucy, the Mathews' maid, was playing on the floor with the child.

"How is he today, Lucy?"

Bobbing a curtsey Lucy grinned. "He's fine, sir. Happy, sweet-tempered little boy he is."

Darnley caught the child up in his arms, tickling him, whereupon the child shrieked with delight.

"Oh, excuse me, sir, but... but well, Madam is ill. I was told to keep him as quiet as I could."

Darnley put Alasdair down on the floor. "Beatrice! What's the matter?"

"Took bad this morning, just after breakfast it were. Master has gone for the doctor himself, she's feverish."

Darnley's brow creased into an anxious frown, remembering the plague that had almost killed his father, the terrible fever that had spread like wilfire, the fever which Alizon had nursed his father through while he had run from it like a terrified animal. He still felt the guilt at that act of cowardice, but pushed it from his mind as he stared down at his son. Suppose... suppose it was the fever? Suppose Alasdair... or himself!

"How long has the master been gone, Lucy?"

"Almost an hour now, sir, I can't think what's keeping him."

As if in answer to her question they heard the front door bang and low voices in the hall. Quickly Darnley left the nursery and went down, meeting Arnold and Doctor Wakefield on the stairs.

"Arnold, Lucy has just told me! What is it?"

"I don't know, but she's feverish, didn't know me when I left. Sarah is sitting with her." The fear in Arnold's eyes matched that in his own, as they both followed the doctor to Beatrice's room. Darnley waited outside, anxiously trying to catch the inaudible words of Arnold and the doctor. Sarah, the Mathews' housekeeper, came out.

"How is she, Sarah, does the doctor know what it is?"

"She's burnin' up, don't know me or even the master." She shook her head sadly as she turned away.

It was Arnold who came out first and one look at his face confirmed all Darnley's fears.

"It... it's the fever, Arnold?"

Arnold nodded dumbly. "But not the plague, another fever. Typhoid, Wakefield called it, but . . . but it's as bad!" He leaned on Darnley's arm, his face suddenly crumpling, and Darnley thought he looked an old, old man. He tried to offer some words of comfort but realised it was useless.

"We can only wait, it's in the hands of the Lord," Arnold muttered brokenly.

Doctor Wakefield appeared. "Send Sarah back up here with a bowl of tepid water and linen cloths, tell her to keep sponging her mistress down. I've managed to give her some physic and I've left you a bottle, we can only hope and pray now."

Arnold shook his head. "No need for Sarah, I'll nurse her myself."

Wakefield nodded his approval, then turned to Darnley. "There is a young child in the house, so I have been told?"

"Yes, my son, Alasdair . . . you don't think . . .?"

"I'd advise you to get him out of the house, and yourself too. I'll be back in a few hours to see how she is, but tell Arnold not to hesitate to call me if he thinks she is becoming worse."

Darnley watched him go down the stairs without really seeing him. His thoughts were upstairs in the nursery. He had to get Alasdair out, but who to? His thoughts were a confused jumble until at last he pulled himself together. Edward Ashe would take them, of that he was certain. He would go straight over now, the sooner he got Alasdair out of the house the better.

Edward Ashe was at home and told him to fetch the child and himself over at once. He had been on his way to the Mathews' house, for it had taken a while for the news of Darnley's miraculous return to circulate. Darnley thanked him profusely.

"It will only be temporary, Edward, I assure you. I don't want to put you out. I've hopes of a business venture and then I'll buy a house of my own, don't want to trouble anyone, be a burden. . . ."

"It's no trouble at all! Stay as long as you wish, Elizabeth will be delighted, she'll be able to practise."

"Practise?"
"Yes, we are expecting a happy event in a few months' time!"
Darnley congratulated him but at the same time felt uneasy. If Elizabeth was so far gone in pregnancy she wouldn't want an active toddler for long, he would tire her and then once her own child was born. . . .
"I'll bring him over now, get him settled. . . ."
"Then we'll have dinner. . . ." Edward interrupted.
"I have a business appointment later tonight, Edward, but it shouldn't take long."
"Good, then you can tell me about your misfortunes."
He was met at the door by a solemn-faced Hopkins. "The doctor's here, sir, he advises you to take the child away at once. Mistress Mathews is much worse, I'm afraid."
"Is Arnold with her still?"
"He's never left her side for a minute, sir."
"Hopkins, I'm taking my son to Mr Ashe's and I, too, shall be staying with him. Will you send word immediately anything. . . ."
"I understand, sir. I'll send word if. . . what I mean is, either way I'll send word."
Darnley stopped outside Beatrice's room, shuddering at the low moans, the hushed voices that issued from within. He packed what few belongings he had into a bag and then went up to Lucy.
"Pack up his clothes, Lucy, we are going to Mr Ashe's on Doctor Wakefield's instructions. Be as quick as you can, girl!"
Lucy did as she was bid, handing him the small bag as he picked up the child. "Sir . . . I . . . what if we all gets it?" She tugged at his sleeve.
"That is something we all risk, Lucy, and no one can tell. I can't give you an answer."
When he arrived back at the Ashes' Elizabeth was waiting to welcome him, and his heart sank as he glanced at the distended belly. She hadn't long to go, he thought. A month, two. . . . "He's a good, quiet little lad, he'll not cause you any trouble, Elizabeth," he began.

"I know he won't, here, give him to me."

"No, he's too heavy, you may injure yourself."

Elizabeth Ashe grimaced impatiently. "When will everyone stop treating me as though I were ill! I'm perfectly healthy and so is my condition, now let me have him!"

Darnley passed the little boy into her arms.

"He resembles you rather than your father, but he has his mother's eyes."

He felt a chill shiver run down his spine at her words. Ignoring her first remark he replied, "Yes, he has Alizon's eyes."

Elizabeth shook her head sadly. "Poor Alizon, if only she'd waited just a few more weeks. You have written to her of course, Darnley?"

"No . . . no, I've not yet had the time, but I shall do," he lied. It was impossible to tell Elizabeth how he hated Alizon or the reasons for his hatred.

After dinner he excused himself and promised Edward that his appointment would take no longer than an hour. He left the house, declining his friend's offer that he take his carriage. He walked quickly down Meeting Street and then towards the wharves. It was a moonless night and there were few people on the streets, a fact for which he was thankful. The Barque Minerva's small latticed windows illuminated the dim, dingy alleyway that bordered the waterfront. Pushing open the door he screwed up his eyes, peering through the haze of tobacco smoke.

In the corner where he had sat earlier that day was Jake, alone, a half-empty tankard in front of him. There was no sign of any of his fellow seafarers or crew, Darnley thought, glancing around the crowded room. He made his way through the throng towards Jake who, spotting him, roughly pushed aside a small dark man who had drunk himself insensible. The man groaned as he slumped onto the floor then slumbered on peacefully, still clutching an empty bottle. Darnley stepped over him without glancing down and sat beside Jake, after catching the eye of the tavern maid.

"Well?"

Jake finished his ale in one gulp. "You weren't tellin' no lies, we checked."

"I knew you would, so?"

"So me and the lads are willin' to take you in with us as long as you leave the business of runnin' the ship to us. How much 'ave you got? How much are you willin' to . . . ?"

"Invest? That depends on whether it's just merchandise or a part in the vessel."

"Merchandise . . . to start with."

"I see, I'm on probation. In that case one hundred guineas, but I buy my own merchandise."

Jake agreed and called for more ale.

It was still risky, too risky, Darnley thought. All he knew about this man was that his name was Jake, nothing else. He had no guarantee that he would ever see him or his money again. He sighed deeply. There was no alternative but to gamble. He must, somehow, obtain a small warehouse and some sort of accommodation, he couldn't stay too long with Edward and Elizabeth.

"Buy your stuff and get it down to the wharves, we'll do the rest. Once you've got your warehouse then we can keep the stuff there until we're ready to sail, that way it will appear all legal." Jake finished his drink. "We sail Monday on the early tide, before dawn."

Darnley rose, wondering whether to offer his hand as he would naturally have done with any of his friends on a gentleman's agreement, but decided against it. Instead he nodded curtly and pushed his way out again into the fresh night air.

Chapter 3

Beatrice Mathews died the next night. The news was brought over by Lucy, sent by Hopkins, with the request that Darnley leave it for a day before visiting as the master was distraught with grief and as Lucy put it "not quite himself, sir, if you understand me?" Edward and Elizabeth were also grieved by the loss, for Beatrice and Elizabeth were distantly related. Darnley was afraid that Alasdair had already caught the disease. He took the child to his room and watched him, searching for any sign of fever, but as the days passed Alasdair remained healthy and he relaxed his vigilance.

After the funeral he set about seriously searching for property, helped by Edward, and at last he found a building that would suit his purpose at the right price. Having put nearly all his money into the joint enterprises there was little left, certainly not enough to purchase or rent a small house. When he broached the subject of leaving Elizabeth demanded hotly how on earth he would cope on his own with the little boy, especially as he would be busy with trade, and promptly declared the matter closed.

His doubts about his gamble were unfounded: Jake Patterson was a shrewd businessman. Why be fool enough to make off with Kirkbride's money when he could have a guaranteed percentage on each trip to add to his own profits? At the beginning of December, early one misty morning the *Gretta* slipped silently past James' Island and into harbour, her hold full of merchandise from Cuba and the French Islands which would find its way into the homes of Charleston's citizens, both rich and poor.

After Patterson's third trip Darnley had enough money to buy a modest house and Elizabeth had given birth. She had had a hard time and was ill and weak, and despite her protests and those of Edward, Darnley moved himself and Alasdair into the new house on Church Street. He engaged a young Irish girl to see to Alasdair while he conducted his business, which continued to thrive. But he soon found that Bridgit preferred to preen herself in front of the mirror than be bothered with the child.

There followed a succession of nurses, but sooner or later he found fault with them all; worse still, he was tired in the evenings and found himself being irritated by the child. What he needed was a wife, he thought, as he sat late one evening after an extremely unappetising supper that the latest housekeeper had put before him. The thought made him uneasy, which was strange. He had been willing, eager to marry Alizon, but he had loved her... once. This would be a marriage of convenience, to someone who would care for Alasdair properly, keep the place clean and cook edible meals at reasonable hours. Grimly he pushed his hands into the pockets of his waistcoat. He could just imagine the polite, embarrassed refusals he would receive from the fathers of the girls and young women idling their time away on the plantations up-river. No one was going to turn him down! He would have to choose the daughter of a tradesman. A decently brought-up but homely girl. He grimaced at the thought, remembering Alizon's liquid brown eyes and long silver-blonde hair. She was a fool to hide herself away in some remote, Godforsaken glen! He eased himself out of the chair and snuffed out the candles. He would have to take what he could get, for convenience's sake.

Since he had become a partner with Patterson he often frequented the Barque Minerva, becoming known to the landlord and his daughter. He had given the girl a few interested glances in the past but his mind had been on other matters of more importance. Today there were not many people in the tavern, for it was not yet noon. After ordering and exchanging a few words with Dick Kerr, the landlord, Darnley took his usual place by the window and watched the activity of the rapidly-growing town. It was Kerr's daughter, Anne, who brought the tankard and set it down on the table. He passed her a coin and then watched her as she walked back to the parlour. He judged her to be about twenty, her hair was very dark, almost blue-black, and curled in tendrils from beneath her cap. She was slim and carried herself with an easy grace, and because she refused to laugh and joke and submit to the rough caresses of her father's customers they had named her "Icy Nan". He called over to Kerr to have his ale replenished and heard him shout into the parlour for her, calling her Nan. It seemed as though everyone called her that.

Looking decidedly annoyed she swept up the tankard and crossed to him, the ale spilling over onto her hands as she set it on the table. Her black brows rushed together in a frown and she muttered a curse under her breath as she wiped her hands on the cotton apron.

"I'm sorry to have put you to so much trouble, Anne."

She stared down at him, still wiping her fingers. No one ever gave her her full name, not since her mother had died, worked to death by that great lazy bastard who preferred to swill back ale with his customers than serve them. Since then she had been forced to take her mother's place and endure the coarse jests, the groping hands and foul mouths of the clientele. It was a long time since she had been called Anne, and some of her annoyance left her. "It's no trouble, there's only yourself in, though give ten minutes and the place will be packed to bursting!" She cast a contemptuous glance through the window towards the men labouring on the quayside.

"Doesn't your father employ enough wenches to serve?"

Another contemptuous glance went in the direction of her father. "No. If he had any sense of decency he wouldn't suffer me to serve the scum we get in here! It killed my mother, she was never strong, but I swear he won't do the same to me!"

"Then why don't you leave? Find yourself a place somewhere else?"

The black brows rushed together again. "Who would have me—I'm trained for nothing! Can you see my applying to the grand ladies to be a governess or a maid servant? For one thing, they can get plenty of girls from the transports as cheap labour. I can read and write, my mother taught me, she'd been a governess herself though what she ever saw in him I'll never know!" The last words were spat with venom in the direction of her father. She held Darnley's frankly interested gaze. He was certainly a cut above the customers who usually frequented the place. He spoke and acted like a gentleman, although his clothes were the dark serviceable ones of those of a man in trade.

"You keep house for your father, too?"

"Yes. I cook and clean though he never notices!"

They stared at each other hard, both sensing the tension

that lay between them, yet the same thoughts were running through each of their minds.

Darnley took a deep breath. "Would you consider a proposition I have to make?"

She sat down on a wooden stool. "That would depend upon what it is."

"I'm not a wealthy man but I do have a thriving business and a modest house on Church Street, I also have a son who will be three years old in the spring."

"You are asking me to be your housekeeper and nursemaid for the child?"

"I've tried numerous housekeepers. I'm asking you to marry me!"

The words hung on the air. She continued to stare at him, and her mouth dropped open. She had been willing to jump at the chance of being housekeeper — but marriage! She closed her mouth, sucking in a deep gulp of air, still holding his steady gaze. She'd vowed that one day she would get away from the tavern and had even, in moments of sheer madness, fancied herself a lady in a carriage. She lowered the thick black lashes over her eyes. Never again to have to put up with her father, the tavern and all it entailed. The wife of a merchant! Respected! Never again to be called Nan or worse!

She raised her lashes and looked at him again: she didn't even know his name. "I'll marry you." The words were spoken. She had committed herself to a man she didn't know. He could beat her, starve her—how could she know what manner of man he was? For a second panic swept over her and she opened her mouth to speak, then she pressed her lips together. This was the heaven-sent chance she had waited for for years; for better or worse she had agreed to marry him. "I don't even know your name." She was surprised to find her voice so steady.

"Darnley Kirkbride. You are quite sure you will have no regrets?"

"I'm sure. I ask nothing of you but that you do not beat or abuse me, although I am sure no gentleman would do either."

"You seem very sure of the manners of gentlemen, Anne Kerr, but you have my promise. In return I ask nothing more than a pleasant companion, a good housekeeper and a considerate stepmother for Alasdair."

She rose unsteadily: the tavern had begun to fill up. "I'll speak to your father this evening."

She picked up the empty tankards, nodded and turned away.

"Anne! After today you will not serve in the tavern, I'll see to that."

A smile now lit her face and Darnley thought he had not made such a bad bargain after all. Anne Kerr was not unattractive; if she was kind to Alasdair it was all he could ask of her. He was still astounded at his lack of consideration in the matter. He had intended to look around at the daughters of some of the merchants, take his time in finding a good homely girl, but some crazy impulse had made him blurt out to a tavern-keeper's daughter his intentions. Still, had he picked some merchant's daughter he would have had to go through the pretence of showing some affection, whereas Anne Kerr expected nothing more than he had clearly stated. He was stuck with her now, he mused, threading his way between the cargoes which lay on the quayside. She must loathe the tavern and all it entailed; presumably she saw him as her only way out. She had courage and determination, and he had to admit he admired her.

If Landlord Kerr was astonished by Darnley's offer he did not show it; he had probably been verbally browbeaten by his daughter, Darnley thought as he discussed the arrangements with him. She had told him that her mother had been a governess, and it seemed likely that she had inherited more from her than from Kerr. Kerr's permission was given and he had completed the arrangements without the other man offering any comment, except to nod or grunt his approval even when Darnley had stated flatly that he did not wish his intended wife to serve any more.

On the first occasion when he called to escort Anne—to a modest supper given by one of his new-found friends—he asked her about her father's seeming complaisance. She stood looking at him calmly. She seemed to have acquired more dignity since their last meeting. The plain dark blue dress was covered by a light shawl and her hair was swept up into a neat chignon and held by a riband of blue velvet. The dark, high-piled hair emphasised the small oval face with the sweeping black brows and lashes, full underlip and determined chin.

"Of course he was surprised. He laughed at me at first, asked me if I'd gone off my head, but I soon put him straight on that score!" She jerked her chin a little higher. "I've always been able to manage Pa, he never has more than a few words to say for himself." She laid her hand lightly upon the arm he proffered. "There was nothing he could do about it. I'm nineteen, nearly twenty, and a free woman, not a bond servant forced to stay and do his bidding!" She saw the quick flash of anger start in his eyes and drew in her breath, wondering why he was suddenly angry. "I have said something to upset you?"

"No. It was merely a memory that prodded me."

The dark eyes narrowed a little. "Forgive me if I seem forward, but what happened to the little boy's mother?"

A breeze was blowing in from the harbour, a warm breeze, yet he shivered. "She's dead."

She said nothing, measuring her steps to his, but sensing that something was troubling him. She was no fool. She had given the matter a great deal of thought, too much thought at times. He could have chosen someone better than she. She was certain that he had not been brought up to be a merchant, he had the manners and speech of a gentleman, and it was very strange that he took such an interest in the child. He could have found some female relative to look after the little boy. These questions she had repeated over and over to herself, finding no satisfactory answers, and now she felt she never would, for he was suddenly taciturn.

They walked on in silence and never once during the supper did he refer to the matter again. She was quite at ease with his friends, though he was obviously not of their class. On the way home she was surprised when after a few minutes of light conversation he said suddenly, "I lied to you, Anne. Alasdair's mother is not dead, but she might as well be."

She stopped and sat down on the small wall that ran around St Michael's churchyard. "I have told you everything that has occurred in my past, I feel it better to start with no illusions. . . ." She paused.

He stood with his thumbs hooked over the pockets of his waistcoat. "My father was a planter on Goose Creek, he died in the hurricane. Alizon . . . Alizon and I could not agree over the boy, so I took him, left for Boston."

"Does he mean so much to you?"

"Yes! We were wrecked off the coast of Maryland and Alizon . . . she sold the plantation and went home to Scotland. She took everything from me except Alasdair. She sold his inheritance and left."

"But she believed you both dead."

He did not miss the note of indignation. "She had no right to Kirkcaldy, no right to anything, it belonged to me! She came here as a bond servant!"

"What was her crime?"

"Attempted murder."

"And you married her?" She was incredulous, wondering if it was a habit of his to pick up strange girls and marry them.

"No, I wanted to. . . ."

She uttered a sharp choked-off laugh. "Don't tell me she refused you?"

"She was no common drab from the transports, she was, she was . . . Alizon!" he finished lamely.

"And you loved her?"

He nodded. "In the beginning I did, now. . . ."

"Now you hate her?"

He stared beyond her, over the top of her head, beyond the brown eyes that looked up questioningly. "I'll get it all back for him one day!"

Suddenly he grasped her wrist tightly and she yelped in pain. "Not a word of anything I have told you must ever pass your lips, you understand me?"

She was on her feet now. Sparks of anger danced in her eyes. "You promised that you would not abuse me!"

He released his grip, but she did not rub the chafed skin or take her gaze from his face. "I'm sorry, Anne. I did not mean to hurt you." He smiled. "You are not afraid of me?"

"No. When you've been forced into contact with some of my father's customers you learn to overcome fear! I'm not afraid of you but I will keep your secret, if such it is, if you keep your promise. Break it and. . . ."

"And what? Are you blackmailing me?"

"Call it my insurance that you will treat me properly."

"Bitch!" he muttered, taking her arm roughly and starting in the direction of the waterfront.

The ceremony was quiet, with few guests, for Darnley had neither the money nor the inclination to celebrate lavishly. Besides, there were other matters pressing him. The French and the Spaniards had recently settled their differences and had become more menacing in their approach towards the British settlement, the Spaniards claiming that Charleston was a part of Florida and therefore legally Spanish property. His business with the privateers was suffering as a result, for there were constantly men-of-war of both countries sailing the channels and islands, and their last cargo had been confiscated by a French galleon, much to Jake's chagrin and Darnley's anger. Anne knew nothing of his business ventures and he intended that the situation should remain that way, for, once installed in the house on Church Street, he had found that far from being a docile, homely wife she was lively, intelligent and self-willed.

During the first week of their marriage she had been even-tempered and had gone out of her way to please him. She had instantly liked Alasdair and the feeling was mutual. She tended to spoil him shamefully and Darnley began to think that this domestic bliss was more than he deserved or had bargained for. The cause of their first quarrel was the arrival, under press of sail, of the ship Governor Johnson had sent out to scout the sea lanes. The ship came into the harbour hard pressed by five French men-of-war. Johnson himself was away at Silk Hope, his plantation, but Colonel William Rhett, who also bore the title of Vice Admiral, took command.

Darnley heard the wild beating of the militia drum as he turned into Meeting Street, which was packed with people. Men and women were standing in small groups, the men talking loudly and seriously. There were signs of fear on the women's faces. He pushed his way through the crowd until he came upon Edward Ashe with a group of other men.

"What's caused this panic?"

"Rhett has called for volunteers for the militia! There are five French warships standing beyond the bar, French and Spanish soldiers aboard!"

"Where's Johnson?"

"Away up-river, but word has been sent and he'll be here to-morrow."

"We could all be dead by then, the Spaniards have allies in the Yemassees," one of his companions reminded him.

Darnley thought bitterly of the cargo aboard the *Gretta* and silently cursed both the French and the Spaniards. "Tell Rhett I'll join him," he said, thinking that even such small resistance as he could put up would somehow help to assuage his frustration and anger at the loss of his cargo.

It was when he had imparted the news to Anne that the trouble started.

"What good will it do for you to go? There will be enough fools who rush to join and follow the drum! What will happen to us if you don't come back?"

"What will happen to you if I don't go? If every man turns out we have a chance, but what if everyone were to heed the whining of their wives? What then?"

Anne's eyes glinted dangerously. "I didn't marry you to become a widow so soon, aye, and worse off than before, for there's the boy! I thought you loved him, yet off you go at the first call! Love, you don't know what the word means!" Her head was tilted back with the weight of the luxuriant hair, her eyes snapped fire and then narrowed, the small chin was thrust out angrily.

"You'll be provided for!"

"But what about your ambitions for Alasdair? Have you forgotten them so soon?"

Anger contorted his face and he raised his hand to strike her.

She jerked up her head and glared at him defiantly. "No wonder she wouldn't have you!" she spat at him.

For an instant his raised hand drew back, then he dropped it to his side. "Remember where you came from, Anne! Don't you even speak of her! I married you!"

She stood there before him, her eyes burning in the paper-white face, her hands twisting in suppressed fury. He saw her as he had never seen her before and she was beautiful. He felt a sudden rush of longing and then swiftly he reached out, catching her by the shoulders and drawing her close to him.

She struggled to free herself at first, twisting and turning to try to escape his lips, until they pressed hard at the base of her throat where her gown was cut away into a deep V, her firm young breasts covered by the lace fichu, then she ceased to struggle. He was young, he was handsome, more than she had ever hoped for in a husband, and as his kisses and caresses became more urgent she pressed herself against his taut body and returned kiss for kiss. The Governor, Colonel Rhett and the impending attack were forgotten as he carried her up the narrow staircase, his head buried in the soft flesh of her breasts.

The sound of the militia drum could still be heard but the beat of her madly racing heart drowned it as his hands sought the soft skin of her thighs. This was the part of the bargain she had thought would never be paid, though she had hoped that in time he would come to love her, just a little. Her head was swimming, shudders of ecstasy were running through her at the feelings his lips and hands evoked. Her hands sought him and she heard him groan. She would make him forget Alizon and every other woman he had known. A feeling of sensuous power surged through her trembling body: his groans turned to harsh, rasping gasps as their bodies rose and fell in unison. She would make him love her, she would enslave him and together... together they would conquer everything, including the past and she... she would see all her dreams fulfilled. She would work for him, scheme for him, they would regain the fortune Alizon had taken from him. From this day he would never be able to deny her, she would make sure of that. She would use her body to gain her ends, she would make him pant after her.

She pressed the hard, pointed nipple against his lips and smiled lazily to herself as his thrusts increased in power and frenzy. When at last he was spent and lay limply upon her, she wound the long strands of black hair around his neck, fastening him to her, and turned and looked contentedly around the room. She had possessed him—he would never be free of her, not now.

She was wrong. Despite his changed attitude towards her, for he could no longer keep his hands from her body, despite their frequent wildly passionate love-making, she could not sway him from joining Rhett. The marauding party that landed on James' Island was quickly put to flight by the bloodthirsty yells of the Indians, but on Wando Neck behind Sullivan's Island a large party who had plundered four plantations were caught unawares as they sat roasting the pigs and cattle they had stolen. Captain Cantey with a hundred men fell on them, killed and captured twenty and the rest were chased to their long boats. Governor Johnson had armed a few small vessels and Colonel Rhett sailed out to attack the French fleet who instantly weighed anchor and made for the open sea. Despite his aversion to the sea Darnley had joined this small fleet, much to Anne's disgust and annoyance, for she had employed every trick and wile she could think of to keep him at home.

The next night word was brought to her that a French ship of force was in Sewee Bay a few miles from the town, and that Rhett had sailed again and Captain Fenwicke had gone by land to launch an attack. She had put Alasdair to bed and stood gazing out of the window in the direction of Sewee Bay, though the darkness hid everything from sight. What would she do if he were killed or badly wounded? She had the house and the business but no knowledge of how to run it, and there was the child. The hours dragged by and at last she lit the candles and sat down, drawing her shawl around her shoulders, preparing to wait for his return or for some news.

It was the jangling of bells that wakened her. She was stiff and her legs were numb. The peals dragged her to wakefulness. They were the bells of St Michael's. She got to her feet and crossed to the window, surprised to see that it was daylight. She shook her head; it was not the single note of the tocsin sounding a warning, but the jubilant peal that was ringing over the waking town. It must all be over! She ran quickly up the staircase and found Alasdair standing by the window.

"Bells! Pretty!" he laughed.

"I know, my little man! Let's get you dressed quickly and then we will go down and see what has happened and where your papa is!" Hastily she dressed the little boy and carried him down the stairs and out into the street. The town seemed to be wide awake now and people were leaning out of windows asking those passing for news. When she reached the east bastion there were already crowds there. No one seemed to know what had happened, only that there had been a victory for the colony.

At last the first of the small vessels was sighted at the harbour entrance and a cheer rang out. Holding Alasdair on her shoulder, Anne laughed to see him wave his small hands and cry out. The flotilla drew nearer and at last weighed anchor. The first man ashore was swamped by the crowd, all demanding news. Holding tightly to the child Anne pushed her way forward. All around her was a sea of faces and the excited babbling of many voices. At last she caught sight of him and once again pushed forward.

"Darnley! Darnley! Over here! HERE!"

Catching her in his arms he kissed her and then hugged Alasdair.

"What happened? Is it all over?" she shouted above the noise. With his arm firmly around her waist and the child perched securely on his other arm, he retraced her steps along the bastion until the crowds had thinned.

"It's all over, hardly a shot was fired and none at all by the Frenchie! Monsieur Arbuset offered a ransom of ten thousand pieces of eight and that was it! And an end of the Spaniards' claim on Carolina!"

"Thank God!"

He looked down into her eyes and smiled teasingly. "You sound as though you mean it!"

"I do! How would I have managed. . . ."

"You'd have managed, Anne, you are one of the most capable and devious women I have ever met!"

She looked at him provocatively from under her lashes, wondering if there was another meaning behind his words.

"That may be true, but I've not yet learned how to manage you properly, you're as stubborn as a mule when you've your mind set on a notion!"

He drew her closer, his fingers creeping upwards towards the swell of her breasts. "And there's a notion I'm set on now, but it will keep for a while, at least until Alasdair goes for his midday nap!"

Chapter 4

Nine months later Anne gave birth to a child: a girl with a fuzz of reddish-gold hair and amber eyes. Almost from the hour of her birth Miss Adeline Kirkbride demanded and got the attention of both her father and mother and a mixture of adoration and jealousy from her half-brother. In those months Darnley's business had prospered so much that when a plantation on the Ashley River went for sale, he purchased it.

"It's run down, after old FitzAlden died his wife had not the heart. The house is dilapidated, the fields slowly going back to swamp and brush, the slaves and bond servants lazy and insolent. Now she's going north to her sister in Maryland." All this he told Anne on his return from the land office.

She put Adeline back in her cradle and straightened

up. "That doesn't matter. It won't take long to sort it all out. Does it have a name?"

He was silent for a second. He had thought of changing the name to Kircaldy, but as his old home was still known as that it would cause some confusion. He had found a new enthusiasm for life with Anne and there were two children now to consider, not just Alasdair. "Chawira."

She repeated it slowly. "A Yemassee word?"

He nodded.

She said it again. "Chawira, it has a good sound to it."

The following day they took a boat up the Ashley river. The weather was hot and sultry and she was glad of the canopy of live oaks with their tendrils of trailing grey moss that blocked out most of the burning rays of the sun. The sluggish waters were dappled with ever-moving spots of golden sunlight and gilt shafts penetrated the rustling, whispering canopy like shimmering locks of angels' hair. The bright beams reminded Anne of the golden down upon Adeline's head. One day her hair would be just such a colour, she thought proudly, glancing down at the sleeping baby. She loved Alasdair but Adeline was her own flesh and blood, the proof of the love she bore Darnley, while Alasdair was proof. . . . She leaned her head against the wooden pole of the canopy erected to give some shade from the glaring sun. Alizon. She had never been able to draw Darnley out any further upon the subject of Alizon and she often wondered what she had looked like, this woman that he now hated. She wondered what had passed between them that he should hate her so, for he had loved her once, Alasdair was the proof. She never allowed herself to ponder too deeply the question, did he really love her? He loved her body, she needed no reminding of that, but was that the extent of their relationship? When thoughts like these preyed upon her mind she would firmly push them away, telling herself she was a fool, why ask for more?

The boat was moored to a small wooden jetty that projected a few feet out into the river and Darnley, after instructing the boatman to make certain the planks were not rotten, turned and offered her his hand. She passed him Alasdair first, then the baby, and when the children were safely on the bank she unsteadily edged her way along the boat and scrambled up the slimy steps onto the jetty. Blossoms of brilliant hues, all growing wild, broke the monotony of straggling green undergrowth until at last they reached the end of the pathway.

They both stopped and stared ahead of them, each with diverse emotions. Darnley's heart sank as he took in the overgrown front yard, the flower beds choked with weeds which even raised impudent tendrils up the front steps. The house of faded pink brick was sadly in need of repair and there was no sign of life. The whole place reminded him of how Kircaldy had looked when he had returned after the hurricane and he had stood overcome with feelings of despair and desolation until he had seen Alizon standing in the pasture, staring at him. Some of his resolve dwindled as he faced the task that lay ahead, months of hard work, a year of back-breaking labour before Chawira's acres would yield their first crop.

In Anne's eyes Chawira was not a rundown plantation rapidly reverting back to the wilderness from which it had been carved. It was a big house, in need of repair, but she was able to visualise how it would be when she had finished with it. The overgrown acres and paddies she saw as a well-tended and thriving estate, an estate over which she would be mistress. Now she understood Darnley's determination to reclaim for his son what was his due. Part of this would belong to Adeline, too. As she stood in the hot sunshine, the baby sleeping peacefully in her arms, she vowed that her daughter would be a lady. Adeline would have the best of everything. She would be beautiful, of that she was certain, and when the time came for her to marry it would be into one of the old families from Goose Creek. Adeline was something very special. Adeline would have everything she had been denied. She looked up at Darnley and was surprised by the expression in his eyes. He looked as though he hated the place.

"It's beautiful, or at least it will be once we've fixed it up!" Her voice was firmly optimistic.

"It will take months of back-breaking work for both of us."

"Not for long, we'll get a couple of girls from the transports for the house and you can buy Negroes for the fields. Within a year you will hardly recognise this place!" Her tone invited no resistance and he offered none. She didn't care what Kircaldy had been, how big or how small or what memories lay there, she would make him forget everything about the place. He was what he had started out to be, what his father had trained him for — a planter. A 'Goose Creek Man', and she would see to it that his son and his daughter would never know the kind of world she came from. Her mother had been gently reared and she had passed some of her manners and breeding on to Anne; she would never disgrace him amongst the wives of his friends. Taking Alasdair by the hand she stepped forward. "Come along, Alasdair, let's have a good look at our new home!"

It was hard work. The Negroes that he had bought with the place had become accustomed to the lackadaisical ways of their previous mistress that they tried Darnley's patience sorely, while the two girls who tended the house were little better than slatterns. After a sharp talking-to with some succinct reminders of their position, given by Anne, they did improve, but there was a great deal of work she undertook herself. Everything had to be brought up-river from Charleston, but this was usually supervised by Darnley on his frequent trips to the town to attend to his warehouse.

In the months that followed the house was repaired and refurnished, the front yard and the pasture cleared of weeds and brambles, the silted-up paddies cleared and new irrigation ditches dug, and the rice crop and the indigo planted. More Negroes were bought and a nurse hired for the children who was also to act as a governess for Alasdair until such time as he needed a better qualified teacher. All this was due to the safe disposal of a certain cargo the *Gretta* had landed in Havana a month previously, which had brought back an undreamed-of profit.

Adeline continued to thrive and for the most part was a placid baby, but as she grew older it became clearer that a fiery temper matched the red-gold curls that clustered around her pale pink cheeks.

Once the plantation and the house were restored in part to their former grandeur and productivity, Anne broached the subject of making the acquaintance of their neighbours. One or two men had called within the first month or so to offer Darnley help and encouragement if he should need it. Their offers had been graciously received and their help repaid, but there had been no official visits, nor had they thought it necessary to bring their wives and daughters on social calls.

"There's still plenty of work to be done here, I've no time to go gadding about the county making polite conversation and listening to the insufferable nonsense you women talk!"

"I was merely thinking of the children. . . ."

"You were merely thinking it was high time you became the lady of the manor—you don't fool me, Anne!"

She glared at him but managed to suppress the sharp words that instantly rose to rebuke him. "Do you want Alasdair growing up without friends of his own age? Do you want to see Adeline shunned? Do you want polite society to look with disdain on your son and daughter?"

The words hit their target as she had intended.

"No, but you will have to arrange the matter yourself, I have too much to do!"

A smile of triumph played around her mouth, but it was short-lived, for turning on his heel he left her. She watched him go quickly down the steps. He threw himself into the saddle and was soon gone, riding briskly down the neat avenue towards the road that led to the town. She watched him go with a sinking feeling in her stomach. As usual she had got her own way, but lately she felt as though she was losing her hold on him. She had quickly dismissed such thoughts as stupid fancies when they had arisen, but recently they had become more frequent. She found herself watching him, searching his face, listening hard for the note of impatience in his voice. He did not come to her bed every night as he had used to do, though his visits were still frequent and at least in their lovemaking nothing seemed to have changed, but at times like this she wondered about their relationship.

She turned away from the window and sat down at the small oak writing-desk, taking out the inlaid box that contained her quills, ink-horn, sand and parchments. Gazing idly out across the green lawns she traced the profile of her nose with the feathered quill. What form of social gathering would be best, she wondered? A small evening supper party, an evening soiree on the lawn at the back of the house where the ladies could sit beneath the arbour lit with small candles? She decided on the supper party. She made a list of prospective guests and then began to write out letters of invitation for the following Sunday evening. By Charleston standards she was determined that it would be a grand affair, not so ostentatious that it would be deemed ill-bred, but with ample varieties of food and wine to ensure that their neighbours were suitably impressed.

The invitations were sent out, the menu decided upon, the food ordered and brought from Charleston, the servants instructed in minute detail as to their duties and behaviour, the house scrubbed and cleaned until she was satisfied and everyone was exhausted and Darnley extremely irritated.

"Is this absolutely necessary? It seems to me that a great deal of money has been spent when a simple supper would have sufficed!"

"Don't be so parsimonious! Do you want everyone to think we are poor?"

"We are not exactly rich. How much did this cost?" He picked up the pale green silk dress frothing at the sleeves and neck with layers of delicate cobwebby lace.

She ignored him but continued to comb out her hair, though she did stare at him irritably through the imported Venetian mirror.

"How much?"

"Enough! Do you want me to wear homespun?" she snapped. Her nerves were on edge and she felt tired, although she would not admit it. She had refused his advances for the past two nights because she was so weary, and now she remembered how coldly he had looked at her before he left her room.

He made an explosive sound but she did not look at him. She heard the latch being lifted on the door and she turned.

"Darnley, please do me the consideration of staying reasonably sober, at least until supper has been served!"

"Don't worry, Anne, I can hold my liquor, if I have to!" was his parting shot. In fact he was nervous, afraid of once more venturing into the old society who — he knew — speculated about the position of Alasdair in his household, and speculated too about his "tavern" wife. He was worried. He had been out of society too long and he felt unsure of himself. He went to the small back parlour and poured himself a glass of brandy. . . .

The front door stood wide open and the sweet cloying scent of magnolias and peach blossom was heavy on the air, mingling with the smell of the candles which illuminated the hallway so that it was almost as bright as day. Those same candles added to the heat of the night. Anne stood beneath the circular wrought-iron chandelier that held a dozen small perfumed lights, each covered by a glass shade. The light played upon the blue-black lights in her high-swept hair. The green silk folds of her skirt billowed around her, caught up at the hemline with knots of white ribbon, like a gently swaying, rippling sea, crested with white wavelets. The deep square neckline was edged with ruffles of lace, the bodice tight, revealing her shapely breasts and small waist, and around her neck she wore a collar of silver filigree interspersed with small emeralds and diamonds, a present from Darnley. She tapped her foot in its high-heeled slipper irritably. There was no sign of Darnley.

The first of the carriages was heard upon the gravelled drive, and with an impatient gesture she sent young Meggy off to find him. Inwardly she fumed, the smile on her face fixed and brittle, only the gently heaving bosom betraying her agitation at being forced to greet her guests alone. Half an hour had passed and there was still no sign of him or Meggy. Her anger mounted, visible only by the two bright spots of colour that burned in her cheeks and the unusual brightness of her eyes.

He was determined to ruin the evening, she thought, he had disagreed with everything she had suggested, when he showed any interest at all! He knew how much the party meant to her and was determined to spoil it out of spite. She excused him to her guests as best she could and then sent another girl to find him. The glasses of Madeira wine were passed around and she realised that she could not delay the supper for much longer, it would be ruined! It was becoming apparent that her guests were whispering amongst themselves, and she caught a few sympathetic looks from the ladies present.

At last she could stand it no longer. Excusing herself upon the pretext of issuing some important but hitherto overlooked instruction to her cook, she left the small room she had made into a salon. Fury now blazed openly in her eyes and she tore viciously at the lace kerchief in her hand. She would never forgive him for this, never! He need not come grovelling to her again when his lust needed satisfying! He had made her look a complete fool in front of half the county and for this she would never forgive him!

She went first to his bedroom and then to his study but both rooms were empty. She ran lightly down the staircase, hearing the chatter of her guests from the room across the hall. The front parlour was already set for supper so she did not try there, instead she went to the small back parlour that they used for everyday. She pushed open the door and then stood stock still, shock and incredulity replacing anger as her eyes took in the scene. On the long settle lay Meggy, her hair tumbled from its cap, the bodice of her dress open to the waist revealing small pointed breasts, her skirts pushed high around her thighs. Lying on top of her, his neckcloth crumpled and stained with wine, his coat discarded and his breeches undone, was Darnley. Neither of them had noticed her. Meggy's eyes were closed and her breath was coming in short bursts while Darnley worked frantically between the slim thighs.

"You bastard! You whoring, drunken bastard!" she yelled, forgetful of her guests.

Meggy's eyes flew open and she uttered a frightened scream, pushing Darnley away from her and trying to cover her naked breasts with her hands. Darnley rolled off her and she jumped to her feet, pulling down her skirts. Anne's eyes never left him as he lay there face downwards, hating himself.

"Get out! By God! I'll see you are flogged for this and sold! Get out!" she yelled at the terrified girl. As Meggy scampered away Anne crossed to the settle and Darnley's prostrate form. She was shaking with anger, but it was anger born of humiliation and hurt. She had loved him, worked with him to build Chawira to what it now was, while he . . . he had thrown it all in her face, tumbling any willing wench under her very nose and across the hall from a room full of guests! Was Meggy the first, she wondered, or had he lain with all the others, even the handsome, statuesque Negro women — it was not unknown? But tonight. . . . "Get up and face me, or haven't you got the courage?" she taunted him.

Slowly he turned over and lay eyeing her, a sneer on his face.

"I suppose you've laid all my maids in turn, probably on the nights you haven't sought my bed?"

"I may have." His guilt and shame suddenly resolved itself into a resentment that she was Anne, and not Alizon.

She wanted to claw out those amber eyes, to rake that handsome, degenerate face with her nails until the blood ran and no woman would ever look at him again. Instead she hit out with the only weapon she could think of. "It's no wonder you were turned down by a bond servant! If she lacked everything else, Alizon certainly did not lack discrimination, she knew you for what you are, didn't she, Darnley? That's why she would have none of you, she knew you for the whoremongering drunkard you are, that's why you could not agree over Alasdair and no wonder!" Her laughter was cutting. "A fine example to your son! No wonder she took everything and left! She had sense, which is more than I can say for myself until this night! Our bargain is broken!"

She knew her words had hit home for as he jumped to his feet, adjusting his breeches, she saw his face contort with rage and hurt.

"You're not fit to speak of her!"

She faced him squarely. "Nor, it seems, are you! If she were above the common drab as you say she was, then it's no wonder she wanted to place an ocean between herself and any memory of you!"

He drew back his arm and she steeled herself for the blow. "Strike me and I'll kill you, Darnley Kirkbride! I've nothing to lose, not now! Strike me and you'll never sleep in peace, you'll be wondering, watching, waiting, never knowing when, but certain that I will come and for you death won't be easy!"

He dropped his arm. She had spoken in the coldest, deadliest of tones and he knew she meant every word. "We had no bargain concerning fidelity."

She wanted to cry out that she had thought there was no need for one, she had loved him and she had thought he loved her: instead she jerked up her chin and eyed him with venom. "No, that's correct, but two can play at that game! I'm attractive, I have a beautiful body — you've told me often enough, and I shall take as many lovers as I please from now on!"

Again she saw the tightening of the muscles in his face and watched his hands clench and unclench.

"What you can do, so can I!"

"You do that and I'll turn you out!"

"Turn me out and the whole of Charleston will know the truth about Alasdair — that he is not your adopted son, but a bastard!"

She thought then that he was going to kill her, and she quailed beneath the force of hatred in his eyes. She paled and her hand went to her throat but she held her head steady, her eyes never leaving his face. Some base instinct of survival told her not to show fear. "In that, then, we do have a bargain! I'll keep my silence as long as you don't interfere with my life. Oh, don't worry, I'll be discreet, after all I have Adeline to think of. Just remember, Darnley, this is one bargain that will be kept!" she hissed. "And now we have guests to attend to, or had you forgotten?" she asked smoothly, indicating his discarded coat before she turned towards the door.

How Anne got through that dreadful evening she never knew. The smile on her face was so set it made her muscles ache to maintain it. She laughed, but the laughter was hollow and too shrill. She feigned interest in the conversation of her guests, but her mind behind the smiling lips and bright eyes was numb. Her head was aching abominably, the leather and bone corset beneath the tight bodice was hot, uncomfortable and made breathing difficult and more than once she thought she would faint. Every now and then she would glance furtively at the clock on the overmantle. How slowly time was passing, would they never go away? She had passed a few over-sweet comments to Darnley at the table but she avoided him whenever possible, not daring to look at him lest her anger break through her mask.

After what seemed an eternity the sound of the last carriage died away in the distance, and she turned and slowly and wearily mounted the staircase, calling for Dora to come and unlace her. Once the restricting corset had been removed she breathed deeply, feeling stronger. Dora brushed out her hair and passed her two pads of cotton soaked in rosewater which she pressed against her throbbing head. Clad only in her chemise she dismissed the girl and pulled a chair close to the open window, leaning her head back on the small herb-filled cushion Dora had brought. She felt drained of all emotions. Numb, confused, rejected and angry. What could she do? She could leave Darnley but where would she go, back to her father and the Barque Minerva?

She had no money of her own, and there were Alasdair and Adeline to think of. She had vowed to have the best for Adeline and what could she hope to give the child if she left Chawira? Nothing. Nothing at all! He was the first and only man she had given her heart to, at first it had been out of gratitude, but then she had grown to love him. What a blind, stupid fool she'd been! A man like Darnley would only take to wife such as she out of sheer necessity. He had never loved her. Their marriage had been for convenience, she had known that from the beginning, but she had soon forgotten it in his arms, listening to and believing his endearments, his lies!

She leaned her arms on the sill and breathed in the heavy perfumes of the night, then rested her still-throbbing head on her arms. What could she hope for now out of life? She had her dream. She was the wife of a planter, a gentleman. She had social position and so did her child, she had everything she had longed for but now it was not enough. Love had not been a part of her dream, ambition only had driven her, but somehow love had crept in and it had destroyed her and her dream.

All she had left was Adeline. The threat of taking a lover had been empty for she wanted no one but him, nor would she spoil her daughter's chances by loose morals. He could go to hell from now on. She would centre all her attention on the children, lavish on them all the love she felt for Darnley. Her life would revolve entirely around Alasdair and Adeline. There was nothing she would not endure for them, not even if it meant years of misery and rejection on his part, for she could never forgive him, it was not in her nature to forgive and forget. She had been hurt too deeply, and the wound would rankle and fester in the years that would follow. Bitter years they would be, she knew that, and how many of them? She was young.

She looked out across the now silent driveway and neat clipped lawns bathed in moonlight. She was condemning herself to perhaps twenty years of misery, but somehow she would survive it. She no longer wondered idly about Alizon. Had Darnley really loved her? Alizon had been hurt as she had been, but even more, for she had had to accept that Darnley and her son were dead. She felt now that she understood the girl whose pale shadow had seemed to stand between herself and Darnley. In a way Alizon was lucky, she thought miserably. She had gone home to Scotland where no doubt she had friends and family, while she . . . she must remain here, for there was nowhere else she could go.

Chapter 5

She leaned forward, gazing intently into the mirror, and scrutinised her reflection. Thirty-five! Where had the years gone? She gently smoothed the fine tracery of lines at the corners of her mouth and eyes. She was still beautiful, her figure was still trim, the years of sorrow and bitterness had not dealt too harshly with her. She drew back from the pool of candlelight illuminating the mirror and sat passively staring at herself as her young maid fastened the necklace around her throat. Fifteen years she had been married, years of unhappiness and a deep loneliness that she had borne with an outward courage and smiling countenance. Fifteen years that had turned her heart to stone and had made the two children the sole reason for her existence.

She thought back to that night, only a vague memory now, and her lips twisted into a bitter smile. She had been so naive, so trusting, so stupid to believe that he would actually come to love her. Oh, how many times over the years had she reminded herself that she had made a bargain, and a favourable one at that. Darnley had bought more and more land and the house had been extended and filled with expensive imported furniture, books, silver and crystal. She wanted for nothing, she held her desired place in society, and since that time he had treated her with courtesy and consideration. What more could she want? She had no right to ask for anything more, yet . . . yet she had been foolish enough to believe that he had loved her, long ago.

He had never slept with her after that night. She tweaked a soft tendril of dark hair further over one ear and her eyes were hard and cold in the mirror, as hard and cold as the diamonds that glistened around her throat. She had upbraided him almost publicly, not caring that her guests across the hallway might have been able to hear every word. It had been in the weeks afterwards that she had suffered for his indiscretion. The stifled sniggers, the looks of pity, embarrassment, the sentences cut short when she came within earshot. But she had weathered all that with her head held high and in time the gossip, the rumours had died away. He was no worse than any other husband.

He had mistresses, she knew that. A seemingly endless string of them. She knew but she ignored it, as other wives in Charleston knew but ignored it. She had also ignored his brief political escapade, "Broughton's Rebellion" as it was called. Colonel Tynte had succeeded Johnson as Governor but unfortunately he had died after a few months in office. The law stated that under such circumstances the Proprietors chose one of themselves to act as Governor and at that time there had only been three of them, Mr Robert Gibbs, Colonel Thomas Broughton (both Goose Creek men) and Mr Forteque Turbeville. Two sessions were called on the same day. At the afternoon session Turbeville voted for Gibbs who was proclaimed the new Governor, but who then had had an apoplexy and died.

It was then discovered that in the morning Turbeville had voted for Broughton, had been bribed during lunch and had changed his vote for Gibbs. Broughton had therefore claimed the office. The consequences were fraught and threatened to be bloody. Darnley had joined Broughton when he had ridden down from Mulberry. Gibbs had closed the gates and raised the drawbridge, but Darnley had been amongst those of the colonel's friends in the town who managed to lower it. There was rioting in the square at the foot of Broad Street and Darnley had been in the forefront. It had not endeared him to Gibbs, who held office until Edward Craven arrived a year later.

Anne had centred all her attention on the two children, supervising their education and their manners and well-being, teaching Adeline her letters herself from a little hornbook, sitting with her as she laboured over the stitches of her sampler and unpicking the tangled mess of silks. She smiled and turned to look at the young girl who was perched on the edge of the bed, her feet tucked beneath her skirts.

"How do I look?" she questioned.

Adeline cocked her head on one side. "You never look any older, Mother."

Anne sighed, fingering the necklace. By the standards of her day she was middle-aged and she had little in life to look forward to. She smiled again at her daughter. Adeline was becoming a beauty, she thought proudly. She was slim like herself, her features were delicate, her skin ivory. She had thick red-gold hair that curled naturally and her eyes were russet with tiny flecks of amber in their depths. The sweeping delicate brows were a shade darker than her hair, and her eyes were fringed with thick deep gold lashes. Adeline was fifteen. Reluctantly Anne realised that soon she would have to think of suitors for her daughter, and once married... she could not pursue that train of thought. She would not, could not bear to contemplate life bereft of Adeline, with her quick spontaneous laughter and equally quick temper.

And there was Alasdair, Alasdair with his father's colouring but his dark eyes, presumably like his mother's. Alasdair whom she loved as her own son. He would marry first and leave her. He had a kind, considerate nature but was not without courage: stubbornness, Darnley called it. Once Alasdair believed in something nothing could shake him from his belief, nothing could shatter his loyalty. She smoothed out the wide skirts of her dress, pushing from her mind the thought of the endless days of loneliness that would face her when these two had gone to live their own lives.

"Why can't I just stay up for supper?" Adeline begged in what she knew was her most appealing tone, one her mother could usually never refuse.

"You know why, you are too young. Next year...."

Adeline's mouth drooped at the corners.

"You know if it was left to me you could take supper with our guests but your father...."

"He's just plain miserable, he wants to keep me locked up forever, he doesn't want me to grow up!"

"Neither do I, I wish . . . I wish you could stay just as you are now."

"I'm fifteen, Mother! Soon I'll be able to go to balls and suppers and be courted by lots of handsome young men."

"Adeline! When I hear you talk like that I wonder if I haven't spoiled you!"

"Alasdair is allowed to stay up."

"Alasdair is almost a man. . . ."

"And old enough to chase after everything in petticoats!"

"Adeline, that's enough!"

Adeline pouted at the reprimand. "It's true."

"Even if it is, I don't want you mentioning it again. Now I must go down, you take supper in your room and I'll look in on you later." Anne picked up the carved ivory fan from the lowboy and turned towards the door. Adeline was sulking, but she went over and kissed her lightly on the forehead. "You'll have your excitement soon, I promise!"

Downstairs a few of the guests had already arrived and she soon forgot her daughter's mood as she went forward to greet them. It was a part she had played so successfully over the years that now it was second nature to her, she hardly noticed it. It had become effortless, and sometimes she admitted to herself that she enjoyed these social occasions, at least they broke the boredom and monotony of her life.

When dinner was over, as the evening was warm, the ladies went out to sit on the front porch, to chat and breathe in the scent and sounds of the night. After a little while the gentlemen followed them and soon everyone was engaged in conversation. It was some time before the noise became audible over their voices: it was the dull thudding of hooves on the turf. Everyone stared into the darkness.

"Who the hell is it at this time of night and cutting across the pastures?" Darnley asked impatiently, voicing the thoughts of his guests. The sound of hooves became louder, accompanied by the grating sound of flying gravel as the rider came up the drive.

Darnley ran quickly down the front steps. "It's Ashe, by God! Hold up there, Edward! Why in God's name are you riding like a madman at this time of night? Is it Elizabeth, has she taken a turn for the worse?" he cried, for Elizabeth's delicate state of health was the reason for their absence at dinner.

Edward Ashe sawed savagely at the bit and slid from the saddle as the horse stopped. Its muzzle was flecked with foam and it was sweating profusely. Darnley called for his groom before taking Ashe by the arm and leading him towards the house.

Their arrival was greeted by a chorus of raised voices. Darnley thrust a glass into his hand, and after taking a deep gulp Ashe explained the reason for his wild ride.

"The Yemassees have risen and are sweeping the country for fifty miles! The Governor was uneasy, he had heard rumours. . . ."

"Yes, we all know that, he sent Nairne to visit Pocotaligo with some other men. . . ."

"The Yemassees slaughtered them all except Burroughs! He swam across the river, ran through the woods to Port Royal and raised the alarm—he saved about three hundred people around St Helena. A merchantman took them aboard. But the Creeks and Cherokees have joined them!" He took another gulp from the glass.

"Where are they now?" Darnley asked.

"Burning and killing between the Combahee and the Stono rivers!"

There were gasps from the ladies and curses from the men, for the Stono river was only ten miles from Charleston, which made the plantations along the Ashley and the Cooper rivers terribly vulnerable.

"What are we to do?" Anne voiced the question that was on the lips of every woman present.

"The Governor is assembling the militia—the outlying plantations are to be fortified as best they can. Wancot, Schinking and Mulberry are already fortified, but if I were you, Darnley, I'd get Anne and the children into Charleston as soon as possible, and I recommend that all you gentlemen do the same!"

"But there are not enough men to repulse large numbers, and if the Creeks and Cherokees are with them. . . ." Richard Seaton interrupted.

"The Governor is sending to North Carolina and Virginia for help and is sending Mde la Conseilliere to New England for arms. Get your families into town, gentlemen, tonight!" Ashe advised.

A strange stillness seemed to hang over them all and for a second they stood as though rooted to the ground, staring blankly at Edward Ashe and Darnley. Anne's heart turned over; the fear that held them temporarily in its grip was almost tangible. Then they were galvanised by the sound of Richard Seaton calling for his carriage. Gone was the conviviality: a mild panic had taken its place.

"Get Alasdair and Adeline and all the servants, pack up what you can! We'll take most of the Negroes in the wagons with us, they hate and fear the Yemassees as much as any of us!"

"How long will it be before we can return here?" Anne asked quietly.

"How do I know! We may never come back, there may not be a house to come back to!" Grimly Darnley thought of the years of labour, the money that had gone into making Chawira what it was now. Would he return to find it a smoking ruin, the fields churned up, the paddies and crops ruined? "Get packed as quickly as you can!" The grim tones of his voice sent shudders down Anne's spine.

Adeline was not in the least bit afraid, she viewed the whole affair as one of great excitement. Alasdair had begged his father to be allowed to stay on, to help fight and subdue Sanute, the Yemassee chief, but Darnley had been firm to the point of anger. They were all going to Charleston. He was to join Colonel Broughton, and Anne, Adeline and Alasdair were to stay with Mrs Ashe, well within the city walls. The boy was rebellious.

"I'm nearly nineteen! I'm a man! The Governor has called for all able-bodied men and I'm old enough!"

Darnley looked at his son and pride tugged at his heart. He was proud and adventurous and would make a good soldier, but not yet. . . . As he watched the boy turn and walk away, his shoulders set firmly back, his head held high, he was reminded forcefully of Alizon. She had never accepted defeat, the mere thought of it was offensive to her, she would fight on for what she believed in. If it were she not Anne who was here with him now she would have refused to go to safety in the town, she would have been obstinate, deaf to all entreaties and demands.

The door opened and for a fraction of a second he looked up expecting to see Alizon standing there. It was Anne, and reason asserted itself.

"Everything is ready. I've packed as much as possible and the Negroes are being shepherded into the wagons, some of them have already run off."

He didn't reply so she continued, "It will be impossible to take any stock with us, best to turn them loose to take their chance in the river bottoms." She looked around the room. The large pieces of furniture it was impossible to take, but she had packed most of her china and silver, her jewels and some smaller pieces. Strangely she felt no sadness, no regret at leaving Chawira undefended. It had been her home now for over fifteen years, but it lacked the one thing that made a house a home: love. She was not sorry to be leaving. The only thing that mattered was that Adeline and Alasdair were safe.

She had heard some of the men talking before they had left, they said there was the possibility that this would be a long and bitter campaign, there was talk that the Governor was sending to England for help. But the English had a new king now, a German, and from what news had filtered through he was not popular and she doubted that he would have time to worry about the Colonies. By the time help arrived from England, if it arrived at all, they might all be dead. She shivered. She had faced it all before, as had all the others. Indian raids, crop failures, disease, hurricane, but that had been before . . . before she had had Adeline. Nothing was going to harm or frighten her daughter; she was not to be subjected to danger. An idea was forming in her mind, one she had toyed with many times before in a half-hearted way, but now, although chaos reigned around her, she calmly made her plans.

They reached Charleston without any hindrance, except for the wagons and carriages of the other planters, for the women and children from plantations twenty miles outside the town were being brought to safety. They were all greeted with open arms by Elizabeth Ashe who, since she had heard the news, had been terrified that they would be overtaken by the savages before they reached the town. Charleston was bustling with activity despite the early hour. The sun, rising in a burst of flaming brilliance, tinted the buildings a delicate shade of pink and turned the waters of the harbour into an expanse of molten gold. Viewed from the bedroom window of the Ashes' house the sunrise was of exquisite beauty, Adeline thought, as she leaned her arms on the sill and cupped her chin in her palms. She looked down into the busy street. At least there was plenty to see and no doubt to do: life in Charleston was going to be far more lively and interesting than at Chawira.

"Sleep, Adeline! Into bed now, you can hardly have had more than two hours all night," Anne admonished.

Adeline turned reluctantly from the window. "I'm not tired, besides, how can I sleep with so much going on? It's so exciting to be here, I much prefer to live in town than out in the country."

Anne smiled wanly. She was tired and aching after the exhausting night and slow bumpy journey over the rough roads. "Well, I'm tired. Now no more complaints, into bed, then later on after lunch we will take a turn around the town. But only if you sleep now!" she threatened, seeing the excited gleam in Adeline's eyes.

"Where has Father gone?"

"To the Governor's house with Edward."

"Has Alasdair gone, too?"

"No!" Anne replied sharply, thinking of the scene that had taken place between Darnley and his son.

"Father thinks he is too young to fight, doesn't he?"

"Yes, and so do I. Eighteen is too young to go out against those . . . those savages. He could be killed!"

"I don't think he's too young!"

"No one asked you for your opinion, miss! Don't let your father hear you airing such views. Now sleep. It's been a long night!"

When Anne awoke it was past lunch-time. Her head felt muzzy and her limbs ached from the jolting journey. She rose, washed and dressed and went down to find Adeline and Alasdair in the parlour with Elizabeth.

"Are you ready to go out now?" Adeline cried as soon as she set eyes on her mother.

"Adeline, dear, your poor mama has only just woken up, let her collect herself, take some tea. . . ."

Adeline sat down again.

"I'll take her," Alasdair offered, eager himself to be out to see what was happening.

Anne looked from one to the other, unsure as to whether either of them could be trusted. She took the cup Elizabeth offered and sipped the tea.

"Please can we go, Mother? I can make sure Alasdair doesn't slip off and join the militia, and he can make sure that I don't get into mischief."

Anne's head was still aching and reluctantly she agreed, covering her ears with her hands to shut out the cries of delight as the two disappeared to summon the carriage.

They came to no harm, so she allowed them to ride each morning. Darnley was away from the house for long spells, and four days later he came home to tell them that the militia was riding out to attack and drive back the Yemassees on the further bank of the Stono. Alasdair was sullen and resentful because he was not going too, and for the first time Adeline felt afraid, wondering what would happen to them if her father were killed, or the whole of Charleston overrun.

Anne knew that the time had come to voice her plans and if possible to gain his approval. She could leave it no longer, for she had no idea when he would next return, if he returned at all. The thought sent fear shooting through her. She had come to rely on him over the years, and although there was no love between them he was her security, a buffer against the world. She shook the mood off. The children came first.

She found him deep in conversation with Edward, who was home for the same reason.

"I'm sorry to interrupt, but could I have a word with you, Darnley, in private? There is something I want to ask you."

He was clearly irritated by her request, thinking it some trivial matter. Edward excused himself and Darnley began gathering together his musket, powder-horn and pouches of shot. "Well, Anne, what is so urgent?"

No word of regret at his departure, she thought. No word of consolation, not even the blatant lie that other husbands were telling their disbelieving wives—that everything would be back to normal in a few days. That it would all be over soon. No word of this kind to her. "This . . . this rising will not be over within a few days, will it, Darnley?"

He looked up at her. It was useless to lie, even if he had the inclination to do so. "No. They have more men than we have, and they have the backing of the Spaniards at St Augustine."

She paled. She had suspected as much, but hearing it spoken aloud unnerved her. "I know. That is why I want your permission to take Alasdair and Adeline on a tour of Europe. You've mentioned it yourself many times. A trip to complete their education. And now is the time!" She saw the look of mistrust in his eyes. "How long do you think I will be able to hold Alasdair here once you have gone? He's fretting and fuming to be away now. Without your restraining hand he will be off to join Rhett, or Moore or Ravenel, and I'll not be able to stop him! He will be safer with me, then when it's all over we will be able to come home."

He could see the sound reasoning in her request. The boy was hot-headed and eager to fight, but what if they never came back? What if he was never to see his son again? The questions were driven away before the other fears that flooded his mind. What if they were to return to find Chawira a smoke-blackened shell amidst the wilderness that would quickly reclaim it, with only the bellow of the alligators in the swamps and the cries of the reed birds to break the eerie stillness. What legacy was that for Alasdair?

"Will he go?" he asked.

"I don't know, I haven't mentioned it to him yet. There will be no trouble with Adeline. She'll view the whole affair as a thrilling adventure and she's becoming nervous here. . . ."

"You spoil her! You'll rue the day, Anne, I warn you! She's headstrong and feather-brained!"

"Headstrong yes, but she has plenty of brains, she's no fool! If Alasdair is agreeable will you let us go?"

He seemed to be studying the powder-horn he held, but she knew that he was fighting himself. Either way he might never see his son again, but at least if he, Darnley, survived and Charleston survived, then when Alasdair came back there would be something here. . . .

"If he refuses, I'll speak to him."

"You'll let us go?"

"On one condition."

"Yes?" She waited expectantly.

"That when this war is over you'll come back at once and bring both children with you?"

"That was my intention from the beginning!"

"You're not lying to me, Anne? I know . . . know there have been times when we. . . ." He spread his hands in a vague gesture.

"I know, but that is between us, it has nothing to do with the future of the children. Charleston is their home and I'll bring them back, whether you are here . . . or not."

"If . . . if I'm not here, then Chawira belongs to Alasdair. He'll be old enough to run it efficiently."

"He will have you to teach him!" she stated firmly, her tone offering no contradiction.

"When will you go?"

"As soon as we can find a ship."

"Where will you go first? You have a choice now that France, Spain and England are no longer at war."

"London, then Paris, then . . . we'll see."

He smiled wryly. "You've been thinking about it for some time, haven't you?"

"Yes. Alasdair is becoming restless, and Adeline will learn how to behave in polite society. And above all, they will be safe."

"I pray they will be! I took Alasdair away once before and we were lucky to escape with our lives."

"Travelling is always hazardous, but it will be more hazardous to stay here."

He had to agree with her. Alasdair would run off to join Rhett as soon as his back was turned, he was better out of harm's way. "Let me know how much money you will need and I will draw up a draft."

She felt deflated; it had all been settled without a cross word. She had expected him to oppose her, she had hoped that he would have made some attempt to persuade her to stay. She shrugged. She had hoped for too much. The only person he cared about was Alasdair, even Adeline, his flesh and blood as much as was Alasdair, drew no concern. It had always been the same. Alizon's child. . . . At times like this she felt resentful and hurt, jealous of the relationship between him and the boy. At times they seemed so close they excluded herself and her daughter from their world. She shrugged again. She knew there would be difficulties from Alasdair, for she had judged correctly that he would run off as soon as her back was turned, but she would leave him to his father to deal with.

She sat down in the armchair and leaned her head wearily against the winged back. London then Paris she had told him, but what if instead of going on to Paris she were to go north to Scotland? She was seized with a burning curiosity to see the woman she felt had stood between herself and Darnley all these years. He would have been happy married to Alizon, she was sure of that. Just what powers did Alizon have and why had she been so determined to go back to Scotland to farm what Darnley had called a wilderness? Alasdair was her son, but a son she believed dead. She had loved and cared for him all these years yet. . . . Bitter resentment grew as she thought about the relationship between Darnley and Alasdair, and of the times that he had hurt and humiliated her. What if the boy were to learn the truth? What would he do then? And Alizon, how would she feel? A fierce determination took hold of her. From London she would go to Edinburgh, not Paris, she would find Alizon and then . . . to hell with Darnley Kirkbride!

Chapter 6

London was a city of contrasts. The bustling crowded streets where beggars rubbed shoulders with the rich and titled; the fine houses of the rich in spacious squares, the alleys and slums that bordered the river, harbouring all manner of human debris. The palaces and churches, the taverns and stews and gin and coffee shops. And the river itself clear and sparkling at Hampton, racing in a polluted, murky torrent between the arches of London Bridge. The Thames was still crowded with craft from barges to lighters, even though the hackney carriage and the sedan chair had taken much of the waterman's business, crowding and choking the thoroughfares. London was noisy, beautiful, exuberant, dirty and corrupt, but to their colonial eyes it was magnificent.

After an uneventful voyage, for which Anne was thankful, they had arrived in the Pool of London at the beginning of August. They had stayed first at The Eagle in Gracechurch Street, but after a few days in the broiling city, suffering the stench that arose from the river and the Fleet Ditch and the gutters, she had moved them all to The Angel in Clerkenwell. The inn was the last stage of the coach route from the north and so its customers did not usually stay long before going on into the city.

They had passed the first week seeing the sights, from

the grim Tower to Wren's masterpiece, St Paul's Cathedral. But the city was uneasy. You could feel it in the air, Anne thought. It wasn't just the heat, the smells, the threat of plague, it was the people's dissatisfaction with their new king. She heard snatches of conversation in the tap room and the gossiping of the maids on the stairs.

The new monarch was unpopular: he was too German in his tastes and made no secret of the fact that he preferred Hanover to England. He spoke only a few words of English and so far had made no attempt to improve his linguistic experience. His callous treatment of his wife, Caroline, was freely discussed and disapproved of. So she had been indiscreet and had taken a lover, was that any excuse to lock her up in some damp castle in Germany? These were the comments expressed by the two maids Anne had heard talking outside her door. He had his mistresses, though his taste in women was appalling, one maid had declared, and this had been followed by an outburst of laughter. The royal pair had been christened the Elephant and the Maypole by the Londoners. One so fat, the other so tall and thin. The king was known to dislike his son intensely and he seemed determined to alienate most of the peers. "We'd have been better off with Scottish James, Papist though he is!" were the words that had finished the conversation.

Anne had been even more disturbed by this. There was talk of an attempt by James Stuart to regain his father's crown; had she brought the youngsters away from one danger only to face another? She gave the matter a great deal of thought. The weather showed no sign of becoming cooler, and sickness was rife. She had seen enough of this city, so huge that it made Charleston look like a hamlet.

She decided to break the news to Alasdair and Adeline at dinner. Alasdair had escorted Adeline on a shopping expedition, but a violent headache had kept Anne in her room, where the stale oppressive air did nothing to alleviate the dull throb in her temples. All her life she had lived in the semi-tropical climate of South Carolina, but in Charleston there was room to breathe, no crowded buildings shut out the sunlight, and the clean air and the breezes that swept in from the ocean were warm, refreshing and free from disease.

The desire to find Alizon had grown until now it was almost an obsession. Anne had convinced herself that it was her duty to tell Alasdair the truth, and to lift some of the burden of grief that Alizon had borne all these years. She had spoken to the landlord who had promised to book seats for them on the next stage to Edinburgh, though he did warn her that it was a long and tiring journey that was sometimes hazardous. She had replied that she had withstood the attacks of plague and Indians and would no doubt find the journey not in the least hazardous, unless of course they had wild heathen savages in Britain? He had laughed and remarked that there were none of those in England but that she might well find some once she crossed the border, for the tales he had heard of the men of the Highlands seemed to correspond with her description of the Yemassee tribe.

Her headache had lifted slightly when Adeline and Alasdair arrived back. Adeline was in transports of excitement over her purchases with which Alasdair was manfully struggling.

"It's the most beautiful dress you have ever seen, Mama! With gloves of the finest, softest kid to match and satin slippers with rosettes on the toes!"

"And where do you think you will be wearing all this finery?"

"Surely we will be invited by someone to dinner?"

"Who? We don't know anyone. You'll have to wait until we get home to wear it all, I told you that when you insisted on buying it!" Alasdair, having spent the whole of the scorching afternoon trailing around after his sister, was hot, tired, hungry and in no mood for one of Adeline's tantrums.

"Alasdair is right, you know, I'm afraid no one is likely to invite us out, and you can't very well wear it for dinner here," Anne agreed.

"Oh! Well! At least I'll be the envy of everyone when we get home. I'm bound to wear it in Paris, we must get invited somewhere by someone, maybe the opera!"

"We are not going to Paris, not yet!" Anne's words had the effect of stirring interest in Alasdair and open annoyance in Adeline.

"Why?"

"Where are we going?" Alasdair had sat up straight in his chair, the weariness gone from him.

"Edinburgh."

"Edinburgh!" Adeline echoed. "That's miles away and I've heard the maid say that Scotland is full of half-wild men who wear skirts like women and burn and kill! We might just as well go home and put up with the Yemassees!"

"Shut up! You listen to too much gossip!"

Adeline glowered at her brother.

"My mother came from Scotland, didn't she?"

Anne nodded.

"She came from a place called Glencoe, my father told me years ago. She had lived through a terrible massacre and because she had tried to kill one of the men who murdered her family she was transported."

Anne noticed the note of pride, the question that lay in his words. Now was the time to tell him! She must do it now! Her heart began to race and the dull throb over her left temple increased. But how was she to tell him without telling him also that he was a bastard? She stared directly at him. He was almost a man now. He was tall for his age and broad-shouldered. He wore his hair unpowdered and tied back with a plain black band, disdaining the curled and powdered wigs. The dark brown eyes regarded her with approbation mingled with a rising expectation.

"Your mother isn't dead, Alasdair. At least, I don't think so!"

His gaze remained steady, but she watched the colour slowly drain from his face until it was ashen and his lips were bloodless.

She rose quickly and eased him down into the chair, ignoring the shriek of surprise uttered by Adeline. "I know it is a shock, but I think it is time the truth were told."

He said nothing, digesting her words while she was

also silent, knowing it best to let him take his time. He was stunned. All his life he had believed that his mother was dead. His father had told him that she had died of the fever, but strangely he had never found her grave, though he had looked in St Michael's churchyard often enough, and now . . . now Anne was telling him that she was alive!

"Why . . . why . . . ?"

"Your father and she quarrelled, and in a fit of anger and to spite her he took you away. Took you on a vessel bound for Boston but the ship was wrecked. Somehow you both escaped, but everyone believed you had died. There was nothing left in Charleston for your mother, so she sold Kircaldy and went back to Scotland."

"I . . . I often wondered why my father was so bitter about Kircaldy. He used to say one day he would get it back for me. I . . . I often wondered what she looked like. Was she pretty, what her voice sounded like. . . ." His words trailed off and the silence hung heavily in the room.

Anne pressed him no further, knowing that soon the question she dreaded would form in his mind and he would give it utterance. She hoped she had the strength to answer without destroying him. She turned to her daughter. "Adeline, dear, go down and see what has happened to dinner. I ordered it to be served up here. Tell Mistress Horsham that we will take a glass of wine before the meal, I think we all need it!"

Without argument Adeline did as she was bid, and as soon as she had gone Anne turned again to face Alasdair. She saw the question in his eyes.

"Then . . . then if my mother is still alive and . . . and my father knew it, he could not have married you?"

"He was never married to your mother, Alasdair. Your mother was married to Bradley Kirkbride."

"Then . . . then Bradley Kirkbride was my father . . . or am I a . . . ?"

"Your mother will be able to explain it all better than I, that is why we are going to Edinburgh, to find her."

He seemed unable to take in her words. He was so confused. Darnley whom he loved and had looked to for confidence and comfort had lied to him. His mother was alive and he... he was a bastard. The word seemed to resound in his head like the loud, jarring sound of the tocsin, sounding out a warning. Don't think about it! Don't think about it, the sound seemed to say.

"Why did you tell me?"

"I have my reasons."

He got slowly to his feet, his shoulders stooped, and reaching out he grasped her wrist. "What reasons? I know you have never been happy, but... but do you hate him so much?"

"No. You must believe that! I loved him once, until he betrayed me, but even the pain of that dulled with time. Your mother has suffered enough, for years she has believed you dead. Can you imagine what her life has been like? Your father hurt her far more than he hurt me and he wanted to go on hurting her, wanting her to believe you dead!"

He dropped her wrist and sat down again, placing his hand over his face. "I don't know what to believe... who to believe!"

"Trust me, Alasdair! I love you, I've always loved you as if you were my own son! I would do nothing to harm you, but I believe that now you have a right to know the truth. You are grown almost to manhood, and a man must know the truth of his origins."

He raised haunted eyes and her heart went out to him. "What... what if she is dead? Fifteen years is a long time.... Then I will never know...."

She took his hand in her own; it was clammy. "You will know. Darnley will tell you. He will tell you the reasons he has lied to you for all this time, and whatever reasons he gives you must believe and be satisfied!"

"Adeline? What will you tell her?"

"Nothing. Not unless you want me to."

"But she'll work it out for herself!"

"Adeline never thinks further ahead than the next trinket or bonnet! She'll not give the matter another thought, except to curse the fact that we are not going to Paris!" She was smiling but her tone was rueful, and he, too, managed a weak attempt at a smile.

"I don't want anything to eat. I will go to my room, I want to think!"

She understood, thankful that he had taken it all so well. There was a strength of character in him that she had only just glimpsed. He had courage, she had often seen evidence of that. Not the hot-headed rashness of youth, but the quiet kind of courage from which a man draws his strength of conviction. She wondered if it was from Alizon that he had inherited this quality.

Adeline returned, followed by a maid bearing a large tray upon which reposed the first course of their meal, a bottle of wine and three glasses.

Anne indicated that she set it down on the table.

"Where's Alasdair?" Adeline asked when the girl had gone.

"He's not hungry, he's gone to his room. He needs time to think . . . to accustom himself to what has come as a shock. . . ."

"Why did Father tell us she was dead? And if she isn't dead why did he marry you?"

The glass shook in Anne's hand and a few drops of the deep red liquid spilled onto the skirt of her dress. Adeline had more sense than she had credited her with. "I don't know why he told us Alizon was dead, only he and Alizon can tell us that. As for the other question, all I can tell you is that my marriage to your father is legal, and Adeline, you'll not mention this to Alasdair!"

Adeline glanced up over the rim of her glass. She knew when she had gone far enough. She could twist her mother around her little finger most of the time, but there were occasions when she knew Anne would stand no nonsense and this was one of them. The stubborn streak in her made her try one last attempt. "Alizon Kirkbride?" she questioned.

"She was Alizon MacDonald from Glencoe when she came to Charleston, she married your grandfather! Now that's enough, Adeline! Let it be! Eat up your supper and then get yourself ready for bed—we have an early start in the morning. It's a long journey to Edinburgh!"

They took the stage for Edinburgh next morning. Although it was August and the air was warm, it was a dull, overcast day that threatened rain.

"Looks like we'll be 'avin' a storm before long!" the coachman said gloomily.

"It may help to clear the air and cool down the temperature," Anne ventured, for he looked decidely morose.

"'Appen it might at that, but it will turn the roads into mud tracks and like as not we'll get bogged down!"

Anne sighed, travel in England was as bad as it was in Charleston. There were other passengers standing on the apron of The Angel, some like themselves boarding the coach for Edinburgh, others for Derby, York and the northern counties. They were soon on their way, jolted and bumped by the rattling of the cumbersome vehicle. Alasdair had persuaded her to let him ride on top beside the coachman and she had agreed, but with the first heavy drops of rain and peal of thunder she had put her head out of the window and demanded that he climb inside, a request he chose either not to hear or to ignore.

"He'll be soaked to the skin and catch a chill!" she muttered irritably.

"He's stupid; he's always doing stupid things!" Adeline cast a contemptuous glance at the roof.

"No, that is something he isn't. He hates being cooped up, and no doubt he'll enjoy the company of the coachman more than listening to our chatter. Besides, it will give him time to think."

"Do you think we'll find her? Papa won't be very pleased."

"Your father had his reasons but they were the wrong ones; keeping the truth from Alasdair all these years was cruel and wrong. We'll find her. We'll enquire in Edinburgh and if we cannot trace her there we will go to the Highlands, to Glencoe."

The further north they travelled the more they became aware of the feelings of hostility the English harboured towards their new king. Even 'the king across the water', James Stuart, had pointed out that there were fifty claimants who had as much right to the throne of England as did the Elector George of Hanover. The northern counties were a stronghold of Catholicism: there were families in Cumberland and Lancashire who had suffered persecution but had continued to cling to their faith, and the further north they travelled, the more noticeable became the atmosphere of suspicion.

After several days of journeying, the lumbering vehicle came within sight of its destination early one bright sunny morning. High up on its sheer escarpment the castle looked down over the waking city: the steeple of St Giles rose like a pale grey tapering needle into the still air. The coach passed through the city gate and Anne, Adeline and Alasdair were as fascinated as Alizon had been all those years ago by the closely packed, precariously leaning, towering buildings with their courts and alleys. The coach had turned into the High Street now and the two women gazed eagerly out of the window.

"Why it's much cleaner and wider than most of the streets in London! Look Mama, there are plenty of fine shops!"

"Do you never think of anything else! I will be glad to take a bath and change my clothes, I don't think I have ever felt so dirty and unkempt or hot!"

"How much longer now?"

"Not far, the coach will set us down in the courtyard of the Thistle."

"But how will we go about finding Alizon?"

"I'll ask the landlord to whom I should go for help," Anne replied confidently, although inwardly her spirits began to drop. Within this teeming city, with so many people packed into it and many more beyond the walls, she had begun to have her doubts. The voices she heard on the street were incomprehensible, almost as if the inhabitants were speaking another language. There were the usual street cries of the vendors but beyond the High Street, for as far as the eye could see, narrow lanes and alleys ran down hill. She began to think that finding Alizon MacDonald Kirkbride in Edinburgh would be like trying to find a needle in a haystack.

She bit her lip. She had promised Alasdair, and now

she realised that he would never return to Charleston until he had found his mother. And would he return ther? Would he want to remain with Alizon? If he did, then she herself would be afraid to return home to have to face Darnley, for Alasdair was his pride and joy. She dismissed the thought as the coach came to a standstill and they clambered awkwardly down, for their legs were stiff.

The landlord stood in the doorway to welcome them: he was a huge broad man with light sandy hair and a ruddy complexion, and his accent was not so pronounced as those she had heard so far. He introduced himself and soon had a half-dozen lackeys running with luggage into the inn while he himself shepherded the family inside, sharply directing the maids in their neat white caps and aprons to take the ladies to their rooms. They must be exhausted, he said, especially the young lassie, and he beamed down at Adeline. Before starting up the stairs Anne turned to him.

"Master McFarlane, we have come this far in search of a woman, a woman of about my age. Perhaps you would be good enough to help me. How might I go about tracing her?"

Sandy McFarlane stroked his chin thoughtfully. "What's her name? Does she live in Edinburgh?"

"Her name is Alizon Kirkbride, but before her marriage she was Alizon MacDonald. . . ."

"If I had a groat for everyone I know called by that name I'd no' be keeping an inn, mistress! Do you know anything else about her?"

"Only that she came from the Highlands, from Glencoe."

The puzzled expression vanished from his eyes. "Ah, then it's the Duke of Argyll you'll be wantin' to see. As head of Clan Campbell he will know of her, he knows nearly every MacDonald, they bein' engaged in the auld feud. The old Duke is dead of course, 'Grim Archie' who they say was one of the instigators of that terrible foul deed done to the MacDonalds, but his son will know. Records were kept of those who escaped and those who didn't. . . ."

"She did, and it was for attempting to kill Campbell of Glenlyon that she was transported to Carolina, but she came home, after gaining her freedom and marrying my husband's father. She came home a wealthy woman."

The man looked interested. "Well, it's His Grace of Argyll you'll be wantin', he'll certainly know of her and where she is. It's none o' ma business but why are ye lookin' for her?"

"Because the boy is her son, whom she has believed dead all these years. He was presumed drowned when he was barely two."

"A fine sentiment, ma'am! To have come so far, too! But be warned," he lowered his voice, "it is not a good time to come, it is not a good time to travel to the Highlands, there is talk that James Stuart is on his way now from France to take what is his. The Clans will follow him to a man and there'll be fighting, burning and looting, for if ever there was a bunch of wild, savage thieves and murderers it's the men of the Highlands!"

Anne paled a little at his words. This was something she had not bargained for! She had left Charleston to escape the Yemassee War but now it looked as though she had walked straight into another one, and a civil one at that, where brother took sides against brother, father against son, clan against clan. She began to ascend the stairs wearily. She was bone-tired and she felt depressed and deflated, but she would not turn back now for even if she wanted to, Alasdair would refuse. He was filled with a burning passion to find the woman who was his mother, and to learn the reasons why his father had lied to him for so many years. Alasdair would not turn back now, not even impending war could deflect him from his quest.

Chapter 7

Anne had made further enquiries that had resulted in an appointment with John, 2nd Duke of Argyll, and as the carriage bore her along the High Street to the grand houses in Canongate she felt apprehensive. She had been told that this man was perhaps the most powerful in Scotland. She had been warned not to trust him, then advised to put her faith in him as he was an honest, fair man, and so she was thoroughly confused and nervous. She had also heard that the Earl of Mar was stirring trouble in the Highlands.

The hackney drew to a halt and the driver called down to her that they had arrived. She stepped down onto the paved street and stared at the grandiose but rather forbidding house before her. She paid the driver, instructing him to wait for her, and then turned and ascended the steps, rapping sharply and confidently upon the heavy brass knocker. Presently she heard the sound of approaching footsteps. The door opened and an erect, stern-featured, straight-backed man clad entirely in black stood before her. She was almost tempted to turn and run back to the carriage.

"I am Mistress Kirkbride, I have an appointment to see His Grace." Fortunately her voice was steady and sounded a little imperious.

The man inclined his head, holding open the door for her. She swept past him with an air of indifference and stood, letting her eyes slowly travel around the portraits and heavy dark oak furniture in the panelled hall.

"Would you have the goodness to follow me, mistress. His Grace is expecting you."

"Thank you," she replied, following him down a narrow, badly-lit corridor until he stopped before a thick door upon which he knocked. The sound from within was almost inaudible, but the duke's manservant opened the door and announced her. "Mistress Kirkbride, from the Colony of South Carolina, Your Grace. I believe she has an appointment."

She walked boldly into the room, holding her head high, with a confidence she was far from feeling. The man who had been sitting in a chair behind a large desk littered with sheets of parchment and books stood up. She was greatly surprised to find herself staring into the faintly amused hazel eyes of a young man dressed in a coat of rich green velvet braided and frogged with gold, a waistcoat of gold-figured damask and a muslin neckcloth tied in intricate folds. The long red-gold curls of his full-bottomed wig spread over his shoulders.

"Mistress Kirkbride, I welcome you."

She regained her composure. "I beg your pardon, Your Grace, but I had expected a much . . . older man."

He laughed. "You were expecting to confront 'Grim Archie' as my father was known! He, alas is dead: you see before you John, 2nd Duke of Argyll and Greenwich, MacCailein Mor, Chief of Clan Campbell. And I hope I can be of some assistance to you?"

"I hope so too, sir."

"Pray sit down, mistress, you have travelled far. Have you a particular reason for leaving the Colony?"

She lowered herself into the chair he indicated, sitting nervously on the edge. "I had promised the children I would bring them to Europe and it seemed an opportune time, there is a war in progress at home. Charleston was being besieged by Indians of the Yemassee, Creek and Cherokee tribes."

He appeared more interested. "Things were desperate, then?"

"Well—I wouldn't say desperate. The Governor had sent for help from North Carolina and Virginia and was purchasing arms from New England. At such times we must help one another. Charleston will survive, it always has before!"

"I'm afraid, mistress, that you have jumped from the griddlepan into the fire, as the saying goes! No doubt you will have heard the rumours flying about the city. We are on the brink of rebellion here. The Earl of Mar with Huntley, General Gordon and some others are trying to rally support for James Francis Edward Stuart, they have no liking for King George."

She thought of the mutterings and complaints she had heard all the way from London. "And you, sir?"

"I, madam, am the loyal servant of his Hanoverian Majesty, as my father was to the late queen. I would advise you, if your business is not pressing, to take yourself and your children back to London if you do not wish to be caught up in our war."

"There is something I must do first, Your Grace."

"What?"

"I must find an old friend. . . ." She was surprised at herself, wondering why she had suddenly become so cautious. Some sixth sense seemed to warn her not to tell this man that Alasdair was not her son.

"When did you last see your friend?"

"I have not seen her for many years."

"And is this reason enough to place yourself between two armies?"

"I have my reasons, sir."

"Does this long-lost friend have a name?"

"Alizon Kirkbride, my sister-in-law," she lied hastily.

He shook his head slowly. "I know no one of that name."

"Before her marriage her name was MacDonald, Alizon MacDonald of the Clan MacDonald of Glencoe."

There was no vestige of a smile now in his eyes or on his lips. Suddenly he was sombre, the expression in his eyes even menacing.

"You know of her and where I can find her?"

He was silent and for a while Anne thought that he was not going to answer.

At last he said, "I know of her!"

"She is well?" She held her head up proudly, determined to show that she was not to be intimidated.

"So far as I know, but I must repeat my warning, madam. Go home. No good can come to you here!"

She ignored his last words. "Where can I find her?"

"You insist in this folly?"

"She is my sister-in-law!"

"But no blood kin. Go back to Charleston while there is still time!"

She rose indignantly to her feet and stood glaring down at him. "Sir, the one thing we in the Colonies do not lack is courage, and no bickering between the government and the Clans is going to drive me home until I have found my sister-in-law!"

"Are you sure you are no blood kin to Alizon MacDonald Stuart? You have the same arrogance, the same unswerving determination!" The hazel eyes were gold and there were flecks of slate-coloured light in them now.

"What did you call her?" Anne felt suddenly uneasy. "Are you sure we are speaking of the same person?"

"She was transported to Charleston after attempting to kill the man who was responsible for the murder of her family, Alasdair MacDonald and his wife, Margaret. MacIan of Glencoe, his sons and daughter-in-law and his grandson! Is this the woman of whom you speak?" She was certain now that she must never reveal to this man or anyone else in Edinburgh that Alasdair was not her son.

"It is."

"But you called her Stuart!"

"She is the natural daughter of King Charles II, a thorn in my side, the constant reminder to my father . . . an instrument in his death!"

She gripped the edge of the table with both hands, trying desperately to hide her emotions.

"You did not know?"

"No!"

"Now you see why I warn you! Nothing has ever been proved against her, but she is the standard around which the Clans will rally. Should she send round the fiery cross the Highlands would be aflame, curse her!"

"You still have not answered my question! Where can I find her?"

"At Rannoch Chase, the house she built on the edge of the Moor of Rannoch, at the northern end of Glencoe."

She began to pull on her gloves. "Thank you for your time and for your advice, Your Grace. I would be telling an untruth if I were to say I hope we shall meet again, for I was not brought up to tell pretty lies!"

Once outside and in the carriage she leaned her head back against the padded seat. Her mind was in a whirl. Stuart! Why had Alizon not told anyone? She was certain Darnley did not know. But what did that make Alasdair? His grandfather had been King of England! It was too much for her to take in—she pressed her fingers tightly over her temples. She had to get him to his mother now at all costs. If Argyll found out about the boy he would imprison him! Even if it meant trekking through battlefields, she would take him to Rannoch. She remembered Argyll's words concerning Alizon: she was the standard around which the Clans would rally, and once they knew she had a son . . . !

For nearly a week Anne tried to find some means of transport and a guide who would take her into the Highlands, but rumours were flying around the city and there seemed to be no one who would risk running into a band of wild clansmen. Some alleged that James Stuart had landed and was even now marching on the city. At last she was so desperate she trebled the price she was willing to pay and again waylaid the landlord.

"Well, mistress . . . it's hard to say! Times are very troubled, but I'm sure you'll have seen that for yoursel'."

"That's why I'm offering three times as much money!"

He rubbed his chin thoughtfully. "It's a long and dangerous journey. . . ."

"If I hear those words once more I'll scream! The journey from the New World is no pleasure trip either!"

He placed a brawny hand across his forehead as though deep in thought, searching his mind for some half-forgotten name. "I think I may know just the man, I'll need time though to find him and persuade him—you couldn't pass over a wee bit o' siller, just to show goodwill?"

"No! I'll not see this friend of yours if I do. He'll be away with my money and I'll still be here! You tell him my requirements and the price and then bring him here!"

The landlord looked a little disgruntled but agreed.

Anne climbed the stairs to her room and found Adeline leaning out of the open latticed window, gazing down into the street below, while Alasdair was idly flipping through the pages of a cheap pamphlet.

"I've told you not to read the trash and sedition they write in those things!"

"Did you have any luck?" His eyes were eager.

"I hope so, the landlord says he knows someone who may take us!"

She wondered for the thousandth time what Alizon looked like. Alasdair had her eyes and she had eyes like those of her father, for she had once seen a miniature of the king from whom Charleston took its name. She shivered involuntarily. If Argyll were to see the boy he would know instantly by those huge dark brown eyes. "He also said that the country is on the verge of civil war, so it won't be easy. It's many miles over rough country with the threat of two armies between here and Loch Leven."

"But we'll still go?" It wasn't really a question, more a statement of fact.

"Of course!"

Adeline looked uncertain. "Wouldn't it be better if we stayed here until things were more . . . peaceful?"

"No! We can't stay here for much longer and Alasdair, I don't want you to leave the inn."

"Why not?"

"Because of something the Duke of Argyll told me."

"What did he tell you?"

"It is not my place to impart the information, your mother will do it!"

"When can we leave?" He sounded disappointed.

"As soon as arrangements have been made. It could take a few more days but in the meantime we can pack up our things. We'll need pack-horses as well as sturdy mounts, the terrain is too wild for a carriage or wagon."

"At least let me see to the provision of the animals?" Alasdair begged.

"No, you must not be seen on the streets. I can't tell you the reason, you must trust me! You'll soon be home amongst your own people."

He stared at her hard. "My own people," he repeated. "My people are in Charleston!"

"No, Alasdair, they are here, you'll know the truth of that very soon now!"

They set out on Tuesday 6th September, 1715, and on that same day the Earl of Mar raised the Stuart standard at Braemar. The Jacobites rallied to him: the Marquises of Huntley and Tulliebardine, the Earl Marischal, the Earls of Erroll, Nithsdale, Traquair, Southesk, Carnwath, Seaforth and Linlithgow; Viscounts Kilseth, Kenmure, Kinston and Stormont, Lords Rollod, Duffus, Drummond, Strathallan and Ogilvy, General Hamilton, General Gordon, MacDonald of Glengarry, Auchterhouse, Aulbar, Sleat, and Glencoe and strangely Campbell of Glendaruel, representing the aged Campbell of Breadalbane. Beneath the blue silk standard that floated in the breeze, on one side emblazoned with the Scottish arms in gold, and on the other the thistle and motto *Nemo me impune lacessit* and the words "No Union", they made a brave sight in shining armour and bright tartans. Attached to the standard were two white pennants, one bearing the inscription "for ourselves and liberty". But Mar's declaration for James Stuart was not even suspected by Anne, Alasdair and Adeline as they passed through the city gates, following the road to the Queen's Ferry as Alizon herself had done.

The man who had agreed to take them was a taciturn, suspicious-looking fellow who, when he spoke at all, they could hardly understand, so broad was his accent, mingled with words of Gaelic. He rode ahead followed by Alasdair, then the two women, then the pack-horses. Without knowing it, they traced Alizon's journey almost step by step, and as the countryside grew more barren and bleak Adeline's complaints increased until Anne lost her temper and told her forcefully to stop behaving like a spoiled brat. This had the effect of causing a fleeting glint of humour to appear in the eyes of their guide.

To Alasdair's eyes the country did not seem hostile. It was different from the humid, swampy lands that verged upon the Ashley and the Cooper rivers, but to his eyes the rugged escarpments with the lichen and straggling bushes clinging to the rocky outcrops, the heather burning purple and blue against the slate grey boulders, the clear, sparkling burns that rushed down the mountainsides, all were beautiful. It was as though despite the harshness of the climate, the howling snow-laden winds of winter, the short springs and mild summer followed quickly by autumn frosts, nature was determined to paint with glowing colours this bare landscape. Purple, blue, saffron, green, clear opalescent waters, still lochans that reflected the blue sky above.

"Amongst your own people", Anne had said. He had denied it, yet he now felt akin to this land: there was something in its very harshness that stirred feelings deep within him. Ever since Anne had told him that his mother was not dead he had tried to picture her. Tried to sort out the tangle of lies his father had told him, but the questions circled round and round in his mind, finding no solution. But the answers would come soon now, he knew it.

Gazing upwards he saw a speck in the sky as an eagle soared on the wind, its flight feathers spread out like fingers. Gracefully it glided on the air currents, high above the crag, always waiting for some movement far far below, then it would drop like a stone upon its prey. He squinted into the watery sunlight, seeing the bird black against the sky, circling its eyrie.

"How much further?" he asked their guide.

The man turned in the saddle. "By morning we should be at Kinghouses on the edge of Rannoch."

He turned away again and Alasdair fell silent. He looked upwards again but the bird had dropped from sight. Tomorrow, then, he would at last see the woman who believed he was dead. Would she recognise him instantly? Would she weep? Would she even want him, after all this time? That was the fear that haunted him day and night. Suppose she should reject him! She might have married again, she might have other children, children who had never left her side from the day of their birth. They might be a complete family with no room or need for someone believed long dead, mourned and forgotten! He had built up his hopes too highly, he told himself. All these years he had looked to Anne for comfort and advice—she had been a mother to him in every sense of the word—how must she feel now, ready to hand him over to a stranger? All the pain and worry she had suffered on his behalf, all the joy, the laughter they had shared, only to find that he did not belong to her, that the woman who had given him life was not dead after all!

But Anne had brought them this far, and since they had left Edinburgh he had noticed a change in her attitude to him. There seemed to be no longer the same light, bantering air between them, she reprimanded him less frequently. It was as though she saw him with new eyes, and he was certain that her visit to Argyll had something to do with it. Tomorrow they would reach the fringes of Rannoch. Tomorrow would hold all the answers for him, be they good, bad or indifferent. Tomorrow he would see his mother again.

Far away at Braemar the cries were loud. "God Save King James!" echoed on all sides, the standard flew proudly, the Clans were gathering slowly to support their rightful king and the liberties of their country. They would fight for the old way of life, the traditions of Gaeldom, they would fight against the Union with England. But their cries were not heard by the small party winding its way up the rough track that led to the inn at Kinghouses, whose scarred door was open to travellers seeking shelter.

Chapter 8

No fire burned in the hearth for the September day was still warm, clinging to the last vestige of summer. The sun streamed in through the window and played like a halo around the head of the woman who sat at the desk. Her hair, taken back into a bunch of thickly curling ringlets, was the colour of moonlight. Her skin was good though it bore lines imposed by harsh experience. She was still a beautiful, striking woman, even in the dark grey woollen dress that had only a small lace collar for decoration. Her large brown eyes were serious as she gazed at the old man who sat in the chair before her, twisting in his gnarled fingers the carved handle of his dirk. His hair was white as was his moustache. He scorned pomades, powders and wigs. His back was straight, and looking across at him she felt a pang of longing. He, that other old man, had looked like that all those years ago. A giant of a man with a mane of white hair, back as stiff as a ramrod and with pride to match. The Highlands would never see the like of him again. They had murdered him, shot down in cold blood that man she had loved, the man she had called "Grandfather MacIan".

"The situation is confused, rumours are rife, nothing definite has been sent in the manner of official orders from Mar," the man informed her.

Alizon Stuart stared across at him. Long ago she had asked him if she could count on him should she ever need his help, and he had answered yes. Now he was here. Ewan Cameron of Locheil, now he was an old man.

"I have heard that the standard was raised yesterday at Braemar but that the king has not arrived. You know as well as I, Locheil, that the money is here to buy arms and men. . . ."

"There will be no need to buy men! Send round the fiery cross and every laird and his tacksmen will rise. . . ."

"That's not what I've heard, there are some who will refuse, prevaricate. . . ."

"Then the old ways will be used against them!"

"Threaten and force them, burn their roof trees over their heads and kill their cattle! What way is that to ensure loyalty?"

"It has served well in the past and will do so now!"

"It's not a method I approve of!"

Old Locheil's eyes softened as he looked at her. "You'll have no need for such measures, they'll not forget who you are. You are the living embodiment of what they remember of the old days, before the Prince of Orange came."

"My father, King Charles, was dead before I was one year old."

"But they don't forget the Stuart name!"

"So what will Mar do now?"

"I don't know, but already hundreds are flocking to him."

"You will take the Lochaber men?"

He assented.

"There are so few left now of Clan Ian Abrach, but they will go to avenge old scores and I wish I could go with them!"

"War and rebellion are not women's business!"

"With that I must agree. We can only stay behind and wait and pray, but at least I can provide the money."

Cameron of Locheil rose stiffly and Alizon rose also. "The Glencoe men will go with you, Locheil, let me know when word comes?"

"That I will do, I'm away now to speak to MacIan."

"You'll have John's support." Never could she think of him as MacIan of Glencoe—for her old Alasdair MacDonald would always bear that title.

When Locheil had gone she sat down again and looked out across the wastes of Rannoch. The heather was in bloom and the moor stretched before her, a burning sheet of smouldering purple, broken only by the few patches of saffrix. After all these years the time had come at last. After all the bitter disappointments, the crushed hopes, at last James Stuart was coming home. She remembered the weeks spent at the court of France, the brief meetings with her uncle when she had pledged her loyalty, her support and her fortune. He had been grateful, calling her niece and treating her as such and not as a bastard of his brother, but she had known even then that he had lost heart, his fervour for the cause was dimming with ill-health. She had returned home to Rannoch Chase to wait in vain for letters that never came, messages that never arrived.

And then he was dead. She had remained hopeful at first, for there was nothing else in life, except her daughter Andrea Charlotte, to interest her, but at last hope had dimmed until it no longer existed. They had been bitter years, the years when she had cried brokenly for Andrew, for Margaret and MacIan and for her baby, Alasdair, lying in his watery grave so far away. She had watched the growing friendship between Gabrielle whom she loved as a sister, and Lieutenant Gowry, the man who had killed

Andrew. She could not hate Gabrielle: it was not always possible to chose whom you fell in love with. She had tried to dissuade her, she had argued, she had raged at the girl calling her a traitor... and never once had Gabrielle hit back, she had stood, her head bent, tears in her eyes, her heart torn between Alizon and Gowry, until at last she had married her redcoated soldier.

Alizon had not attended the wedding. She had refused to see Gabrielle for a year until Sarah, her kinswoman, had made her relent, for she had missed Gabrielle's companionship more than she would ever admit to herself. She would not allow Robert Gowry into her house without a warrant, and it was his embarrassing and uncomfortable duty upon two occasions to enter and search Rannoch Chase for arms, seditious literature and wanted men. But the day had come when he had entered without his scarlet coat and white breeches that she hated so much, and hat in hand had begged her to be godmother to his son Phillip. She had been astounded at his temerity.

"You killed the man I loved, you killed the father of my child, and now you come to me and ask that I be godmother to your son!" she had cried.

It had been Sarah again who had been the mediator. "Alizon, you must learn to forget. Think of Gabrielle! You miss her, don't deny it, I know you do! You will be hurting her, not him!" She had fixed eyes on Alizon for Sarah, too, hated the soldiers. Remembering, always remembering that night she had staggered through the blizzard with her baby in her arms while all around her her friends and relations were being butchered. "Think of Gabrielle!"

And so Alizon had agreed, and afterwards she was glad, for Gabrielle came more frequently from the Black Garrison, now called Fort William, bringing the baby with her.

The old look of hatred returned to her dark eyes. Fort William, named for the dead William of Orange, the man on whose orders, carried out by Argyll, Breadalbane, and Glenlyon, half of Clan Ian Abrach had been murdered in cold blood. She hated the name of Campbell. Old Argyll, too, was dead and Breadalbane an old sick man, but she had taken great pleasure in hearing of Argyll's death, for she had reminded him of his guilt and had prayed that MacCailein Mor would burn in hell for ever.

During the reign of Queen Anne she had turned her attention to her lands and her daughter and the people of the glen who would have starved to death without her aid. They had been left with nothing. They had been beaten, terrorised, subdued by fear and hunger until she had returned to Glencoe, until she had seen her dream rise in the form of Rannoch Chase. A smile played about her lips as she remembered the looks of horror that had come when she had announced her plans for farming the barren wastes.

Rannoch was marshy, the people of the glen cut the turf for their fires and grazed their cattle in summer on the moor, but the plans she outlined to them were sheer madness, of that they were convinced. She was going to drain part of the marshy ground. This in itself they considered folly. Patiently she had explained the methods of drainage and irrigation on the plantations of the Colonies, and how the drainage system could be employed here. In vain did she advocate the use of better seed than the bere barley and grey oats which gave little or no yield, even in good years. She had explained that straw and silage, even turnips, could be fed to the animals in winter. The livestock of the glen had previously had to exist on a meagre winter diet of boiled chaff, and when spring came they were so weak they had to be lifted onto their feet and put out to grass.

Alizon had argued fiercely against the old traditions: the reason they could not start ploughing before spring was that the land was undrained, many did not start to plough what little patches of productive land they had until March. The grey oats were not sown until April, and it was May before the 'bigg' four-rowed barley was put in, consequently the crops were not ripe before the autumn when the gales and early frosts were upon them.

The first year they had refused to follow her advice. Autumn came and her crops were in, her fodder piled in the barns and her animals well-fed, healthy and sleek throughout the winter. They had come to her next spring and asked her advice. She smiled again, knowing the effort swallowing their pride had cost them, but no one had starved in the glen after that, nor on the moor either. Famine frequently stalked the Highlands and even the Lowlands, starvation was no stranger to the Scots, but neither she nor her people felt the ravages of hunger again. She had prospered and the remnants of Clan Ian Abrach had rallied under the leadership of John MacDonald. But the soldiers still remained at the Black Garrison, Clan MacGregor was still outlawed, each man broken and hunted like an animal, and now there was a foreigner on the throne that belonged to her cousin. A German with appalling manners and tastes, so she had heard, and he had been accepted without a sword being raised in England. Even despite the Act of Union, Scotland would never follow the English in their docility.

"Has Locheil gone?"

Alizon raised her head and shook away the cobwebs of the past. "Yes, he's gone to see John." She smiled, her eyes softening as they always did when she looked at her daughter. Andrea Charlotte was fourteen now and lovely. Her hair, which fell about her shoulders in loose curls, was rich gold, the colour of ripe corn, while her eyes were large and brown. Alizon could never look into those eyes without being reminded of Andrew, her dead lover. If only they had let her marry him there would be no bitterness, no hatred, no eternal longing tearing at her heart.

"Then it's true? The Earl of Mar has raised the standard for King James?"

"He has, but no one seems to know what exactly is going on. Locheil will go with the Lochaber men, he promised me that long ago, and John will go with what men of the glen will follow him. Glengarry, Appin and Keppoch also, from what I've heard."

The young girl's eyes danced with excitement. "Then this time we will win! I know we will!"

"The king has not arrived yet."

"But we will drive out the soldiers and send the fat German running back to Hanover!"

"Don't be too hasty, Andrea. There has been no official war declared yet, and what of your Aunt Gabrielle? If the soldiers are driven out, what about Phillip?"

Some of the excitement died, replaced by confusion. "Why did Aunt Gabrielle have to marry a redcoat? It makes everything so complicated! I love her and Phillip is like a brother, but. . . ."

"I can't explain it to you. She loved him and that was that. She was like a sister to me, yet for a time I would not speak to her. Robert Gowry is a soldier, he does his duty according to the oath he swore. He is an honest man, a fair man and had he worn plaid instead of scarlet broadcloth and white buckskin I would have welcomed him with open arms. But life plays strange tricks, it does not always fulfill its promises." Her voice was low and sorrowful and Andrea knew she was thinking of her father, Andrew MacDonald. He had been an outlaw, hunted by Gowry when she had been born, he had never been wed to her mother and she knew what that made her, yet she was proud for her grandfather had been a king—a Stuart king. King of Scotland and England.

"What can we do?"

"Nothing, only wait. Always it is a woman's place to wait and wonder and pray."

"I'll not wait! If I had the chance I would ride with them!"

"Don't be a fool, Andrea! War is not for women!"

"You are growing old, Mother. Once you fought with every weapon at your disposal. . . ."

"And I lost! Disillusionment and bitterness were the spoils of my private war, I hope they will never be yours!"

"If Scotland has a Stuart king again and is free from the rule of the English, then I'll ask no more of life!"

Alizon laughed. "Brave words, but will you never love a man and marry and have bairns?"

A faint colour rose to Andrea's cheeks. "Maybe, but I'll not marry a soldier and that's what Phillip says he will be!"

"Ah, you are very fond of Phillip. . . ."

"Not if he joins the army of the Hanoverian!"

"You are still only children, both of you, and all boys want to be soldiers and fight wars, especially if their father happens to be a lieutenant in a gaudy shiny uniform! Now away with you, I'm going to see your Aunt Sarah!"

"Can I come?"

"Yes—fetch your shawl."

Alizon smiled again and shook her head as Andrea ran off. Was it fourteen years? It seemed like yesterday. She had loved and lost, Andrew had died in her arms, and thinking of her daughter's fondness for Phillip Gowry she prayed that no divided love or loyalties would tear her child apart.

Their visit to Alizon's kinswoman Sarah and her quiet, dreamy son was the occasion for a spirited outburst from Andrea. As she had told her mother, she wished to fight alongside her countrymen to right Scotland's wrongs. She made no bones about saying so to her aunt and cousin.

On the journey back to Rannoch Andrea was silent and preoccupied, but Alizon judged her mood correctly. "If you are entertaining any thoughts about slipping away to join the Clans, miss, then forget them!"

"You've always been able to read my thoughts!" the girl laughed.

"That's because you are like me. Once I was filled with a hatred that kept me alive. I wouldn't call it hatred now, the years have dampened the fury, but it still smoulders."

"If I had been a boy you would have let me go!"

"No! Even had you been a boy I would not have let you go, you are too young and too dear. . . ." She had been only two years older than Andrea now was when she had fallen in love with Andrew, but she had not thought of herself as a child.

"We've visitors! It's not Locheil, or Glengarry, I've not seen those horses before and there are pack animals too!"

Andrea's words and her outstretched arm brought Alizon's gaze to the front of the house. There were three horses tethered, a sheltie, and four pack-horses all loaded with boxes and bundles.

"Whoever it is looks as though they've come to stay!"

Andrea's voice was rising with excitement. "Do you think it could be. . . ."

"Don't be a fool, Andrea! Why would King James come here? He'd be too far from Braemar, too far from his forces."

"To see you?"

Alizon tutted impatiently. "Why? I've sent money and the men will be going tomorrow, there is no reason. . . ."

"You are his cousin."

"Half-cousin. All will remember that, especially he. He was born in wedlock, I was not!"

Andrea remained silent, staring intently at the tethered beasts. She herself was a bastard. Oh, they had told her pretty tales when she had been a child about how her father had been murdered by the soldiers of the Black Garrison on the orders of Argyll, but they had implied that her father and mother had been married. It wasn't until she had heard two of the maids whispering together that she had been faced with the truth. And the truth had hurt. She had gone crying to Alizon, demanding an answer to her questions, and that day she learnt many things, including her relationship of second cousin to "the king across the Water".

"Whoever it is they will be welcome, no one is turned away from my door. . . ."

"Unless their name is Campbell!" Andrea finished with venom.

Chapter 9

As they turned their horses into the stable-yard they saw that another horse was tethered to the hitching-post.

"Gabrielle is here!" Alizon exclaimed, but in her voice was an edge of fear. Had Gabrielle come to warn her that soldiers were on their way? They dismounted and went into the house through the kitchen where Jeannie was kneading bread in the shallow trough.

"Mistress Gowry is here, I see, Jeannie, but who do

all the other horses belong to?" Alizon threw her cloak across a chair and absentmindedly patted her hair.

"A lady with a lassie about Andrea's age and a fine lad a wee bit older, she's come from Edinburgh, with Duncan MacLeod as her ghillie. I didn't know what to do with them but then Mistress Gabrielle came and she's tendin' to them now."

"Wipe your hands, Jeannie, and go and whisper that I've come back and that I'd like to see her. Oh, I know it's not polite to whisper in front of folk but I want more information."

With a nod Jeannie wiped her hands on her apron, then untied it and went in search of Gabrielle, returning with her in a few minutes. Gabrielle had been Alizon's maid in Charleston, a girl transported as Alizon herself had been. One look at Gabrielle's white face and shocked eyes made her run the few steps across the kitchen and clutch Gabrielle's arm.

"What's the matter? Who are they and why have they come here?"

"Alizon! Oh! Alizon! I . . . I'm confused! I hope I am wrong, yet at the same time I hope I am right!"

"Who is she?" Alizon shook her friend. "What do you mean? Sit down, you look faint."

Pushing Gabrielle into a chair, she bade Andrea bring a cup of water, but Gabrielle pushed it away. "No. It's the boy, Alizon! Oh! Should I tell you or not? Dear God, help me! I could swear it is but. . . ."

Alizon exchanged glances with her daughter, both wondering if Gabrielle had lost her wits.

"Who is she?"

"Anne Kirkbride."

"Anne Kirkbride!" Now it was Alizon's turn to stammer. "She is . . . she is. . . ."

"Darnley Kirkbride's wife, so she said."

Alizon sank down onto a stool, her legs suddenly feeling like jelly. "He's dead! He's been dead for years! He died at sea with. . . ." She rose to her feet unsteadily, stretching out one hand as though she were feeling her way through a fog. Andrea ran to her side and caught hold of her.

"This is the man you told me of, when you lived in the Colonies?"

Alizon could not answer her. A large lump constricted her throat as she remembered Jeannie's words, "a lassie and a fine lad a wee bit older". It couldn't be! It wasn't possible! Not after all this time, not after hope had long since died! "Gabrielle, take me to her!" she managed to whisper.

Gabrielle had pulled herself together and now held her firmly by the arm while Andrea followed them down the hall. She paused before the door. Supposing it wasn't?

Andrea opened the door. The room was bathed in sunlight, making the heavy carved furniture glow darkly, yet bringing into brilliance the rose and gold draperies and upholstery. The prisms of the large chandelier sent rays of rainbow lights across the room. Beside the large fireplace stood a girl of Andrea's age with red-gold hair, a delicate complexion and large amber eyes. Seated in the chair next to the hearth was an attractive woman, elegantly dressed, a fashionable hat placed on her shining blue-black curls. But it was on the boy who stood with his back to the window that Alizon's eyes were riveted. She could not see his features clearly because of the sunlight that dazzled her. She shaded her eyes with her hand and her heart leaped into her throat. It was so long ago and he had only been a baby, but his hair, his eyes. . . .

Anne Kirkbride rose, extending her hand. "I'm sorry we could not let you know of our arrival but communications are difficult. I'm Anne Kirkbride, Darnley's wife." She paused, her words echoing in the silent room.

Alizon stared at her, then her eyes moved again to the boy by the window.

"Darnley . . . he did not die?"

"No."

"And . . . and my son . . . ?"

Anne did not reply. She raised her hand to her eyes, unable to stand the agony in the other woman's face.

"This is my daughter, Adeline," she whispered.

"And my son?" The fierce brown eyes bored into her. "What of my son?"

Blindly, unable to answer, Anne raised her hand and pointed to Alasdair.

"He's alive . . . my son. . . ." No longer the baby she had mourned so deeply for so long, but a strapping eighteen-year-old with large brown eyes and tawny hair. She seemed to be paralysed, unable to move a muscle. "Alasdair!" she whispered, and sank slowly into a chair.

Bending over her, Anne took her hands in her own and pulled her to her feet, but they felt like lead. She was unable to move them. "I have brought him back to you, Alizon." Anne's own voice was hoarse and tears glinted on her lashes. She loved him as if he were her own son, but the look on Alizon's face was worth all the heart-searching, all the doubts, all the pain.

Still she could not move, she stood holding Anne's hands as if they were a lifeline, staring at the boy.

"We've come a long way to find you, they told me . . . they told me you were dead!" Alasdair's voice cracked and finally the leaden heaviness lifted.

Alizon skimmed the few feet that separated them and threw her arms around him. Tears coursed down her cheeks and mingled with his as they both wept unashamedly. Anne dabbed at her eyes with her kerchief, and Gabrielle sniffed loudly. Only Andrea Charlotte and Adeline remained dry-eyed staring suspiciously at each other from opposite sides of the room.

When the first moments of shock had passed, Alizon, having introduced her daughter, sat on the long settle with Alasdair whose hand was firmly in her own, and Andrea who was looking slightly rebellious, while Anne proceeded haltingly to tell them of the reasons why she had come to Scotland. When she came to her visit to the Duke of Argyll, Alizon, Gabrielle and Andrea exchanged uneasy glances.

"You went to MacCailean Mor to ask of me?"

"He was most helpful, he seemed a pleasant enough young man!"

"You forget, mother, 'Grim Archie' is dead," Andrea reminded her.

"He is still head of Clan Campbell and the son of the devil!"

"It was he who told me that you are Alizon Stuart."

"But . . . why Stuart," faltered Alasdair. "Why do you use the name Stuart?"

Alizon did not answer. She stared at Gabrielle who finally said, very quietly to Alasdair and to Andrea Charlotte, "Though born of different fathers you have the same mother." She looked directly at the boy. "And your mother's father was King Charles II."

He was even more confused; he stared at Alizon, then Andrea, and began to stutter.

"It's true, I am the bastard daughter of King Charles II and you are both his grandchildren." There was a note of sadness and of pride in Alizon's voice.

Alasdair turned in confusion. "You bear his name, Charlotte?"

"And you bear the name of old MacIan, though I doubt it means much to you!" For a second anger flared between them.

"How do you know that?"

"How can it? You know nothing of what my mother suffered, nothing of Clan Ian Abrach or the customs of Gaeldom!"

"But I can learn and I will learn! This is my country now!"

Alizon made peace between them while Anne looked sadly on. With those last words she knew she had lost him forever, and now she doubted the wisdom of bringing him back here.

During this Adeline had remained silent until Gabrielle addressed her. "How old are you, Adeline? Such a pretty name for such a pretty girl!"

"I'm fifteen, madam."

"Ah, the same age as my son, Phillip. I'm sure you will all become friends, at least I hope you will!"

At the praise Adeline's attitude thawed a little and she smiled.

"That's better, you have such a pretty smile, always you

should smile!" Gabrielle laughed, still with tears in her eyes. They should all laugh, she thought, they should all be happy, there had been so little happiness in all their lives. She loved her husband dearly and during the first months of her marriage she had felt ill with grief because it had caused a rift between herself and Alizon, but Phillip's birth had changed all that. Gradually Alizon had become less frigidly icy towards Robert, though Gabrielle knew that Alizon would never forgive or forget her marriage to a redcoat. Looking at the dark-haired woman in her elegant London clothes, Gabrielle guessed that her life had not been without sorrow also. She remembered Darnley Kirkbride and she had not been fond of him. The girl, Adeline, was like him and she suspected that she had her father's ways, too. Watching Anne closely she saw the deep grief buried beneath the smiles. It must have cost her a great deal to bring Alasdair back, for she obviously loved him a great deal, but then perhaps she hated Darnley so much that it was not much of a price to pay!

They sat talking of the past, of what had happened in Scotland and in Charleston, Alizon asking Anne so many questions that they hardly noticed darkness falling. The three young people had remained silent for most of the time, suspicious of each other, each a little jealous of the other. When Gabrielle declared she must leave and Alizon said she would show Anne to her room, they were left alone.

There was an awkward silence.

"Was the voyage good?" Andrea asked at last.

"Quite fair. I've only travelled by sea twice before and I don't remember much about. . . ." Alasdair's voice trailed off, for it reminded everyone of the reason they were here.

"I thought it was tedious and the cabin smelled!" Adeline wrinkled her nose as she remembered the odours of bilge-water and close-packed humanity and musty bedding.

Again there was an ominous silence.

"As we are all related I suggest that we at least make an effort to be friendly," Alasdair remarked awkwardly.

Andrea nodded slowly. "I suppose I was jealous of you. . . ."

"And Adeline was jealous of us both, admit it, you were!"

Adeline pouted, then smiled. "Well, everyone was fussing, and crying, I felt . . . abandoned!"

"I, too," said Andrea. "I felt that somehow you had taken my mother away from me. Did you mean it about Scotland being your country now?" she shot at him, somewhat resentfully.

"I meant it. I intend to stay but I know Mother and Adeline will go back, when the Yemassee war is over."

"Why didn't you stay behind and fight? I would have done."

"Because my father said I was too young!"

"I get the same answer." Andrea sighed.

"You can't fight, you're a girl, unless women fight here! Do they?"

"No! But if I were a boy I'd be off to join the Earl of Mar no matter what Mother said!"

"There will be a war here?" Adeline asked, her voice rising a little.

"Yes. The Earl of Mar has raised the standard of King James at Braemar and all the Clans are flocking to join him, even some of the Campbells!" She spat out the last word with venom, while Adeline gazed at her in horror.

"I knew we should have stayed at home! At least in Charleston you knew it was the Indians you were fighting, but here Scot fights Scot, you don't know who your enemy is!"

"Our enemies are the English soldiers, their German king, and Argyll and his Campbells, who've always been traitors to their king and country!"

"When the king lands I will join him!" Alasdair cried, his face flushed with the emotion of discovery of a new cause.

Andrea looked at him with open envy.

"Why should you go and get yourself killed, this is not your fight! I'll tell Mama and she won't let you!" Adeline almost screamed the words.

"You've forgotten, Adeline, Anne isn't my mama. Do you think Alizon will stop me?" He addressed himself to Andrea.

"I don't know. She's only just found you again after so long, yet she hates Argyll and has pledged her support in money, arms and men to the king. MacIan and the men of Clan Ian Abrach go at first light tomorrow! MacIan's son is going with them and he is only two years older than you; they are going to avenge what happened in Glencoe in 1668."

"I've heard the story. I've read some of the pamphlets, old ones, in Edinburgh. It was the king, William of Orange, who gave the order, wasn't it?"

Andrea nodded bitterly. "And who can fight kings! But now we'll have our chance, this time we will win! Why do you want to go?"

"Because . . . ," he paused. "I know that all these years I've considered myself the son of a planter, but now . . . now I know who my grandfather was!"

"Our grandfather!" Andrea corrected him.

"Oh! Does it matter? What's Phillip Gowry like?" Adeline changed the subject, for she could see no logic in Alasdair's statement and she was growing bored with the entire conversation.

"He's not so bad, considering his father is a redcoat soldier. A Scot in the English army, and he was responsible for the death of my father!"

"Yet you still remain friends with him?"

"It wasn't Phillip's fault, and Gabrielle came from Charleston with my mother years ago, they were close friends, though it broke Mother's heart when she married Robert Gowry. But that's all over now. Phillip and I were brought up together, and we don't see much of his father!"

"Will Phillip go to war with his father?" Adeline asked.

"No. Not this time. But he's been saying lately that he will join the army and I've told him that if he does I shall never speak to him again!"

Adeline tutted impatiently—they were back on that subject again.

"I think I'll go for a ride out on the moor," Alasdair said, suddenly wishing to be alone.

"Take care. It's marshy in places! Do you want me to come with you?" Andrea offered.

"No, I'd sooner go alone, I have much to think about."

"Then I'll take Adeline up to her room and help her unpack, and she can wash and change for dinner," Andrea offered.

Thankful that at last she could wash the grime of the journey from her body and change into one of the expensive dresses she had cajoled Anne into buying her in London, Adeline's good humour was restored and the war forgotten, in her mind, at least.

Chapter 10

Rumours still flew thick and fast, often conflicting. First it was said that James had landed, then that he had had to turn back for France because of English gunboats and storms. There was confusion throughout the country but more so in the remote Highlands where news took days to travel. The Jacobite headquarters was at Perth where Mar wasted his time issuing edicts which he had not the power to enforce, practicing war games and fortifying a camp, and men were heard to complain that under the Great Montrose the whole country would be marching south by now, instead of wasting time. A daring attempt was made to take Edinburgh Castle by Lord Drummond, Charles Forbes of Brux and MacGregor of Ballhaldy, but even this was mismanaged and ended in disaster.

Between the four young people a strong bond of companionship had grown, for Phillip Gowry seemed to spend more time at Rannoch Chase than he did at the Fort, and both Anne and Alizon agreed that this was due to the presence of Adeline. The four youngsters paired off, Andrea and Alasdair bound by the stronger tie of blood. In many ways her two children were alike, Alizon thought as she watched them ride out across Rannoch together. They were both strong-willed, neither lacked courage, and since Andrea had spent long hours relating to her half-brother Scotland's woes under the Union of the Crowns the boy had also developed a strong sense of nationalism, feeling for the first time that he was at home, that here was something worth fighting for. He had been unable however to persuade Alizon to let him go to Perth, and when he had tried to enlist Anne's aid all he had received was a determined shake of the head.

Most of the news that reached them came from Phillip, who heard it from the soldiers in the garrison, or the occasional group of Highlanders on their way to join the ever-increasing army. All four of them had been walking one day along the banks of the Coe, leading their horses along the reed-strewn bank until they had come to the remains of a cottage near the Signal Rock. It was one of those rare days in early November when a first sharp frost had powdered the bare trees and hard ground with a shimmering cloak. The sun, high in the pale bluish-green sky, burnished the waters of the Coe and shone gently on the upturned faces of the little group.

"Is there more news, Phillip?" Alasdair asked.

"Not much," came the guarded reply as Phillip placed the roll of cloth carried on the back of his saddle for Adeline to sit on. She smiled her thanks and indicated that he should sit next to her. Andrea perched upon the fallen hearthstone in what Adeline thought a very uncouth manner: she wore no hat and her long blonde hair streamed about her shoulders, cascading over the rough brown plaid cloak she wore over her dress.

Alasdair knew that Mar's army consisted of 917 horse and 2,666 foot and that most of the Clans had not yet joined the earl in Perth. "When the Chevalier lands he will have the whole of Fife, Forfar, Kincardine, Aberdeen, Banff and Moray as well as Perth and Inverness, and one hundred and sixty miles of sea coast. Skye and all the other western Isles will be his, and all the MacDonald lands and those of Appin. Only Argyll's Clan will not follow him and even they are divided."

Phillip shrugged. He liked Alasdair, Andrea he looked upon almost as a sister, but he was completely enchanted by Adeline. It was because of her that he avoided such arguments. Often he would lie awake at night thinking of her, her lovely hair and eyes, the petite figure, the tiny hands and waist. Part of him was torn between the growing feelings he had for her and the loyalty he owed to his father, and there were times when he knew that if he was faced with the need to choose, he could not be sure of his reaction.

"The Lowlands and all the country around Glasgow support King George, and there are rumours that troops are being brought north. . . ." He stopped abruptly, silently cursing the situation that had him trapped. "And I hear Mar has increased the taxes, and with the winter approaching many of the Clansmen will not be able to pay. Brigadier MacIntosh has crossed the Forth and is marching south, and the men of Northumberland have joined him and are pressing on into Cumberland and Lancashire!"

"Then where is King James? Why doesn't he come? If he came now it would only need the sight of him to spur on the Clans and they could be in London by Christmas!" Andrea snapped a dry, hollow reed between her fingers. "Is he coming or isn't he?"

"He will come," Alasdair declared firmly.

"But it may be too late," Phillip replied.

Seeing the danger signs in Andrea's eyes Adeline interrupted quickly, lest the conversation degenerate into an argument. "Why don't we do something exciting instead of sitting day after day talking of war?"

Andrea shot her a disdainful glance but Alasdair laughed.

"Poor Adeline, you have no interest in politics do you?"

"No, and I never shall!"

Phillip got to his feet. "What would you like to do?"

She pretended to ponder for a minute. "I'd like to hunt the stag!"

Both Phillip and Andrea looked anxious. "It's dangerous, a wounded stag can turn when at bay, and it can tear open a horse's belly with its antlers! How well do you ride?"

"As well as you do!"

"No, she doesn't! She's used to riding the flat, spongy pastures of Chawira. . . ."

"And the uneven, muddy river bottoms with mangrove roots that can trip up even the best horse and rider!" Adeline cried.

"We've no weapons!" Alasdair declared thankfully.

"We could always go back to the house. . . ." Andrea could have bitten off her tongue as she encountered the black looks of both Phillip and Alasdair.

"No hunting!" Alasdair's tone was firm, and knowing him of old Adeline realised that she would have no sport. Instead she jumped up, ran to her horse and quickly threw herself into the saddle, unhindered by her long skirt. Hammering her heels into the horse's flank she urged it into a canter. She would show them that she was as good a rider as any of them. She shortened the reins and leaned forward in the saddle, almost standing in the stirrups, the weight of her body taken on her small feet. She whipped the horse into a gallop, her hood slipped down and her hair streamed out behind her.

Faster and faster she rode, following the river bank up the glen towards the Herdsmen of Etive and Rannoch itself. Behind her she could faintly hear her name being called, but she could not distinguish whether it was Phillip's voice or that of Alasdair. She drew level with the Devil's Staircase and the horse was sweating now, the valley floor was widening out and she could see the waters of Loch Rannoch in the far distance. The house came into sight. At last she slowed her mount down, then she wheeled him round and held him in check. It was Phillip who was in the lead, beating his horse with a short whip; as yet there was no sgin of either Alasdair or Andrea.

As he pulled up beside her he was breathless and his cheeks were red. "Damn you, Adeline! Why did you do that? You could have been killed if you'd fallen at that speed!"

"Because I could see that no one believed that I could

ride as well as all of you, but I can!"

"You could have been killed!" Now there was anger in his voice. She looked at him coyly from beneath lowered lashes. "Would it have mattered so much to you, Phillip?"

He leaned over and caught the bridle of her horse. "Yes, it would have mattered to me and there's no need to play the prissy miss with me, you know it would."

She blushed but offered no reply, letting him lead her towards the house. He helped her dismount and for a few minutes they remained standing together, his arms about her waist, her hands on his shoulders. She looked up into his eyes. "I'm sorry, Phillip! I didn't mean. . . ." She tilted her head back expectantly, feeling excitement tingling through her, he was going to kiss her, she was sure of it. . . .

"So you've finally come home! Phillip, I've had word from your father. You are to go back to the garrison at once!" Alizon's voice broke the spell and he released her. Alizon's sharp eyes had missed nothing. "Adeline, I suggest you dress your hair before your mother sees you."

"Did my father say why he wants me so urgently?"

"No. Remember, Phillip, to your father I represent a grave threat, the message only said you were to return at once."

He remounted his lathered horse.

"When will I . . . we see you again?" Adeline could not keep the note of disappointment from her voice.

"I don't know. But I'll come as soon as I can!" With a spurt of gravel he was riding through the gate, out towards the moor and the road to the Black Garrison.

"Adeline, my child, you should be careful . . . you should not become too . . . friendly with Phillip Gowry. I do not want you to be hurt."

"Why do you say that? What do you mean?" There was real puzzlement in Adeline's eyes.

"Because his father is my sworn enemy, even though we have maintained an uneasy truce all these years for the sake of Gabrielle and Phillip, but not with the king coming home. It is Robert Gowry's sworn duty to fight against me and mine. He could be killed, the men of the glen could be cut down to the last man, I could be killed, at least imprisoned. . . ."

Adeline's eyes grew wide with horror. "No! Could Phillip be killed?"

"He could, and his father, by Highlanders who would tear the Black Garrison down stone by stone with their bare hands, given the chance, and if what I hear of the size of Mar's army is true, nearly eighteen thousand men, they could do it!"

She knew they had a chance. Only this morning she had heard that the two armies were encamped, facing each other in battle array, Argyll on the heights of Kippendavie between Dunblame and Sheriffmuir, and the Jacobite army at a small place called Kinbuck. It was only a matter of time now. It would take days to hear the outcome and all she could do was wait.

All her life she seemed to have been waiting. She remembered her words spoken long ago when Andrea was a baby, when the tiny fingers had plucked at the ribbons of her bonnet. "One day you will wear such ribbons in your hair, you will be the envy of every girl in the Highlands, but I pray you will never suffer as I have. I pray you will live to see your cousin restored and Scotland free of soldiers."

Jeannie had promised that one day her prayer would be granted and she had replied, "If not, then we will all die for that dream!" As she walked back to the house with the silent girl beside her she longed for a favourable outcome, for an end to bloody war. Would Scotland be free again by tomorrow, or would she have to die for that dream? Would Alasdair and Andrea also die for that dream? "Oh God! Let news come soon and let it be good!" she prayed.

A week had passed. A week during which she had fretted and worried. A week during which Alasdair and Andrea paced restlessly like two caged cats. A week during which Anne was formulating her plans to go back to Charleston, and Adeline was miserable because Phillip was in danger and she knew of her mother's plans to return home.

Then it came, in the form of the first group of men returning to the glen with John MacDonald at their head. She had seen them coming from the long gallery. She had stood rooted to the spot, clutching the window-ledge as she had so often before when watching small groups of redcoats approaching. But as soon as she realised who they were she ran down the stairs, grabbed a plaid and threw it hastily around her head and shoulders and ran down the drive and out of the gate to meet them. Her heart was pounding the nearer she drew to them. They were tired, their faces dirty, and around John's arm was a strip of bloody cloth, but they still had their muskets, their targes and their claymores!

"John! What happened? What happened?"

He shook his head wearily. "It's all over, Alizon."

"You mean. . . ." Her eyes were dancing, sparks were glittering in their dark depths, her cheeks were flushed with excitement.

"No! Alizon! All is lost! It was a stramash!"

The bubbling excitement, the surging pride and joy were instantly quelled. Tears started in her eyes, her mouth drooped at the corners and John thought she looked like an old, beaten woman. She had lived for this day, as they all had. They had carried hope and revenge like a burning torch over the years, and now that torch had been extinguished. Sheriffmuir had been a debacle. They had far outnumbered Argyll's troops, but Argyll had chosen the ground and he was no fool. There had been bitter fighting, the courage and stamina of the Highlanders had not faltered, good men had been slain, but it had all been grossly mismanaged. Mar was no general: if only they had had Montrose or Claverhouse, the "Bonnie Dundee" of the old songs!

"You're hurt." At last she found her voice. "You must all be tired, cold and hungry—come into the house." Her shoulders drooped and her head was bent as she led them inside. By this time Alasdair had seen them and was racing down the staircase, followed by Andrea. The expectation in their eyes died as they took in Alizon's haggard features, the dejection that sat on the shoulders of the group like carrion crows, the bloody rag on John's arm.

"We . . . we . . . ?" The question formed on Alasdair's lips.

"We lost!" John's voice was flat and cold, but all the misery of dashed and trampled hopes and dreams was portrayed in those two words.

"Why? Why? We had everything! We had the men, the arms, the hopes—Scotland's future was in our grasp, why did we let it slip away?" Andrea's eyes blazed and her voice rose almost to a shriek. "We have all lived for this day, prayed for it! We were betrayed! Betrayed by Mar, betrayed by our own prince! Where is he? Why has he not come? Does he not want his crown? Has he grown idle and apathetic in his old age?"

"Andrea! That's enough! There is nothing we can do now, except hope that there will be no reprisals!"

John sat down at the table, staring morosely into the goblet of whisky he held before him. "Already they've written a ballad, the Ballad of Sheriffmuir!"

Andrea crossed to the table. "What kind of a ballad?"

"A very explicit one!"

"Well, what does it say?" Alasdair asked.

"There are twenty verses, do you want to hear them all?"

"No. One or two will do!"

John took a swig of the whisky and began to recite in a low, toneless voice.

"There's some say that we wan, and some that
  they wan,
And some say that name wan at a' man!
But one thing I'm sure, that at Sherra-muir
A battle there was that I saw, man.
And we ran and they ran, and they ran and we
  ran,
But Florence ran fastest of a' man."

He took another drink and continued, his voice bitter now,

"Strathmore and Clanranald cried still 'Advance Donald'
Till both of those heroes did fa', man
For there was such a hashing and broad swords a-
  clashing,
Brave Forfar himself had a claw, man,
And we ran and they ran, and they ran and we ran...."

"Stop it! Stop it!" Alizon cried.

"Rob Roy McGregor was there," John said.

"Rob Roy there stood watch on a hill for to catch,
The booty, for aught a' saw, man
For he ne'er advanced from the place he was stanc'd...
He took no part, he never moved an inch!"

Alizon groaned and sat down weakly beside John. It seemed as though all the energy had been drained from her, she could have laid her head on the table and slept forever, but she held her head up, encouraged by the blazing anger in her daughter's eyes. She had named her well. Andrea Charlotte named for Charles, was all Stuart.

John pushed a grimy piece of torn parchment towards her and Andrea held it close, peering at it. "Is this the last verse?"

He nodded.

In her clear biting tone she read the words aloud.

"Whether we ran or they ran, or we wan or they wan
Or if there was winning at a', man
There no man can tell, save our brave general,
Who first began running of a', man!"

She ripped the parchment to shreds and threw them down on the table. "Mar! I hope he hangs for it!"

In the days that followed a melancholy settled upon the household. Voices seemed to be hushed, Jeannie no longer sang in the kitchen, the spinet was silent, even the dogs in the yard lay with their heads on their paws or crept around with their tails between their legs. Going out into the yard one night, seeing them lying close to the barn door in the moonlight, Alizon was reminded of the Grey Dogs of the Feinn that came before death struck a MacDonald. She shuddered, remembering the last time she had seen those grey forms, the night before . . . before the Campbell soldiers had risen against them!

It was with real regret that Anne told Alizon some days later that she must make plans for their return to Charleston. During the few months they had spent together they had become very close and were sad to part. With a deep sigh Alizon told Anne she must hurry before the passes were closed with the heavy snows of winter.

"What will you tell Darnley?"

"You mean why Alasdair has not returned with me?"

"Yes. If I remember him, Anne, he will be furious and will never forgive you. He will want to hurt you. Take care of Adeline! Don't let her out of your sight!"

"Adeline is not a baby, he could not abduct her so easily! Leave Darnley to me. Alasdair has told me he will never leave you now, that this is his country, it is where he belongs. . . ."

Tears started in Alizon's eyes. "Anne . . . never can I thank you enough, words are not enough. . . ."

Anne patted the trembling hand that tightly gripped a kerchief. "I will miss him, I would be lying if I said I would not, but I have Adeline, she is mine, but even she is reluctant to go. . . ."

"Because of Phillip?"

"She's only a child, she will forget him once she has been home for a month or so. He is the first boy who ever had any affection for her, and it was so obvious. She was flattered, and she has the vanity of youth. I've spoiled her, I'm afraid, but she'll soon forget him!"

Alizon agreed with her, putting all thoughts of her own childhood sweetheart and the love that was denied them from her mind. Adeline was a spoilt child and she would forget. Darnley was a wealthy man and now that the danger of the Yemassees had passed, the social gatherings would resume. With her fragile beauty Adeline would soon become the most sought-after girl in Charleston, and Phillip Gowry would be just a memory. It was for the best. She wondered to herself how she could receive the boy now, knowing that his father had played his part once again in her heartbreak. Her friendship with Gabrielle was somehow protected from all outside forces, nothing would change between them, but Phillip. . . .

Her thoughts turned to her children. Alasdair spent most of his time away from the house; his friends were the sons of the tacksmen and she doubted if he could find again that friendship with Phillip and Andrea. . . . Oh, Andrea. . . . She could see the hatred and frustration that had burned within herself after Andrew's death, burning now in her child and she prayed that it would not consume all the capacity for love in Andrea. She was too young to hate with such consuming ferocity, but for that Alizon must blame herself, she had brought Andrea up to hate the gaudy uniform, the men who wore it, and the name of Campbell.

It was she who had sown in her daughter the seeds of a hatred that could destroy her. She had only meant to keep Andrew's memory alive, and remain intensely loyal to the old ways. Instead she had kindled the raging fire of a hatred that threatened to destroy as it grew with the years. If only Andrea could find a love as she herself had, at least some of the hatred would melt. She was still a child, only the same age as Adeline, yet she seemed years older. The thought crossed her mind to ask Anne to take Andrea to Charleston with her, but she realised the girl would never go, and besides Anne would have enough to contend with when she faced Darnley on her return.

"I don't suppose we shall meet again, Anne, but I will always remember you, and I shall write and tell you how Alasdair is. . . ."

"And I shall write back to you and tell you my news, that I promise!"

They both rose and left the room, Alizon to find Andrea and Anne to prepare Adeline for their departure.

Four days later, after the tearful farewells had been

said, the small group trotted out of the gateway and onto the moor. They were to pick up an escort at Fort William, Gabrielle had arranged that, and from there they would take ship from Leith back to the warmth of Carolina, to the fresh winds that blew in from the ocean, to the long peaceful evenings Alizon remembered so well. She raised her hand to wave and Alasdair placed his arm about her shoulders while Andrea slipped her hand into Alizon's. Hope raised its head again. She had her son and her daughter.

Chapter 11

Charleston had survived the attacks of the Indians as it had survived, hurricane, fever, and flood. Darnley had increased his acreage and was now one of the richest and most respected men in the town. On her return without Alasdair, Anne had borne his fury with head held high and in silence, though she had quaked inside. He had not spoken to her for nearly two months, but at length an uneasy truce had come to pass between them. All this Alizon learned from the letters that went regularly to and fro between Charleston and Rannoch. Another thing she learned from Anne was that the Colony was loyal to German George, but, Anne added, they had wept for King Charles and praised King James II, had accepted William and Mary, and Queen Anne had been their Dear Sovereign Lady. In fact the people of the Colony were so involved in their own affairs that the significance of Stuart or Hanoverian rule largely escaped them.

After the defeat of the uprising of 1715, Alizon once more turned her attention to her family. As the years passed hope dwindled again. The Union seemed to have been strengthened, not weakened, by the rebellion. Scotland would always be the poor relation, and she felt that now there would be no future for her country. Alasdair had soon adopted their way of life as his own, and his friends were the sons of the lairds and chiefs of the septs of the MacDonalds and the young men of Glencoe. He was a quiet boy who, although he had little to say at the many discussions, was respected and liked by all. His Stuart blood set him a little apart, although he always strove never to take advantage of this.

Andrea was still a lively, strong willed spitfire, but she had grown into a beautiful young woman who had learned to curb her waspish tongue, and to smile sweetly when provoked instead of becoming vituperative. Alizon was amused when she witnessed such instances. Andrea had a woman's wiles, and was aware that there were more ways of getting her own way than by bullying and argument. There were times when Alizon worried about her: she was of marriageable age, yet she showed no inclination to take a husband. She confided her thoughts in her letters to Anne, who was having problems of her own with Adeline.

Andrea was seventeen when they visited Inverness and she encountered Ian MacIntosh for the first time. Their meeting did not begin well. He was leaving the Royal Arms and was not very steady on his feet when she happened to pass by. They collided.

"My dear lady! I beg your pardon!" he gallantly apologised, though his words were rather slurred.

"I am not your dear lady and you, sir, are drunk!" Andrea's eyes were blazing as she straightened her bonnet which had been knocked askew, and prepared to pick up her purse and the parcel she had been carrying. He too bent to retrieve the articles and in doing so stumbled, falling heavily and pushing her backwards. They lay sprawled together upon the ground which, fortunately, was dry for there had been no rain for a week. With a hefty shove Andrea pushed him off her skirts and rose to her feet, her cheeks burning. She shook with anger. What a sight she must appear, sprawling on the street with this drunken idiot! There was a large rent in her skirt and she had a smudge of dust on her nose. Her bonnet had slipped off entirely and was hanging around her neck, secured only by its ribbons.

"How dare you! You drunken, ignorant lout!" she

shouted, forgetting her manners and position, and oblivious to the fact that quite a crowd had gathered.

"I can't apologise enough madam! It was an accident." He seemed, suddenly, to have sobered. "We were both bent on retrieving your purse and goods. I'm afraid I've ruined your dress."

Her attention was drawn once more to the rent in her skirt and she exploded with anger, calling him all the unsavoury names she could think of, not caring if she sounded like a woman of the Grassmarket in Edinburgh. The crowd was getting bigger, and smiles and titters only added to her anger.

"What's happening, Andrea?"

She turned to find Alasdair elbowing his way through the crowd, and pointing a finger at the dishevelled youth she started to enumerate the insults she had suffered at his hands.

Alasdair tried to quieten her. "Do you not realise what a spectacle you are making of yourself?"

"It is he who has made a spectacle of me!" she cried, glaring at his offending personage.

"I've apologised most profusely!" MacIntosh declared heatedly.

"Who are you, sir?"

"Ian MacIntosh, and you?"

"Alasdair MacDonald Stuart and this . . . this lady is my sister, Andrea Charlotte."

Ian MacIntosh blinked rapidly. "Not the Stuarts who live on Rannoch?"

"The same."

"Then, sir, may I double my apologies to the lady. I of course will pay for all damage . . ." he added, as Andrea tried to hide her torn skirts with her shawl.

Glancing around him at the grinning crowd, Alasdair thought it prudent to remove Andrea from the scene. "Accepted—now I think we had better leave before the town guard take it into their heads that we are starting a riot."

Young MacIntosh nodded solemnly as Alasdair took

Andrea by the arm and propelled her forcefully to where their horses were tethered. She fumed in silence all the way home, after berating her half-brother for not at least horse-whipping the ignorant, drunken sot.

"He seemed quite a gentleman, Andrea. It was after all, an accident and he did offer to pay for any damage."

"Decent! Staggering from a tavern, pushing me into the gutter, then knocking me off my feet and having me sprawling in the dust! You call that the conduct of a gentleman?"

"It was not deliberate, Andrea! He's no drunken lout. He is a gentleman—as far as I can see it was accidental and you should have had the good grace to accept his apology. Now let that be an end to it!"

She had related the tale to Alizon on their arrival at Rannoch. Alizon in turn heard Alasdair's version and decided that Andrea was taking the matter too much at heart. But she, as much as Andrea, was startled when the very next evening a rider came trotting into the courtyard and presented himself at the front door, bearing a large parcel.

He was received by Alizon herself.

"Are you Mistress Stuart?"

"I am and you, if I am correct in my judgement, are Ian MacIntosh from the description my son gave me."

"Aye, mistress, I am Ian MacIntosh. I've come to make amends with this." He held out the parcel.

"What is it?"

"Fifteen yards of fine silk, to . . . to replace the dress that was er . . . ruined."

Alizon tried unsuccessfully to hide a smile. "I'm sure it will more than make up . . . silk, that must have cost a fair amount of silver?"

"Well . . . yes. . . ."

"You must give it to her yourself, if you can brave her. I'm afraid she has a fierce temper!"

He grinned. "I know that already!"

Alizon smiled back. She liked him. He was about twenty years of age she judged, tall but not thickset. His unpowdered hair was reddish-gold and his eyes clear blue, but by the cut of his clothes and his manners she judged him to be the son of a MacIntosh laird. "Who is your father?"

"Ewan MacIntosh."

She had been right in part. Ewan MacIntosh was head of the MacIntosh Clan and loyal to the Hanoverian.

"Well, make your peace, if you can. But let me tell you now that I oppose your father's views! Are you of the same opinions as he?"

"I am, mistress, I'll not deny it!"

"You know who I am and what I stand for?"

"I know."

"Yet you come here with gifts for my daughter? The apology in Inverness was enough!" Her manner towards him had grown cool.

"I'm a man who speaks his mind, Mistress Stuart. I hold faith with my own beliefs and those of my father, and no man or woman will change that. But I am here to ask leave to court your daughter with a view to taking her for my wife, for she is the most beautiful girl I've ever seen!"

This was the last thing she had expected! She was completely astounded, and against her own judgement found herself liking the young man, even though she certainly did not approve of his politics or loyalties. His honesty, his audacity, was somehow courageous. "You . . . you astound me. . . . What makes you think I should accept you as a suitor for my daughter?"

"I'm a determined man!"

"And my daughter is a most headstrong, self-willed young woman. I doubt that you would suit each other! But you may stay for dinner at least." Never let it be said the Stuarts lacked hospitality. She turned and walked, trying to conceal a smile, towards the room in which the table was set for the evening meal.

Alasdair was leaning on the mantle while Andrea was fondling the ears of a small lapdog, both waiting their mother's appearance for dinner. When Andrea saw who it was who accompanied Alizon she froze, and the smile on her face vanished.

"What's he doing here?" she snapped.

"He has come to make reparation for yesterday and he has ridden a long way. He also has something for you." Alizon went to the side table and poured out a glass of wine for herself and a dram for their guest.

Suspicion was apparent in Andrea's eyes, while Alasdair looked on, grinning to himself.

"It... it's some silk to replace the dress I ruined, take it...."

Andrea eyed the parcel as though it were full of repulsive insects.

"Andrea!" Alizon's voice held a note of reprimand, and very slowly and reluctantly Andrea took the parcel from him and placed it on a chair.

"As he has come so far I have invited him to stay for dinner. Andrea, you may tell Jeannie to lay another place."

Throughout the meal Andrea remained silent, picking at her food, her mouth set in stubborn, sulky lines. Occasionally she would shoot a sly look at Ian from beneath her lashes. He was quite handsome, for such a boor! But watching him now when sober she had to admit he was a gentleman. She thought of the other young men she knew and with some chagrin realised that she had seen many of them in a far worse state than Ian MacIntosh had been the previous morning. Some of the cold fury seemed to depart and the glances in his direction became more frequent. He seemed, most certainly, more of a man than any of her clansmen. And there was something in the way his blue eyes twinkled that made her feel suddenly breathless.

Alizon did not eat much either. She watched the two young people, feeling sad and strangely old. Why him? she asked herself. Why, of all the eligible men, did he have to come along? What could she do? What should she do, for he was sure to call again. She tried to calm her racing thoughts. She must remain impartial, at all costs. Andrea must choose for herself. The choice of husband had been denied Alizon. She had never been allowed to marry the man she had loved and she had sworn long ago that she would never impose such a restriction upon Andrea. But MacIntosh of MacIntosh! Dear God! Let her find him repugnant! She prayed silently, though as she watched the anger fade from her daughter's eyes to be replaced with a hesitant admiration she already knew that prayer was one which would not be answered.

At first, after the dinner, she stormed and raged at her mother for even allowing him into the house. When he came the second time she refused to see him, but after he had gone she felt disappointed and miserable. Alizon declined to give any indication of her feelings towards him, which confused Andrea even more, but when he came again she went to meet him and consented to walk with him for a short way on the moor. His visits became more and more frequent and as she watched them Alizon knew that soon she would have to give her permission to a marriage that she violently disapproved of. Andrea was a fervent supporter of the Stuarts, she believed in Scotland's freedom from the Union, she was quick-tempered and obstinate, but in Ian MacIntosh she had met her match, for he could handle her as no one else could simply because he loved her.

There were frequent arguments and quarrels, usually about their differences of politics, but other than that they seemed to have been made for each other. When the day came when he asked Alizon's official permission to wed Andrea she had to agree. When she saw the radiance in her daughter's face, the happiness shining in her eyes, she could do nothing else. Once, years ago, she had loved like that and had been forced to the bed of another man. That was never going to happen to Andrea.

The house that was to be their home, Glenmoy, was on the MacIntosh estates near Inverness, and this was Andrea's one regret, that she would be so far away from Alizon.

"But I have Alasdair!" was Alizon's reply to Andrea's misgivings about moving so far away from the glen and the moor.

"I do not want to go away . . . to have to live near Inverness. . . ."

"With your husband, where you belong from now on!"

Alizon had said firmly, although she dreaded being parted from this child to whom she had been so close. She loved Alasdair, but he was Darnley's son. Andrea was Andrew's child and she had loved Andrew all her life, she still loved him, even death and the passing of the years had not deadened the pain, the longing. Always the ache would be there until she, too, was dead.

So Andrea had gone north to Inverness at the head of the great glen, to be mistress of her own home. It was not as big or as lavishly furnished as Rannoch Chase, but comfortable enough, with pleasant views of the towering crags and the deep waters of Loch Ness. And in time Alizon came to accept, in peace, that her beloved daughter was now a woman. . . .

It seemed, by contrast, that the wooing and wedding of Alasdair passed without trouble, without excitement, almost without notice.

The girl was as quiet and gentle as a mountain faun and was, moreover, a MacDonald of Glengarry. Alizon had known her for years, and yet not known her, for she was as retiring and shy as Andrea was spirited and rebellious. Alizon realised one day, with a sense of pleasant surprise, that Alasdair and young Janet were together for much of the time. They seemed to have drifted together without anyone noticing and their marriage passed in the same way. Janet moved into the house with Alizon and Alasdair, and seemed never to mind, never to want the independence of a home alone with Alasdair. In the same way that she had won his heart, she won Alizon's. Gentle, quiet, biddable, she was a girl who was never noticed, but who yet became an integral part of Rannoch Chase.

Sometimes it seemed to Alizon that the years had telescoped — rushed past so quickly that she had not noticed them until one day she realised she was no longer young, was no longer yearning like a young woman for her dead love. Life, which had been passionate and anguished, became tranquil and filled with the pleasures and contentment of her family. Andrea gave birth within the first two years of her marriage to two sons, the first she called

Andrew after her father, and the second son, Robert.

Then Alasdair and quiet little Janet also provided her with grandchildren, two girls, Catherine and Margaret. Alizon, caring for her two little grand-daughters who brought back life and energy into Rannoch Chase, sometimes wondered what had happened to the young tempestuous girl she had once been. Is this what happened to everyone as they grew older? Did grandchildren, the changing of the seasons, the quiet pleasures of living in a house with those one loved take the place of youthful passion?

It did not really matter, for she was content.

Alasdair's son was born before Andrea's third child. They named him Alexander Douglas, Douglas in memory of Margaret Douglas, Countess of Lennox in the reign of Elizabeth Tudor, who was herself the daughter of a Scottish queen. Andrea's third child was yet another son, whom they called Ewan, for his MacIntosh grandfather. When Andrea was recovered enough from childbirth she took the children on the long journey to Rannoch, for although she heard regularly from Alizon she had not seen her for nearly four years. As she threw herself into her mother's arms she noticed the new lines around her eyes, the new furrows in her forehead. Alizon was growing old, she thought sadly.

"Are you lonely, Mother?"

"Lonely! Why should I be lonely? I have Alasdair and Janet and the children, there is no time for loneliness!"

Andrea stood studying Alizon closely. "Not even when you lie awake at night?"

She saw the pain in Alizon's dark eyes and regretted her words.

"Even in a crowd one can be lonely, even with one's own family constantly around you there are times when you feel alone, terribly alone. I do."

Alizon's expression changed to one of concern. "You are not happy with Ian? Has something happened to damage your marriage?" Had her fears been confirmed? She had thought them well suited but she had always doubted his false loyalties. Had they now become the cause of such a wide rift between them that Andrea had brought her children and come home?

"We are happy, that I promise you! I've not run away from him, if that's what you're thinking! He promised that after the baby was born and I was well enough to travel I should come home to see you. . . ." Strange, she thought, of how she referred to Rannoch Chase as home, even though she had a house of her own. In her mind she would always think of Rannoch as her home, a place of safety, security and love.

Alizon smiled with relief. Janet was such a gentle, docile girl that she hardly ever raised her voice, even to her own children, and she could see that Alasdair was happy, but she had no way of knowing if Andrea spoke the truth.

"How long can you stay? It's been so long. . . ."

"For over a sennight, if I wish. Ian told me I could stay as long as I liked, but the children will miss him. . . ."

Alizon picked up Robert in her arms. "They are all like Ian. Will there be more, Andrea? You have, both you and Alasdair, made me a grandmother so quickly! Six grandchildren. . . ."

"There will be more, God willing. I want a daughter. In the end sons grow away from you, but girls . . . though I'm far away from you now. . . ." Suddenly there was a lump in her throat and she couldn't continue.

"Distance is nothing! You are always in my thoughts! Come. Let's go find Janet and the children. Alasdair is away down the glen with John, but he'll be back for dinner."

The house seemed to be bursting at the seams with laughter and noise. There was the thump of small feet, the squeals of delight, the howls of rage, as the children played and fought together while Andrea, Alizon and Janet watched over them with pride and joy. Seeing them playing in the pasture at the back of the house, Alizon thought that this was what she had built Rannoch for. It was meant to be filled with the sounds of children playing, their laughter, their singing, not left to grow stagnant, empty, and filled with loneliness until at last its former magnificence fell into disrepair and finally ruin. Catherine, Margaret, Andrew and Robert were all running about, the September sunshine glinting on the varied hues of their hair which ranged from the silver-blonde of Margaret's to the deep auburn of Robert. Each one of them had the huge, dark, melancholy eyes that she herself had inherited from her father, Charles Stuart.

Alizon sighed. If only her father had had one legitimate son there would have been no wars, they would have lived peacefully all these years under the reign of a Stuart king. James Stuart was growing old but he had a son, a young man with her father's name and, from what she heard, some of his temperament. Did their hopes lie in that direction, she wondered. Would Prince Charles Edward Stuart ever come to claim his grandfather's crown? Would these children playing now in the sunshine grow up in peace or would war and rebellion disrupt their lives?

She looked up as she heard the shout and saw Alasdair running across the grass towards them, in his hand a parchment. Her heart plummeted down to her stomach. What news? What had happened now?

Chapter 12

Janet rose to her feet, a tiny dart of fear stabbing her as she saw the look on Alasdair's face. "What's has happened? What is it?"

He passed the parchment to Alizon. "Darnley is dead, and Anne herself is ill with the fever. There is another epidemic . . ."

Janet stared up at him, seeing grief and worry struggling in his face with something else. Was it regret, she wondered, as she laid her hand gently on his arm.

Alizon didn't really see the words, they were just a dancing mass of squirls that seemed to roll into each other with fluidity. He was dead. He, too, had gone now. She remembered the day she had seen him return to Kircaldy after the hurricane, and she remembered the hatred she had felt when she had discovered Alasdair gone, and then all those years of grief. She should feel no pity for him, but strangely she did. And Anne? How long ago the letter had been written she did not know, it took weeks, months for mail to travel. Anne, too, might be dead by now, and Adeline would be alone. Alone in the huge house on the river, listening to the silence broken only by the alligators in the swamps. She looked up at her son. "What will you do? Adeline begs you to go back."

"I don't want to go back, this is my home now, Scotland is my country."

"They both loved you, Alasdair. He enough to take you from me because he thought it was right for you, and Anne—hers was a deeper love because you were not her own flesh and blood and she took great risks to bring you back to me. She faced his anger when she returned without you. Her life may have been a living hell for all we know, because of that one act of compassion. I think that only I understand what it cost her to leave you."

The time had come. There had been a week of frantic packing by Janet and Alizon with the help of Jeannie the maid, while Alasdair had made the necessary arrangements. And now all the trunks and bags were loaded onto the pack animals and the two little girls were astride the sure-footed docile Shelties. Janet stood with young Alexander in her arms, while Alasdair was in conversation with John MacDonald who was to take them to Edinburgh and from there to Leith.

"We shan't be away long, Alizon!" said Janet. "And we shall come to no harm. I am very certain of that, otherwise I would not risk it."

Alizon took her in her arms and kissed her. "If he had travelled the length and breadth of Scotland he could have found no better wife, Janet!" There were tears in her eyes as she kissed Alexander, then crossed to hug and kiss Catherine and Margaret. John helped Janet up onto Alasdair's horse and Alizon handed her the baby. It remained only for Alasdair to mount now, for Janet was to ride pillion.

"It's time to go, Mother. . . ."

She looked at him, loath to let him from her sight. Once before he had left her, and he had by some miracle been restored to her. This time she might not be so lucky. "Take care of them all, and give my love to Anne. See that your father has a decent burial, for he loved you."

"I promise!" He bent down and kissed her cheek as she held him close to her.

"Come back soon, Alasdair! Come back soon!"

They were too late, even though they had taken the fastest packet out of Leith. They were three days too late. Anne was dead. The epidemic of yellow fever had claimed many lives, as it so often did. They sat in the small parlour of Chawira and heard Adeline's pitiful tale of how Anne had called in vain for Darnley and herself, and had not recognized Adeline though she was with her almost day and night.

"Poor Adeline," Janet thought, seeing the dark circles of fatigue beneath eyes swollen and red from weeping, and cheeks hollow with anxiety and fear.

"She is still here?" Alasdair managed to control his voice.

Adeline shook her head.

"Too late even for that!" he muttered bitterly.

"She lies beside him in St Phillip's, they were both taken by river. She . . . she loved him so much, even though he hardly spoke to her after we came home. It was as though at times he didn't even notice that she was there in the same room!"

"Because she gave me back my mother and a new life!"

"She did that because she loved you, too!" Janet reminded him.

"Oh Janet, I'm so glad you came! I've been so afraid, so lonely. There was no one to turn to. . . ." Adeline broke down and wept while Janet signalled for Alasdair to take the children to the nursery and begin to supervise the servants. Adeline hardly remembered Janet from her visit to Scotland years before, but already Janet's quiet sympathy had made the girl turn to her for support and comfort. Janet led Adeline, sobbing, into the small library, where shades cut out the glare of the sun and the room was reasonably cool.

"Tell me, Adeline, why did she do it? Why did Anne bring Alasdair back to Scotland? She knew what Darnley's reactions would be. Why did she bring Alasdair back to Rannoch?"

"Because although she loved my father, yet she hated him! It sounds foolish, but she wanted to hurt him for what she had endured. Her sufferings started years ago. They thought I didn't know, but I did. . . . There were always women, overdressed, painted women, and he gambled. We have lost a lot of land and slaves because of his gaming." The sobs were renewed and Janet stroked the golden curls that lay in her lap as though Adeline were one of her little daughters, Catherine or Margaret. Anne was better off now, she thought sadly. She was past all the pain and humiliations and at least Darnley had died before his gambling had made paupers of them all, leaving Adeline destitute.

Adeline raised a tear-stained face. "You will stay, Janet? I've been so lonely and afraid. . . ."

"Of course we will!"

"You won't ever go and leave me alone again, all alone in this great silent house!" She shuddered.

Janet was thoughtful. It would not be fair to bolster Adeline's courage with lies. "We will stay for as long as you need us, but Alasdair does not look upon Chawira as his home now. Rannoch Chase is where he belongs."

"But what about Chawira? My father built it up from nothing, all for Alasdair!"

"Hush now, let us not look too far ahead. . . . We have plenty of time to sort everything out when . . . when you are calmer and in better health. You are so thin! When did you last eat a hearty meal?"

"I don't know. I've had no appetite, I've cared for nothing . . . all I did was pray that you would come soon!"

"We're here now and that is all that matters. You will

never be alone again, I promise you!"

Adeline wiped her eyes with the corner of her skirt. "Did . . . did you see Phillip before you left?"

Janet was surprised and taken off-guard for an instant. "Phillip?" She said the name as though she had never heard it before.

"Phillip Gowry."

"Oh! No, he . . . he doesn't come to Rannoch Chase now. He joined his father's regiment and since then came twice. Alasdair made it clear that he would not welcome that uniform in his mother's house. He did not come again, though Gabrielle still visits. Andrea was with us when your letter came, she helped me pack before she returned home with her children."

"Alizon did not approve of her marriage, did she?"

"No, but Andrea is happy despite the occasional difference of opinion. She sent word just before we left to tell you to have courage."

"Andrea would not have been afraid. . . ."

"Maybe she would, who knows? Beneath that hard exterior I suspect there is a soft heart that could be easily hurt. Would you consider coming back with us, Adeline?"

"I don't know . . . I've not thought about it. Charleston is my home, I felt . . . I felt unsure of myself, at Rannoch. The manners and customs are so different, but . . . but I may think about it."

Janet wisely left the subject there. The choice was up to Alasdair. Chawira belonged to him now, to sell or retain as he saw fit. She would leave the decision to him and if he decided to sell, then she was sure she could persuade Adeline to return to Scotland with them. She had been surprised about the enquiry after Phillip Gowry. She thought Adeline had long forgotten him, but obviously she had not.

Alasdair rode the flourishing acres of Chawira and something akin to pride rose within him. As a child he remembered the small house on Church Street which had no back yard, yet Darnley had worked and schemed to buy this place and make it into one of the richest and most flourishing plantations along the river. He was aware, having gone through his father's books, that a great deal of land and nearly fifty slaves had been lost through Darnley's gaming, but there were still acres and acres of rice and indigo. Strange, he thought, there could be no two places on earth that contrasted so sharply as Chawira and Rannoch Chase. The first was set amongst luxuriant vegetation in a semi-tropical climate, where jessamine, magnolia, myrtle, dogwood, honeysuckle, the blossoms of the peach, orange and plum trees gave riotous colour and sweet perfumes with the changing seasons. At Rannoch, from November to March and sometimes later, the moor and the hostile bare mountains were covered in a white blanket that stretched as far as the eye could see, broken here and there by the black outline of a tree, its branches a fine tracery against a grey sky. In summer and spring it was beautiful, not in the same way as Carolina, but more gentle, more muted.

Chawira was the young, slightly brash and vividly colourful girl dancing in brilliant sunlight, while Rannoch Chase was the older, more subtly beautiful, gentle-voiced woman who had experienced much more of life. His loyalties were torn. In Charleston he had spent his childhood and most of his youth. It was the place of his birth, and at Chawira under Darnley's supervision and Anne's devotion he had spent his formative years. Yet in Scotland, a foreign land with its alien culture and language, where he had spent such a short time, he had become so completely engrossed and absorbed that it felt as though he had been born and raised there.

He remembered Andrea's bitter words after the news of the failure of the rebellion had been brought to them. They were part of an old Gaelic saying and she had repeated them often. Now he murmured them to himself, 'Cha Till, Cha Till!' No return, No return, I will never return! But he would return, one day, as Alizon had done, drawn back by blood ties and memories and the rights of a prince who, like himself, had had a king for a grandfather. Memories and blood ties worth fighting for, worth dying for!

He drew rein and stared ahead of him at the house, the bricks faded now to a rosy pink and covered with the clinging clematis and wisteria. He shivered. He was not superstitious, but an odd feeling flooded over him and he shivered again, though the sun was hot on his back. Suddenly it was important to him: he must rename Chawira. It would become Rannoch: that name must live on. He had his fears for his mother and Andrea and the house on the moor that he loved so much. He must go back, one day he must go back, but the grey moss above his head seemed to mock him, whispering, always whispering, 'Cha Till, Cha Till no me Tuille!'

Alasdair had intended to sell Chawira as soon as possible and return to Scotland, but somehow running the place had produced a certain pride of ownership in him. He would go to Scotland —one day—but now the urgency to sell had gone. Janet had suddenly blossomed as the young matron of the plantation and the children thrived in the warm air. They had all settled far quicker than he had thought. The only restless one, strangely enough, was Adeline. . . .

There was something different about Adeline, he thought. He had only just noticed it but he could not put his finger on it. At first she had been shocked and grieved at the deaths of both her parents and the ordeal of being alone on the plantation until he had returned with his new family. She had quickly recovered and had soon become her old self again, but sometimes he thought she was too bright, her conversation too forced, her smile too sweet. This was especially noticeable in the company of the other girls and young men at the increasing number of social functions they attended.

He sighed. It was only to be expected. The plantation was large and flourishing and Charleston, too, was becoming more settled and cultured. There were many fine buildings of stone now. The old church of St Phillip had been replaced by a splendid stone edifice. Broadcloth, carpets, silk, gloves, ribbons, silver plate, books, china, pictures, prints and fine furniture were all imported weekly. There were frequent productions of Shakespeare's work in the two new theatres in Church Street and Dock Street, there were the St Cecilia Balls and there was the Jockey Club. At first only a small strong breed of horse called the Chickasaw was entered, but as time had passed stock was imported from England. The races held at the New Market course just outside the town were the social event of the year, culminating in a ball. The shopkeepers put up their shutters, the law courts were closed, the schools gave a holiday and everyone rode out to the race course.

Alasdair was trying to sort out the administrative matters of the plantation. Reluctantly he drew the papers that had been awaiting his attention for some time, towards him. Those who thought that the life of a planter was one of idleness and pleasure should become one, he thought. Mistakes had been made in the beginning, and they had been made at great cost. At least Darnley had laid out his fields and irrigation system correctly, and had taught his overseer who in turn had taught the Negro slaves the correct procedures for the growing and harvesting of rice and indigo, their main crops, and also the few fields planted with cotton. All building work, however, had to be directed by Alasdair. The domestic concerns were Janet's, but she was capable and had said that she found running a large house just as easy as a small one. Her only problem was with Adeline.

He frowned. His own three children were growing up; they would in time acquire Charleston manners and adopt Charleston's way of life. Little Alexander would have no memory of the country he had been born in. But Adeline. . . . After she had overcome her grief she seemed to fling herself into a whirl of social functions, collecting about her a group of fervent admirers. She appeared to be thoroughly enjoying herself and yet there was something wild and untamed about her. The months had slipped by and as a family, they were putting down roots.

Janet particularly had become more self-assured and confident. The children were thriving and whenever he mentioned Scotland to his wife she would brush aside the question adroitly or turn the conversation in another direction. It seemed they had all of them grown comfortable and happy there. And so life drifted along until a year had gone, and then two, and still Adeline bothered him.

Adeline worried Janet, too. She knew that there was something driving the girl, but her attempts to draw Adeline out had all failed. She had watched her at balls and parties; Adeline's laughter was too shrill, her eyes too bright, the witty remarks too forced, the smile too brittle as though she were hiding something. She had many suitors: four young men of good family had proposed but she had refused them, preferring, so Janet thought, to be surrounded by admiring, flattering young men, rather like a queen bee. Janet wondered if she were secretly afraid of marriage and one day she tried to speak to her about the matter.

The afternoon was warm, the insects droned lazily in the flowers and for once Adeline was sitting in the garden alone. She sat beneath the huge old cypress tree where it was cooler—her eyes were closed and at first Janet thought she was asleep. Adeline heard her approach. She had hoped to spend a few hours alone, to think, to remember him, the words he had spoken to her, but obviously it was not to be. Perhaps if she feigned sleep Janet would go away. She wished—fleetingly—everyone would leave her alone, but she was bound to admit that she would be tormented to the point of misery if left by herself with those memories.

Phillip. How often had she whispered that name, how often had she remembered that look of pure adoration she had seen in his eyes. Before she had been forced to return home she had told him that she would come back to him one day. They had both sworn never to forget each other or let their love die. Oh, she knew everyone thought they were only children, but she had loved him and he her and she would go back to him, she would! At first, after the shock of her parents' death, she had wanted to stay at

Chawira (which Alasdair had now renamed Rannoch) forever, but as the weeks had turned to months and both Alasdair and Janet seemed to be settling there, her thoughts turned more and more to her childhood sweetheart. She began to remember Scotland with nostalgia, thinking of the happiness she had known there, wondering how she could return there.

She had once or twice mentioned the matter to Janet but the answers she received from her sister-in-law were discouraging. "But Adeline, there is so much work to be done here!" and "Adeline, you said you wanted to stay here!" Slowly she opened her eyes and stared up at Janet. The climate of the Colony suited Janet, she looked well, happy and contented, Adeline thought.

"I thought you were asleep, I was just about to leave you . . ."

Silently Adeline cursed herself. "No, I was just resting. It is so warm today and as I was needed for nothing and have no engagement I thought I would sit here."

"I don't know where you get your energy from at times, you seem to whirl and dance from place to place and in this heat. . . ." Janet fanned herself with a palmetto leaf.

"You forget I was born here."

"True. I'm becoming acclimatised now and so are the children, they are blossoming!"

"Was there something you wanted to say . . . ?" Adeline enquired before Janet could launch forth into an account of the virtues of the climate of Carolina and those of her children.

"Yes. Henry Grant came to see Alasdair yesterday."

"I know and I know the reason and the answer is no!"

"Adeline, he was the fifth! What are you trying to do? You have dismissed the sons of some of the best families in the county. Are you cutting notches in a candle to keep count? What is the matter with Henry Grant? I thought you were very fond of him, he has been forever at your side for the past month!"

"There is nothing wrong with him, I just don't love him!"

"Adeline, my dear, what are you waiting for, a knight

in shining armour to come and sweep you off your feet? That only happens in fairy stories, children's tales. You are old enough for marriage. Don't you wish for a husband of your own? Do you not *want* to marry?"

"No! I would willingly wed the man I love. . . ."

"There is someone?"

Adeline glanced at Janet, trying to judge her mood. If she told Janet would she laugh at the childish romance and tell her to forget Phillip Gowry? Tell her that she would never see him again and that she must be sensible and choose one of the young men of Charleston? "Janet. . . ." she began.

"Yes?"

"Janet, if you loved someone and you were forced to leave him would you . . . what would you do?"

Understanding dawned on Janet. . . . All this time Adeline had been thinking of young Gowry. All this time, while she had been courted by so many suitors, her heart had been far away with a young soldier who wore the uniform that Alasdair hated so much. "I . . . I would try to be reasonable, sensible about it. If there were no chance of ever seeing him again and . . . there isn't, Adeline! Alasdair has settled down again here and I . . . I love the place, it is so good for the children. . . ."

"I thought Alasdair had promised one day to return to Scotland! I thought that he intended to sell this place?"

"He did, at first, perhaps in his heart he still does, but Adeline, be sensible! This is where you belong—marry Henry Grant, Carolina is your home!"

"No!"

"Alasdair would never let you marry Phillip Gowry! You know he has enlisted in the king's army and you know that his father killed Andrea's father. You know where Alasdair's loyalties lie—he would never let you marry him! Be sensible!"

"I don't want to be sensible! I don't want to spend my life mouldering away in some stagnant plantation on some equally stagnant backwater! I hate Henry Grant! I hate them all! I love Phillip and I will have him! One day I will! You can stay here with your children and your everlasting dull, boring soirées, balls and concerts, I'd sooner wander barefoot through the heather if I could have Phillip!"

She had said too much, she knew it. Janet would repeat it all to Alasdair and she would never get a chance to go back... she should have curbed her unruly tongue! She jumped to her feet and holding up her skirts she ran lightly over the green turf towards the house. At least in her bedroom she could think of Phillip. The tears were stinging her eyes, her vision was blurred by them and she stumbled but kept on. Someday, somehow, she would go back, they could not force her to marry someone she did not love. She would go back!

Chapter 13

Governor Glenn had gone, and had been glad to do so for there was trouble brewing again with the Indians. He left the flourishing town fair and fortified, so he claimed, but the fortifications would be of little use in a full-scale Cherokee attack. This was the feeling of most of the gentlemen of Charleston at that time, and was Alasdair's view also. Only the year before the town had been devastated by a terrible fire that had gutted great numbers of buildings, but it was recovering, seeming to have a tenacity that even nature herself could not overcome. The Cherokees and Tuscaroras, however, were a different matter.

Alasdair was well content with his family: Catherine, Margaret and Alexander were sturdy healthy young people. Alexander was nearing his fifteenth birthday while the two girls were already attracting suitors. Adeline still had not married and both Janet and Alasdair, indeed the whole county, now assumed that she never would. She was still beautiful, though past her prime. She had been so foolish, everyone said. She could have had any of the young men in Charleston, but now Adeline was looked upon as a confirmed spinster.

The new Governor, Lyttleton, found the Colony in turmoil, with Occonostata and the Cherokees on their doorsteps and in an ugly mood. Lyttleton at once summoned the chiefs to give up those of their tribes who had already murdered the inhabitants on the outlying plantations. Occonostata sued for peace, but Lyttleton was a military man and told the great chief that he would receive their submission in their own country and at the point of his bayonet.

"The man's a fool!" Alasdair exploded when Edward Ashe rode out to explain the situation to him. "Doesn't he know what he is subjecting us to? How the hell are we to defend our homes? Dear God! This is a private house, we have no cannon here!"

"He's escorting the delegation back to their lands, then he has told everyone to meet him at the Congaree river."

"He's mad! He's going out with an untrained rabble against Occonostata and Attakullakulla!"

Ashe nodded.

"Then I'll have to go with him. I'll send the women and Alex back into the town. Are you joining this madness?"

"I've no choice, neither has any man who values his home and family!"

"I don't suppose there will be help from the other Colonies?"

"Can't say, but I don't think he's asked for any."

"Damn the man!"

Alasdair was preoccupied with his preparations for joining Lyttleton and moving his family into the safer confines of the town. He failed to note the sudden decisive change in Adeline, a look of speculation and secrecy in her face that became more and more apparent as the family move to Charleston was discussed.

Catherine and Margaret were truculent, complaining that it was hot and sticky and dirty in the town, but Adeline reminded them that there were far more social events there than out on the creek. This seemed to cheer them a little and she hoped that they would not realise that all the young men would be away with the Governor and that there would be little social life of any kind. This prospect did not worry her at all.

The plan had been fermenting in her head for a long, long time, and now, suddenly, she found the courage and the opportunity to carry it through. Young Alex was furious that he was not allowed to go with his father and the other men to fight the Indians, but Janet forbade it and after a most serious talk with his father, which lasted almost an hour, he did not mention the subject again, but fumed in silence.

They had left the plantation, Janet with tears in her eyes, for it had become her home and she loved and cherished everything in it.

Adeline was glad to go. The sooner she reached the town the sooner she could be away. Alasdair accompanied them and saw them settled in with Elizabeth Ashe, then he and Edward rode off to the Congaree river. They were rather cramped, there being four young Ashes as well as themselves, and when a friend of Adeline's offered her room in her home Adeline gratefully accepted, feeling that fate was on her side—everything was conspiring to make her escape more easy.

There was sparse news in the town of what was going on out at the Congaree, but Adeline had little interest in the rumours and gossip that were inevitably flying around. She went down to the wharves and gained the information she required, then she paid the captain and arranged her passage. She had been saving her allowance ever since the plan had formulated in her mind. She called to see Janet, thinking that it would be the last time for many years, perhaps forever, that she would see her.

"Rumour has it that Attakullakulla wishes to make peace, and that the men will soon be home and the danger will be over!" Janet told her with some relief in her voice.

"When did you hear that? How long do you think it will be?"

"I don't know. I don't even think there's been any fighting, thank God!"

Adeline's voice was urgent. "But how soon will the men

be home? Has this treaty been signed already?"

"I don't know, Adeline! If it *has* been signed then the men will already be on their way back—I hope so!"

Adeline managed a half-smile but her brain was racing. The journey back from the Congaree would not take long, and she prayed they would not return before tomorrow night, for if they did that would be the end of everything! Alasdair would drag them all back to the plantation and she would never get the chance again. She rose. "Well, I hope it's all true!" she managed to say calmly.

"Oh! So do I, Elizabeth has been so kind, but... well... things have been a little complicated and nerves have begun to become a little frayed.... I'll be glad to get home. Thank God there has been no fighting!"

It was almost blasphemy, but Adeline wished there had been some sort of a skirmish that would have held the men up. "I'll be ready," she said, rising.

"Of course, dear!" came Janet's unsuspecting reply.

The wharves were mainly in darkness but here and there a torch flared in a bracket upon the wall. By the dim light Adeline picked her way between the boxes, bales and casks, startled occasionally by the dim outlines of the rats that scuttled away at her approach. The ships tied up at the wharves were mainly silent, but there were muffled laughs and feminine voices coming from a few. Lanterns glowed from their mainmasts and as she furtively walked the length of the wharf she prayed that she would meet no one, for after dark it was not the sort of place where a lady was safe. At last she stopped and let out a deep sigh of relief as the lettering on the bows became clearer. The *Heron*, she read. "And bound for Leith!" she said aloud. The ship had more lights than the others and there were plenty of signs of activity, for she was due to sail at two o'clock.

"Excuse me, mistress, are you the lady we 'as been waitin' for?" The voice came from behind her and she spun around.

"Yes. You are from the *Heron* bound for Leith in Scotland? Captain Huger is expecting me."

The man nodded solemnly and led her across the gang-plank and onto the deck. "You wait 'ere, mistress, I'll see the captain, then I'll be back to show you your quarters, cabin that is."

She looked back at the town. Just a few feet of dark water separated her from it. She could see the lights in the many windows, the steeple of St Phillips, and she felt the wind warm on her cheeks. She gripped the rail and looked down into the inky depths. She hoped the wind would freshen once they were beyond the harbour. Captain Huger had assured her that the ship was one of the fastest packets that sailed out of Charleston. By morning she hoped to be well clear of the harbour and on her way to Leith, long before Alasdair came home and found her gone.

Oh! She had waited so long for this day. Eleven years! Eleven long miserable years. Why had she not escaped before? Almost at once the old fear, the old nightmare was on her. What if he had forgotten her? What if he had married someone else long ago? She had faced this question time and again and she knew the answer. She would make him love her again. Whether or not he was married, she would become the woman in his life. He would still love her, she was certain! That thought alone had carried her through the years.

She looked up to where the stars hung in the sky, making a dancing path of silver that led out of the harbour. "I'll make him love me!" she repeated. She was going back to reclaim the lovers' vows they had made years ago. If Phillip Gowry was already married then she would become his mistress, she would feel no shame, for she had loved him first, when they were hardly more than children.

Lyttleton and his army were back. Attakullakulla, the little carpenter, had made peace, signed a treaty he had every intention of breaking and watched with cunning in his dark eyes as the Governor marched his men back towards the town. They were greeted as conquering heroes. A great banquet was given in the Governor's honour, the clergy presented him with an address of commendation, the Library Society made a speech in which they declared him not only their Governor and protector but the patron of Literature and President of the Society.

Janet greeted Alasdair with open arms. "Thank God you are safe. Thank God there was no fighting!"

"There were a few uneasy moments but Lyttleton kept his head. He's a fine man and a good soldier from all accounts."

Janet at last untangled herself from his arms. "When can we go home?"

"Just as soon as you are packed up. Has it been so bad?"

"No, Elizabeth has been very kind, the girls have been rather bored though and of course Alex. . . ."

"What about Adeline?"

"Oh, she's over with Helen Montaigne, they are old friends and it made more room here. . . ."

Alasdair took Janet in his arms again and stroked her hair. "I love you, Janet, have I made life too difficult for you?"

"No, I love you and wherever you are then I am happy. I love Charleston. . . ."

Her words brought back the old conflict. Years ago he had vowed to return to Scotland. How quickly those years had passed by, and always there had been some reason why he had not gone. Janet felt Charleston to be her home now and the children had been brought up here with every comfort. He could imagine the cries of horror if he suggested the long and hazardous journey by sea, the cold climate, the almost non-existent social life of the Highlands. Only young Alex would be content, he thought. The boy was very like him and he was glad of it. Alex needed a firm hand to guide him, but he would be at home amidst the rugged mountains, would find companionship amongst the boys of the glen with their hunting and their fierce game of shinty and their pride.

He looked at Janet again as she nestled her head into his shoulder. His heart was torn in two. To ask her to leave all this would be to break her heart and yet it had been so long now . . . too long. He remembered how Alizon had looked as he had kissed her goodbye and the proud set of her head, the determination not to cry. She would be an old woman now, he thought. It surprised him, for he could never imagine her as being old. And Andrea... the determined, headstrong half-sister who loved her country almost to the point of obsession, Andrea in whose veins ran the same Stuart blood that coursed through his own body.

Suddenly he felt intensely ashamed, he who had been happy to stay here and grow rich. He knew that Alizon and the people of the glen were not starving, neither was Andrea and her family. But there were thousands of Scots who were. Thousands of Highlanders who were only waiting, praying for the return of their rightful king who, they trusted, would put everything right. Still holding Janet in his arms, he wondered about Scotland. Poor by English standards, destitute by the plentiful standards of Carolina where even the Negro slaves had full bellies all year round. And their rightful king? Prince Charles Edward Stuart, the 'Young Chevalier' as he was called, for his father was dead. It all seemed so far away, like a dream from the past. He held Janet closer. He could never ask her to return to that.

"If we are to return home we'd better make a start!" she said, drawing away from the circle of his arms. "Though now that the men are back I doubt if Catherine and Margaret will be in such a hurry to leave!"

Alasdair laughed. "I must be getting old, I forget that they are almost of age to be wed!"

Janet laughed with him. "I'll send someone over to tell Adeline to get ready."

"What do you mean, gone?" Alasdair questioned the Ashes' boy.

"That's what Miss Montaigne said, sir! She's gone. All her things have gone and her bed ain't been slept in!"

"When was the last time Miss Montaigne saw my sister? Did she say?"

"She said she last saw her at supper last night. She said Miss Kirkbride had a bad headache and went up to her room early, but that's all she said, sir!"

"Alright, go back to your work. Where could she go?

What's got into her? She's usually so sensible. . . ."

"I think we've misjudged her, Alasdair!"

"She's fooled us, you mean!"

"I know where she'll be, or at least where she will be heading for."

Alasdair clutched Janet by the shoulders. Although she was only his half-sister he loved Adeline dearly. "Where? Where has she gone and why?"

"If I'm right she'll be on her way to Scotland by now. It's my fault! I knew she was planning something—I sensed it. She has never forgotten Phillip Gowry!"

Alasdair stared at her. Phillip Gowry! God, he hardly remembered what he looked like! How long must it be . . . nine . . . ten years, more than that. Adeline couldn't be so stupid. "But she surely can't still love him after all this time?" he asked slowly.

"She does. Or at least she thinks she does. That is the reason why she rejected every proposal!"

He was incredulous. "He will have forgotten her and married someone else by now and will probably have half a dozen children too!"

"I tried to tell her that a long time ago and I thought that she had at last become aware . . . but I see she hasn't! She . . . she once told me she would have him by any means she could, even if it meant becoming his mistress!"

There was anger now in Alasdair's eyes. "She'll never be his whore! I'd kill her first!"

Janet was frightened. "What will you do? What can you do?"

"I'm going after her!"

"You will be too late! Alasdair, listen to me, she's been denied love for so long—let her be! Let her take what happiness she can before it's too late! He may not be married. . . ."

"It doesn't matter if he is married or not, he'll not have her!"

"Because of what his father did? That was not his fault, nor has it anything to do with Adeline!"

"He is in the army of German George! She'll never have him!"

Janet shrank away from him, frightened by the intense hatred that she saw in his face. "Alasdair . . . Alasdair, for my sake don't go after her! Stay here, stay with us, we need you! What if there is more trouble. . . . ? I won't be able to hold Alex here with you gone, he'll go off. . . . Oh, Alasdair, please, please don't go, it will only cause more misery. We have all been so happy. . . ." There were tears in Janet's eyes. But she knew nothing she could say would make him change his mind. His pride, his position as head of the family had been challenged. "Oh! Adeline! Adeline! Why?" she murmured.

There was no ship leaving for Leith or for any English port for four days and while Alasdair fumed, Janet tried to soften his attitude. She knew nothing would divert him from chasing after Adeline, but perhaps she could make him view her behavior with more kindness, more tolerance. She dreaded what would happen when they met.

Catherine and Margaret had persuaded her to let them stay on in Charleston under the care of Elizabeth Ashe, for neither of them wished to return to the tranquillity of plantation life when the town was filled with so many handsome young men and every night there was some form of entertainment. Janet had agreed only because if there were another attack by the Indians they would at least be safer in the town. The thought of being alone on the estate did not upset her. It was her home and she loved it. Saunders was a good man who would deal aptly with the running of the plantation, while her time would be taken up with the household, and there would be her son, Alex, and there were her friends to visit. The time would pass quickly until Alasdair returned, though she doubted that he would return with Adeline.

The year 1744 was drawing to its close, the weather would be rough, the storms frequent and violent and Adeline had five days' start. Janet pressed her hand to her aching head. Life had previously been so simple, but ever since the Governor had called for men everything had been turned upside down! She had ceased trying to dissuade Alasdair from going these past few days. All she could do was pray that he would meet his sister calmly and return soon, with or without her.

Adeline had waited long enough for love and she hoped Phillip Gowry was not married, for Adeline's sake, and that Alasdair would not kill him as he threatened to do. It was an old feud now, why couldn't they let it lie! Sixty years had passed since that terrible February night when, in a blizzard, the Campbells had fallen on the MacDonalds and massacred them. Alizon was an old, old woman and Andrea a mature wife and mother, as was she, Janet. Why could they not let the spirits lie at peace instead of digging up old grudges, old hatreds, old wounds? She herself was a Scot but she would never return. At first she had been homesick but life here was so much better. Her daughters had far more than they could ever hope for in Scotland.

He was down on the wharf now, securing a passage for himself. She paused, holding the shirt she was packing close to her. What if he didn't come back? He had escaped the sea when he was a baby, but what if... what if once he arrived in Scotland he forgot about the plantation just as he had forgotten his vow to return to Rannoch.... She shook herself. No, he would not do that, he loved her far too much. He would only stay a short time, however long it took to find Adeline. Adeline had always been difficult, spoilt by her mother. Looking back over the years Janet saw another person. A shy, docile, timid creature that she hardly recognised as herself. Now she was capable of running a large plantation alone, unafraid of their vulnerable position should Attakullakulla attack.

She put the shirt in the trunk, listening with nostalgia to the sound of laughter that came from the room Catherine and Margaret shared. Oh, to be as young and as carefree as they were, she sighed. But it was best that they should have their time of laughter and gaiety, for all too soon they would marry and have families and with that went anxiety and pain, hand in hand with love and happiness. She closed the lid of the trunk firmly and turned to the window. Only the masts and rigging of the ships in the harbour were visible, but the sight of them made a heaviness drag at her heart. "Let them come back safely, dear God! Give Adeline her chance of happiness as you gave it to me, but most of all protect him and send him home soon!"

Chapter 14

She was frozen to the bone. Her fingers and toes were numb. The journey by sea had been bad but this was worse. She had been sick, very sick, not caring for almost a week whether she lived or died. At times she had begged for death to release her from the eternal rolling and plunging of the vessel, but she had recovered. Even in Edinburgh it had been cold, and she had been warned against trying to travel to the Highlands in such weather, for most of the roads were blocked by snowdrifts of ten feet or more, but she had come so far that she would not turn back.

She huddled closer to the fire, pulling her woollen shawl around her. It had been the first thing she had purchased, that and the heavy dress she wore, for she had arrived with a trunk full of flimsy dresses and shawls and dainty shoes with thin leather soles, all of which were utterly useless, and she had had to buy more clothing. She had found a man to act as her guide but he had demanded an extortionate rate. She had grudgingly paid him, but once their journey had started she realised that he would earn his money for they had to circle miles out of their way to avoid great drifts of snow. The passes were blocked, the rivers frozen, but she had somehow managed to arrive safely at Fort William.

She had sat still in the saddle and gazed down on the small town that clustered around the old stone garrison. She would go to him first, for to struggle on to Rannoch meant at least another day journeying through this freezing white wilderness. Her guide insisted that she put up at an inn, otherwise she would die from cold, not being used to such a rigorous climate. She had sent a letter to the fort by the young boy who ran errands and tended the horses, and now she sat huddled by the small fire, praying that he would come soon, excited yet afraid.

Had he changed? Had he forgotten her? And that most dreaded of all questions—was he already married? Would he still find her attractive? She touched her cheek, then let her finger slide slowly down her jawline to her neck. The two warm dresses she had hastily purchased were of drab colours and with little style. Her hand crept upwards to her hair. At least that had not dimmed in its colour or lustre.

The knock was loud and made her start up quickly. Her heart was pounding, beating at three times its normal pace, so loudly she thought the sound filled the room. She put out a hand to steady herself for suddenly the room swam before her, and her voice sounded as though it belonged to someone else as she called out "Enter!"

No longer was he a dream, he was real. He was older, his hair seemed darker, his skin weatherbeaten with lines cut deeply round his eyes from habitually peering into the distance.

"Phillip." Her voice sounded strangely hollow.

He stared at her in silence and all manner of thoughts flew around in her mind, then he smiled, his eyes crinkling at the corners. "Adeline, at first I couldn't believe it was true, but the boy was adamant, so. . . ."

She had visualised this moment in so many dreams, she had lived each second of it, she would rush into his arms while he would hold her tightly and cover her face with kisses; instead they just stood staring at each other, almost like strangers. All the prepared speeches had disappeared from her mind, her heart still beat madly but she seemed to be frozen to the ground, and still they stared at each other.

"You have come so far alone?" At last he had spoken and she breathed again.

"Yes, but by now my brother will be following me and if the snowdrifts and frozen tracks did not deter me. . . ."

"Then knowing Alasdair, they will not deter him either! Why did you come?"

Her eyes widened and she felt as though he had slapped

her across the cheek. Surely she couldn't have heard correctly? He was asking her why she had come—it couldn't be true! "I . . . I did not think you would ask, I . . . I thought you would know . . . there is . . . someone. . . ."

"No! I am not wed, unless it's to my regiment!" He had crossed to where she stood, her head bent, her fingers toying with the fringe of the shawl. "Adeline, we are no longer children."

"That is something I am reminded of each time I look in the mirror." Her words were uttered in such a low voice that he barely heard them.

He took one cold hand in his. "I did not mean that to sound like a rebuff. I had given up hope years ago. I never visit Rannoch now, not since my mother died two years ago. So I did not know you were coming back."

"No one knows except you. I did not write to Alizon or Andrea. I came, I came because. . . ." Now that the moment had actually come she could not say the words, they stuck in her throat, her voice died away, but she looked up at him, her heart in her eyes. He still held her hand but it did not seem to be a part of her any longer. This was not how she had planned it.

"You came because you still love me?"

"Yes." It was a whisper of a sound, and she could not look at him.

He cupped her chin in his other hand and raised her head. "Adeline, I never thought you would come back! I thought you would be married by now with a small brood of bairns! I thought. . . ."

There was no longer any need for words between them. She was in his arms and he was kissing her and she was babbling like a child of how she had never forgotten him, of the long years of waiting before her final flight.

"But Alasdair?" he questioned, his words slightly muffled as he kissed the base of her throat.

"I don't care what he says! I'm of age, I'm not a child! Beside it will take him at least three weeks to catch up with me, if he can get through at all!" Her heart still thumped but now her legs felt weak and she clung to him for support. "I thought when you first came in that . . . that

I had wasted my time, that it was all for nothing. . . ." His mouth cut off the rest of her sentence and the blood began to pound in her head. It was as though they were in a vacuum, that they had drifted into space, and she felt his body taut against her own. His hands were moving over her breasts and now she knew what he had meant when he had said they were no longer children. She wanted him, she had waited eleven years for this moment, she was a woman and she needed to be loved. The shawl had fallen to the floor and she pulled away from him, her eyes still fixed upon his face.

"Adeline?" It was a question.

She nodded and began to unbutton the front of her dress, her fingers shaking so much that they fumbled in their task. Quickly he picked her up and carried her to the bed. The years rolled back as though they had never been apart—she pressed his head down to her breasts. After today no one would ever part them. She had at last freed herself from her bodice and skirt but the air was not cold on her naked limbs. He drew away from her and drank in her body with his eyes before lowering himself on to her. There was some pain, instantly replaced by a feeling of such pleasure that she thought she would lose her senses. His body against hers was shaking, or was it her own body that was beyond her control? She cried out as his lips bruised her breasts but she thrust herself hard against him, biting into the flesh of his shoulder, worrying his throat with teeth and lips. The sensation intensified until she could no longer remember even where she was or who she was—the only thought in her mind was that at last he belonged to her!

"Phillip." Gently she touched his shoulder. He opened his eyes and turned towards her, pulling her to him.

"Is something troubling you?"

"No, nothing can trouble me now . . . nothing!"

He brushed his lips against her hair. "Not even Alasdair?"

"No. Least of all him."

"But suppose he offers violence? I'm a soldier, a man of violence by profession, but he is your brother. . . ."

"Half-brother," she corrected.

"No matter, he still loves and cares for you and he made it clear that he found my presence, to say nothing of my uniform and loyalties, objectionable."

"I'm not a child! He can't take me back to Charleston."

"He won't. There is no law that allows a married woman to be forcefully separated from her husband by her brother."

The small spectre of fear that had been nagging her disappeared. She had known that they would marry but he had not mentioned it during their love-making, and the doubt had nagged. She nestled closer to him.

"I'll make all the arrangements, my love. . . ." He rose and reached for his shirt.

"Must you leave now?"

"I'm afraid so, but the sooner I can get everything settled the better, then we will never have to be apart again for long!" He leaned over and kissed her again and she clung to his mouth.

"I don't know if I was made to follow the drum!"

He laughed. "You've proved that you are, Adeline! You've crossed the ocean at the mercy of the wind and waves, forced your way through snow and ice—following the drum will be dull by comparison. You will probably never need to move from here; we are not at war and the Highlands are quiet."

"Until Alasdair arrives, that is!" She laughed and grimaced.

"I'll leave Alasdair to you!" he quipped, pulling on his scarlet coat—the uniform that was the cause of so much trouble.

"When will you come back?"

"This evening, and I should have some news by then."

They were married two days later by the chaplain at the fort, and Adeline had never been happier in her life. They rented a small house at the foot of the walls of the fort and even though it lacked almost everything she had taken so much for granted in Charleston, she was happy.

Just as she had expected, Alasdair arrived three weeks

later. He had enquired at the inns he passed until he had eventually been given the information he sought. Now he stood in the small cramped parlour, and despite all her resolves, she shrank at the anger in his face.

"Alasdair, I am married to Phillip and there is nothing you can do. I love him, I've always loved him! Janet knew it—I thought you did too!"

"I would sooner see you dead than married to a red-coated soldier!"

"Be reasonable! Can't you forget all the old anger? It isn't your cause!"

"No! This is my country just as much as Carolina, more, even! Only an accident of birth caused me to be born in the Colonies but I have my grandfather's blood in me! I can't forget, I won't forget!"

"Why? It does not affect you! I can understand Alizon's hatred and Andrea's, but not yours. You did not live here. . . ."

"Their hatreds are mine, their fight is mine and you, my sister, have betrayed everything by marrying Gowry!"

"I love him! I don't care about your hatreds or your politics, I only know that I love him and he loves me! Wherever he goes I will go!"

"Then you are no longer my sister. . . ."

Adeline stood her ground, her eyes blazing. "You will kindly remove yourself from my house, you are trespassing!" She deliberately made her tone calm and icy, and turning away from him, she stood staring into the hearth until she heard the door slam behind him, then she gripped the mantleshelf as her control snapped and she began to cry. Alasdair, who had always protected her from babyhood, who had come when she was alone and frightened after Darnley and Anne had died, and now. . . . Oh, if only he would forget, it was not his fight! He was a Colonist, not a Scot. She wished Anne had never brought them here all those years ago, but then she remembered that she would never have met Phillip. Alasdair was stubborn, she knew that, and he was proud. She had severed at one stroke all the love and loyalty they had shared. She had only Phillip now. She drew the sleeve of her dress across her eyes and straightened up. What did it matter, he was the only person she needed!

"Is she happy?" It was Alizon who asked the question quietly, after she had listened to the long tirade Alasdair had launched into after their initial meeting.

"So she says, but she'll regret it!"

"Why, because he wears a red coat? Gabrielle was my closest friend and I miss her sorely, yet she loved the man who killed Andrew. I could never hate her for that. I hated him, but Gabrielle, and Phillip . . . how well I remember him as a child." She looked out of the window as though expecting to see Gabrielle and her child riding towards the house. "I'm an old woman, Alasdair, and I've seen enough bitterness and hatred in my life. Hate Gowry as much as you like, but not Adeline! A woman cannot always choose. . . . I could not, which is why Andrea. . . ."

"Is she happy? You do not like MacIntosh, do you?"

"No, but despite that I don't love Andrea any less, and she is happy—they have their quarrels but who does not?" She shrugged her frail shoulders. She had always been slim but she had aged so much, Alasdair thought. Her eyes were still beautiful, large and luminous, like two pools of water with deep brown leaves in their depths, but her hair was grey now and her hands gnarled, and she walked with the aid of a stick.

She had indeed seen enough hatred in her life, she thought. The bitterness that once had filled her had gone. All her hopes, so fresh and vibrant they had been all those years ago, were dead now. She was old and knew that there was little time left for her. Never in her lifetime would she see the Highlands free from soldiers, never would she see a Stuart king on the throne: she had realised that, these past winter months. She must leave those things to Andrea and to Alasdair. The people of the glen had clung on to the old ways of the Gael, and they would never relinquish them unless they were killed down to the last child. She could never forget that night, though it was decades ago now, when she had run terrified through the swirling white flakes while all around her there had echoed screams and flashes of gunfire. Those deaths had never been avenged as she had sworn they would be, but not for her now the task, but for Andrea and Alasdair.

"Go back to her and tell her you are sorry."

"Never!"

"Then you'll regret it." Suddenly she felt very weak and tired. "Help me to a chair—I can't stand for very long now."

Alasdair felt the fragile bones beneath her skin as he guided her to the chair by the blazing fire. Bones so brittle that he felt they would snap like matchwood if she were ever to fall.

"Mother, are you ill?"

"No, just old and tired."

"How long is it since you last saw Andrea?"

"She came in October, before the snows. She brought the children with her, fine and bonny they are too. They look like MacIntosh himself except Mairaid, she is a Stuart! Alasdair, go to her when the thaw comes, she will be pleased to see you again."

He had not thought about how long he would remain; he had not intended a long stay. "I will go as soon as the passes are open again," he promised. She seemed to have drifted into sleep and he bent and gently kissed the white hair. It would be two months at least before the thaw came, he thought as he stared out over the white wastes of Rannoch Moor. Had he really imagined that he could take Adeline home with him? Or had he just used it as an excuse to come back? Was there some reason fate had in store for his returning?

The snows melted early that year. By mid-March the passes were open, and for this Alasdair was thankful. Alizon was very ill: for the past few days she had slept almost continuously and he had walked the floor, frustrated and grieving. There was nothing he could do for her but keep her warm and try to force a little gruel down her. He had silently raged at the weather which kept help beyond his reach, but now the thaw had set in: patches of brown sodden earth had begun to appear on the moor and bare spots of stone on the lower slopes of the mountains. He had sent a ghillie to Inverness for Andrea and another to the fort for a doctor. He had not seen or heard of his sister in all the time he had spent at Rannoch Chase, but with the messenger going to Andrea he had sent a letter explaining everything to Janet. The journey to Inverness and back would still take some time, he thought, but at least the doctor should arrive soon.

He came in the next afternoon, and after seeing Alizon shook his head sadly.

"There's nothing I can do for her now, laddie! Let her go peacefully, she'll not feel any pain."

"What is it? Is there nothing I can do?"

"Nothing. It is a lung fever, you hear the rasping sound when she breathes, the fluid . . . she's not strong enough. . . ."

Alasdair thanked him and asked him to stay the night, for it was a long journey back and the wind was still freezing. The physician accepted gladly.

It was nearly noon of the next day when Andrea arrived. A heavy cloak lined with the fleece of sheep swathed her almost from head to toe. Her horse was sweating profusely, a cloud of steam arising from its coat into the sharp air.

Alasdair shouted for the stable boy to take the horse and rub it down, then he took Andrea into the house.

"Why didn't you let me know you were here and that she was so ill?" Andrea demanded, her cheeks ruddy from her long ride. The hood of the cloak was turned back, revealing the silver-blonde hair neatly coiled on the top of her head.

"Because of the weather. I see you are well!"

"Never mind me, how is she? What ails her?"

"A lung fever, the doctor said. She finds it difficult to breathe, there is nothing we can do. . . ."

"There must be something!" She refused to believe that Alizon could be so ill. Alizon, the mother who had always been so strong, so purposeful, from whom she had learned so much, drawn so much of her own strength and resolve. It couldn't be true! As soon as she saw the figure in the bed, like a child asleep amidst the pillows and blankets, she knew Alasdair had been right. She bit deeply into her lip to stop herself from crying out and blinked rapidly, in a vain effort to fight back the tears that had sprung to her eyes.

She knelt down by the bed and took one wasted hand in her own. Alizon did not move and Andrea buried her head in the fur coverlet and cried. Part of her life was passing away with Alizon; she had always relied on her mother. Alasdair reached down and touched her shoulder in a futile attempt to comfort her, and she clutched at his hand. She hardly knew him, this brother who had eyes like her own, like Alizon's . . . yet she was drawn to him by their mutual grief. "I . . . I can't help it . . . she . . . was always so strong. . . ."

"Her strength was in her love for both of us—we were her future, we *are* her future! She's suffered enough in her life for ten women. . . ."

He stopped, for Alizon had opened her eyes and was gazing at them.

"Mother! I will nurse you back to health . . . soon we will have you up again. . . ." Andrea's tears fell freely.

Alizon shook her head. Her voice was so low that they both had to lean close to her to hear her words. "Too late for that, besides, I have lived too long. I've waited for this day, I've been so alone all these years, after he had gone. . . ." The effort was too much for her and she began to gasp. Alasdair quickly held her up in his arms.

"Don't try to talk, save your strength!"

Again she shook her head. "Promise me. . . ."

"Anything! Anything!" Andrea cried.

"Promise me you will never forget the Stuart blood in your veins! Promise you will fight for your kinsman's rights when he comes. . . ."

"Yes! Yes! We both promise! Oh, Mother, stay with us, we need you!" Andrea was sobbing now and Alasdair was fighting back his own tears. They both stayed with her all night, one either side of the bed. Andrea was sitting on the floor with her head against the bed, still holding Alizon's hand, but she must have fallen asleep for she was jerked awake by Alasdair who was gently taking Alizon's hand from hers. The cold grey March dawn was filtering through the window, the room was quiet and cold for the fire was out and she herself was stiff and numb. She tried to cling on to Alizon's hand but Alasdair shook his head, firmly prising open her fingers.

"She's gone, Andrea! We must face life without her now!"

Chapter 15

They had lain her on Eilean Munde beside Andrew MacDonald, MacIan and Margaret, the three people she had loved most in the early period of her life. The journey back across the still bleak water of the Loch was a silent one. Already rumours were abroad that there was to be another rebellion. Andrea had not told Alizon of this, for word had only come within the last few days. There had been no need for Andrea to remember the Jacobite cause, it was instilled into her, and now she must do what Alizon had done in the '15. She would supply arms, food, horses, and men, the men of Glencoe. If necessary, she would rally the other MacDonalds should they show signs of faltering. She thought of her husband and a spasm of agony twisted her heart. She had known that this day would come, sonner or later. The day when their divided loyalties would threaten to tear them apart. She could see no way for them to avoid a conflict, for MacIntosh was a Loyal Union man.

She looked at her own sons, Andrew, Robert and Ewan, all of them old enough now to fight. Something tugged at her heart, a small voice whispered "not Ewan, not Ewan, he's too young!" He was nearly fifteen—how could she keep him at home when there would be other boys of his own age marching beside their fathers? A horrifying thought crept into her mind and made her shiver. Suppose their father decided to march in the ranks of the Union army and took his sons with him? They were old enough to make the choice for themselves, she told herself, the decision was theirs alone, but she prayed that it would be the white cockade they would wear, and not the red coats.

Alasdair was silent too; he had heard the talk of rebellion and despite the feelings of guilt that possessed him for leaving Janet for so long, he knew he must stay on, even if it were only to ascertain that the rumours were unfounded. He looked across at his sister: she was staring ahead of her towards Invercoe and the look in her eyes frightened him. He remembered what she had once said, all those years ago when they had been children, and she had asked him why he had not gone with his father to fight the Cherokees. She had said that she would fight, he remembered clearly, and looking at her he wondered if she, too, was remembering. His gaze wandered over his three nephews. He knew that if rebellion came Andrea, like the women of Sparta, would send out her boys to return with their shields or on them. He would have to write and explain to Janet but he was sure she would understand why he must stay; after all, this was her birthplace too.

As the boat scraped on the shingle of the shore he could see a solitary figure awaiting their return. Shading his eyes with his hand, he realised that it was Adeline. As the small funeral party drew closer she walked slowly towards them. It was the first time he had seen her since the day she had told him to leave her house.

"Alasdair . . . Alasdair . . . I'm sorry. I would have come sooner . . . but . . . Andrea, you understand, don't you?" Her last words were a plea, a cry to be once more accepted.

"I understand and so did she, she more than anyone. Come back with us to Rannoch? All families quarrel at times and Highland families more often than others, but we must give the appearance of being united."

"Then you have heard?"

Andrea was instantly alert, remembering Phillip. "Heard what?"

"Rumours that the Young Pretender is on his way."

"I've heard no such thing, that is probably all it is—rumour!"

No more was spoken on their journey up the glen. When they were at home, seated round the roaring fire, Adeline announced that she thought she was to have a child.

"So soon! Are you sure?" Andrea sounded doubtful.

"Almost sure."

There was a brief moment of silence.

"Adeline, will you think of returning to Janet to have the child? If you go now before your condition is... advanced, you will not be uncomfortable." Alasdair had spoken quietly with no hint of uneasiness in his voice.

"Why? What are you trying to tell me? You know more than I do. The rumours are true!"

"They are rumours, I know no more than you or Phillip. I thought... I thought you would be easier with Janet, the weather is kinder, you would be amongst friends, while here...."

"While here I am in an alien country surrounded by hostile people! Does that include you and Andrea? I go where my husband goes! I will not go back to Charleston—my child will be born here!"

Alasdair shrugged, and Andrea put her hand on Adeline's arm.

"You are not among hostile strangers! Despite all our differences we are still a family! Remember that, Adeline! Alasdair does not approve of my husband's views as he does not approve of your choice of husband, but that is not to say that he has disowned you or me. Phillip's father killed mine, yet my mother and Gabrielle never let hatred come between them, and neither should we!"

Adeline felt the tears well up in her eyes and angrily she wiped them away.

"When your time is near you will come to me at Inverness, but please don't think that you cannot come at any other time, my house is yours."

Alasdair put a hand on her shoulder. "There is always a place... a home for you here at Rannoch, should you ever need it."

For a few hours they were a family content to be together, all differences, all bitterness forgotten as they sat before the huge peat fire. Andrea told some of the old stories passed on from Alizon, who in her turn had heard them at Margaret's knee. She told of Fingal and the sleeping sons of Feinn, and of Somerled whose name struck fear into the black hearts of even the Viking raiders, and of the Grey Dogs of Death that came silently before the death of a MacDonald. The firelight danced upon their faces, tranquil now as they listened to Andrea's soft musical tones. Alasdair relaxed, his broad shoulders hunched in the chair, at his feet Alizon's deer hounds. Jeannie, the maid, sat on a low stool behind Alasdair's chair, her eyes fixed upon Andrea. Adeline rested her head on a cushion, her eyelids drooping with fatigue. They formed a circle round Andrea: the firelight had turned her hair into reddish-gold, and accentuated the dark eyes, the finely-drawn features, the high cheekbones. Although she was slight, as Alizon had been, there was a quality of toughness in her, a streak of guile, a strange mixture of courage, cunning, recklessness and tenderness all mixed together: all qualities inherited from her grandfather, Charles Stuart.

Spring came again to Rannoch to be swiftly followed by the warmth of summer and the cattle were driven out to the sheilings as they had always been, by the young men and girls of the glen. But pitifully small were their numbers now, Alasdair thought as he watched them pass by, amidst the deep lowing, the laughter, the barking of the dogs. He had heard of how it had been in that summer so long ago when Alizon had first fallen in love with Andrew MacDonald. He turned away from the laughter and youthfulness. The rumours were rumours no longer. There was still much speculation at the fort and at Inverness, but he was one of the few who knew the truth.

Charles Edward Stuart would come in July. The date was uncertain at this stage, yet all was ready. Andrea and he had discussed their plans to the last detail. The fortune Alizon had brought with her from Charleston had not diminished, for Rannoch was self-sufficient and even the money spent in the '15 had almost been recovered. Andrea would hear of no stinting; she knew this time they would need every piece of silver that she and Alasdair owned. Janet was managing in Charleston as he had known she would, but she did beg him to remember his children: already Alex was asking to come to Scotland. This last request he firmly discouraged, in fact he wrote a separate letter to the boy absolutely forbidding him to leave Carolina.

How slowly the weeks seemed to pass with nothing to do but wait. His impatience made him nervous. How soon would news come? How many more weeks of this frustration were yet to be borne? He had already picked out the ghillies who would carry the charred wood bound in the shape of a cross through the glens and mountains. That charred wood be their signal to take out the targes, claymores, dirks and muskets and the wicked Lockber axes from their hiding-places in the thatch or beneath the stone cairns, and rise against the Hanoverian and his sons. The first George was dead but his son was equally hated in the Highlands.

Alasdair wondered what Andrea would do. Her misery was apparent in every letter that came. But the answer to that question he knew: MacIntosh might plead, command, beat her, lock her up, disown her, but he would never change Andrea's loyalty. And then there was Adeline. He would go to war against his brother-in-law. The thought sickened him. This would be the most terrible of all rebellions, for families would be fighting against each other, there were Clans divided. There were the men of the Am Freuceadab Dubb, Highlanders who had taken service in the King's Watch, the Black Watch, because of the dark tartan they wore, traitors to their Clans, yet many had joined their ranks until now there were four companies.

He had tried again to persuade Adeline to leave the fort and return to Charleston but she vehemently refused, and this, most of all, caused him anxiety. If Phillip were killed where would she go, what would she do? Plunder and pillage would be the order of the day for the victors, and he shuddered to think of what would happen to her, for her pregnancy would not protect her, she was the wife of a hated redcoated soldier. Somehow he must get her to Rannoch, she would be safer here than at the fort; if the garrison were besieged she could starve, or the child might come before its time with no one to help her.

The weeks merged together into one long drawn-out agonising space of time until at last the day came in July when the handsome, reckless young boy set foot on the white sands at Arisaig, accompanied by a handful of ageing men who had supported his father.

The news ran like the wind through the glens and mountains. The fiery cross was borne by the running ghillies from Clan to Clan, from Harris and Lewis the MacLeods, from the smaller Isles of Rum and Eigg Clanranald with their brothers on the mainland, Mackenzies, Munros, Grants, Frazers, the Appin Stewarts, the Camerons of Lochaber, and the septs of Clan Donald, those of Sleat, Glengarry, Keppoch, and Glencoe. It was borne too by Campbells from Inveraray throughout Argyllshire, and the old hatreds of Clan Donald and Clan Dairmaid burst forth again, as Argyll's men joined the Royalist army.

For Andrea Charlotte Stuart there was no decision to be made. The long-awaited day had dawned. This time it would be different: the prince was a young man come to start a rebellion, not an old man who had only appeared when it was over, as his father had done in 1715. He had a manner about him, a way of charming people so that, wherever he went, men flocked to his banner. Her plans had been made months ago: beneath old rugs and skins in the attic were some small chests filled with white ribbon, and soon the MacIntosh women had sore fingers from plying their needles.

There had been the one terrible, anguished quarrel with Ian, more violent this time than ever before. He had accused her of being a fool, of sacrificing her years as a wife, and his love to a hopeless cause. She had screamed at him that he was a traitor to his country and natural king and that never, never would she be wife to him again if he went to join Argyll. He had stood his ground before the blazing anger in her dark eyes, anger that was more vehement than it should have been because of the misery in her heart, and he had seen that she was no longer the woman he had lived with for nineteen years. She was a Stuart. Sometimes—often—he had been able to forget that, but before the bitter passion in those eyes he was reminded forcefully of the pictures he had seen of her grandfather and, unable to speak, he had turned away. All those years between them were as nothing. He had left her, striding out into the courtyard, mounted his horse and accompanied by a dozen of his servants had ridden out to join with Argyll and his Campbells, not caring if he were to be killed in the forthcoming conflict.

An hour after his departure Andrea herself stepped out into the sunlight. Over her dress of pale blue silk, the best she owned, was pinned a length of plaid caught on the shoulder with a small targe, her hair was dressed in long ringlets that hung over her shoulders and above the shining curls was a blue bonnet with the white eagle feathers of a chieftain. Pinned to it was the white cockade of Prince Charles Edward Stuart. She smiled at the handful of men who had refused to follow MacIntosh. The white ribbon was in their bonnets, their weapons stuck into the belts of their kilts.

"Annie, have you brought out all the boxes?" she asked of her maid.

"Aye, mistress."

"Then there is no need for us to stay here any longer."

Through the length and breadth of the MacIntosh lands she rode, herself pinning the white ribbons to the bonnets of her husband's tacksmen who would follow her. Most came willingly, swearing they would go with her to hell and back, and she had laughed and tossed the bonnet with the eagle feathers high in the air, as they gave her a new name, "Colonel Charlotte." A name that was to bring her to the notice of William, Duke of Cumberland. And on that fine July day she could not envisage tragedy or failure. Her only regret was that Alizon had not lived to see it.

When they had all gone Andrea turned her horse and rode south towards Rannoch. She would see Alasdair before she rode back to join Clan MacIntosh. She would make sure that Adeline was safely installed at Rannoch

Chase and she would entrust to Adeline the care of her own daughter Mairaid. Her prayers had been answered, in part, for Andrew, Robert and Ewan had all declared for the prince and had left to join the clans. As she rode to Rannoch Chase she remembered who she was—a Stuart—of the Royal House, and she sat straighter in the saddle. But beneath the plaid her heart was breaking, for her sons, and for her husband. . . .

At Rannoch Chase she found Alasdair and the tacksmen of Glencoe ready to depart.

"Andrea! I hear you have been busy since Ian left!" Alasdair greeted her, catching her as she slid from her horse.

"I've brought Mairaid with me. The boys have all gone to join the Clans. Adeline is here?"

"Not yet, but I've sent to the fort, begging her to come and begging Phillip to think of her safety!"

"I thought she would be here by now! I didn't intend to stay—I must go back after my tacksmen!"

"You can't! Andrea, you've done everything you can—you can't leave Mairaid, you can't fight, I won't let you!"

"I swore years ago that if this day ever came I would go and that no one or nothing would stop me! I'm going!"

"You can't! What of Mairaid?"

"She'll be safe with Jeannie!"

Alasdair caught her firmly by the shoulders and stared down at her.

"This is the last thing that Alizon would have wanted! She did not go in '15 and you can't go now!"

"She hated them! She hated them all for what they did to Clan Ian Abrach! She hated them for what they did to her! She never gained revenge and now it is too late for her, but not for me!" She caught her breath and faltered. "I have wrecked my life for this cause, Alasdair. Ian and I are sworn enemies—and I loved him. Don't stop me now. I must do this for our mother."

"You think I don't know how much she hated them, but it is I who must go, not you! You will be needed here;

the women of the glen will look to you for strength and comfort, as Adeline will. You can't go!"

The sullenness showed in her eyes and in the drooping corners of her mouth, but then she knew he was right. Alizon would have made her stay at home and she couldn't leave Adeline or the other women, for there were bound to be casualties. There would be women widowed, children orphaned and they would need her help. At last she nodded in agreement. "I'll stay."

"That's better! There is much you can do here. We are almost ready. As soon as I hear from the fort we will go."

"Where is the prince now?"

"At Glenfinnan—the standard has been raised and thousands are flocking to it!"

"But not the Campbells?"

"There are a few, but most are with Argyll."

"I curse them all!"

"Don't worry, the old scores will be settled this time. Margaret, MacIan and all the others did not die in vain, they will be remembered!"

"I trust you to make sure of it, Alasdair, or before God I'll go to Argyll myself and kill him!"

The next day Adeline arrived, accompanied by two men from the fort who wore no uniform. Her pregnancy was beginning to become apparent and she was tired and aching from the long hard journey through the rough country of the Lochaber Camerons.

"Andrea, I'm so glad to see you! I was afraid you would have gone with Alasdair, despite his letter. Mairaid is here, too?"

"Yes, we thought it safer." Andrea smiled ruefully. "You have more success with your husband than I have with mine," she said sadly.

"There is not the division of loyalties between Phillip and I; I am a Colonist, not a Scot. All Phillip cares for is my safety, and he could see the sense in me staying here rather than at the fort."

Andrea looked out through the window to where the towering peaks of the Herdsmen of Etive were outlined against the summer sky. "We are a society of women."

"All the men have gone?"

"One hundred and thirty: every boy over fourteen and every man under seventy, and some went despite the fact that they were too old or too young. I would have gone too. . . . Damn Alasdair!"

"Why?"

"Because he made me see reason! Because he made me stay here and wait!"

"You intended to go with Clan MacIntosh?"

Andrea nodded.

"War is not for women!"

"That's what he said—you are alike at times, you two!"

"He is my half-brother!"

Andrea managed a smile. "And mine, and God go with them all!"

When his army had been fully assembled Prince Charles Edward Stuart made his way to the Stirling plain and then on eastwards to the Firth of Forth, and at Prestonpans on September 21st the Highland Army won a resounding victory over the only Government Army in Scotland, that of Sir John Cope. Sir John had arrived at Inverness on the 4th but had found no recruits, and he had urgently sent for transport to take his men to protect the Lowlands. On September 16th Edinburgh was taken by the prince's army without bloodshed, although the garrison at the castle held out. The fortress high up on the rock was as it had always been—impregnable.

On September 20th the prince marched his men from Duddingston, crossed the Eske and the Highlanders were on the site of the old battle of Pinkie when they came into full view of Cope's army. On the next day, at Prestonpans, the Highland Army had slaughtered and routed the Government forces, for in the mists of dawn they had risen like screaming demons with the wailing and skirling of the pipes in their ears and run against the enemy. Firing their pistols when within musket reach, they then had drawn their swords, throwing down their guns, and with targe and dirk in their hands darted through the smoke and flames.

With a quick, deadly thrust of the claymore and they were through the lines and before this onslaught the raw Hanoverian forces turned and fled. Four hundred were killed and five hundred wounded and 1,500 prisoners taken, to the Jacobite total of only six officers killed. Nothing remained to stop them now, but for five weeks they remained in Edinburgh, though urged by Lord George Murray to march south at once. When this news reached Rannoch Andrea fumed and fretted again.

"Why don't they go on? The fools! The stupid fools, why don't they listen to Murray? If they went now they could be in London by Christmas! Why waste so much time while the English are bringing back their troops from Flanders?"

"I suppose they are doing what they think is best!" Adeline tried to calm her, but she stalked the floor in impotent anger and frustration.

"Is it best to dance in the Palace of Holyrood when they could dance in the Palace of Whitehall at Christmas? The fools should go on!"

"They'll go soon, Mother. They are not all fools," Mairaid said quietly.

Andrea smiled at her. Mairaid was a quiet, shy child of thirteen who promised to grow to be a beauty, but there was plenty of good sound sense in her head. "Then I hope the prince does not waste any more time."

Chapter 16

It was not until November 8th that the prince's army crossed the Esk and rode into England, marching onward through Carlisle, then Preston and Manchester. Here a regiment was raised who marched with tartan sashes and the white cockade, but no other Englishmen joined the Highland Army. They were jubilant; at last they were in the enemy lands where there was food aplenty, fat cattle and sheep and horses. But two English armies had now amassed against them, one at Newcastle under George Wade and the other across the London road commanded by the King's young son, William, Duke of Cumberland. The Highland Army pressed further south and reached Derby on December 5th. Now they were confident of being in the capital by Christmas!

As this news travelled back to Scotland it was received in the Highlands with cries of joy and tears of happiness. At Exeter House the young prince, exuberant with his victory at Prestonpans and his unhindered march so far south into England, urged his council of war to go on. Murray warned him it would be too dangerous; obviously there was to be no support from the English themselves and neither was aid forthcoming from France. They had approximately six thousand men against three armies, for a third was now assembling on Finchley Common to protect the City of London. Murray and the Clan chiefs were afraid of having their line of retreat cut, with two armies between them and the border, and to all the prince's entreaties they turned a deaf ear. Finally they turned back.

As she had been after Prestonpans, Andrea was furious. "They should go on! They should go on!" she almost screamed at Mairaid and Jeannie when the news was brought. "They can't turn back now! They will lose everything! Everything we have suffered for, hoped for, lived and died for over all these years will be lost forever if they turn back now!"

"Hush, Mother! You'll wake Adeline!" Mairaid pleaded.

Andrea resumed her pacing in silence. Adeline's child had been born a month ago, and although young Mitchell was a healthy baby he had cost his mother a great deal in strength and health. Adeline, still far from recovered, was resting in bed upstairs in the room that had been Alizon's.

Although she had been angry and frustrated after the time wasted in Edinburgh, now a sense of desolation seemed to take hold of Andrea. Nothing mattered except that the prince's army should go on. She even considered the idea of riding herself to Derby to urge them forward.

But she would be too late, already they had turned back. She shivered suddenly; it was as though icy water had been poured down her back, and she wondered if it were a premonition. She could not go, she could not leave Adeline and the baby, or Mairaid and Jeannie or the other women. She could only wait. Wait, wait, wait! she fumed to herself, was there to be no end to the waiting?

Murray with the MacPhersons and Glengarry MacDonalds fought a gallant rearguard action against the Hanoverian Dragoons at Clifton, and the Manchester Regiment were left behind at Carlisle to defend the town, but they could not hold out. Those who did not end their days at the end of a rope ended them in the transports to the Colonies.

The year had turned, and with it the luck of the prince's men. By late February the dwindling army turned north into the Highlands. By March the passes were open again, and Adeline sufficiently recovered to travel. Andrea had waited long enough. She had decided to take Jeannie, Mairaid, Adeline and the baby and as many of the women of the glen who wished to go, to her own home in Inverness.

"I'll be able to hear the news more quickly—we will be quite safe. I'll be amongst friends on MacIntosh lands," she assured them.

Mairaid said nothing. Secretly she was afraid, but she knew her mother. She had watched her through the long winter days, anxious, restless and impatient for news. The girl glanced at Adeline with the baby in her arms. The weather was still bitter and raw and although Adeline was strong and well again Mairaid wondered if the journey would prove too much for her. A few of the Glencoe women had asked to go, but the majority remained in the glen awaiting the return of their men, or at least news of them, be it good or bad.

On April 4th they set out: a week of fresh snow and sleet had delayed them, but that day the sun shone bravely. It was one of those fine spring mornings when the sky was a cloudless blue and the countryside looked as though it had been washed clean by the winter's storms.

New leaves were beginning to appear on the trees, the burns rushed rapidly down the sides of the mountains, swelling the lochs in the valleys, cascading over steep rock falls in a rush of white churning water, and the air was filled with birdsong.

Glancing around her, Mairaid thought that the world was too beautiful for it to be overshadowed by the horror of war. She had never witnessed bloodshed, but she had heard the tales, and it seemed to her that war, for whatever cause, was ugly, wasteful butchery. Today, when the first warmth of spring was seeping into the Highlands, should be carefree and joyful, yet they rode towards a battlefield—where it would be she did not know—where men would die horribly, women would be left to weep with their children, mothers for their sons. She looked at her mother who rode with her head held high, her shoulders set proudly, and she thought of her father and Phillip Gowry. What if her father were to kill his own sons, her brothers? Loyalties were so divided throughout Scotland, and nowhere was this more evident, she thought, than amongst her own family. She felt miserable. She wished they could have stayed at Rannoch, far away from the battlefield, safe in the old house her grandmother had built.

They were cold, wet, hungry and bone-weary to the point of exhaustion. They were lucky that they were mounted, for the depleted infantry could hardly place one foot before the other but shuffled along like men walking in a dream, seeing nothing, hearing nothing, feeling nothing, driven onwards only by the beat of the drum and the thin wailing of the pibroch. They rode together with the Glencoe men amongst the rest of Clan Donald.

Alasdair sat hunched in the saddle, his plaid sodden, his blue bonnet dripping. On his left rode his nephews, Andrew, silent and morose, and then Robert and young Ewan. The boy was reeling in the saddle with exhaustion, and from time to time Robert would reach out and pull him forward across the neck of his horse. Then Ewan would jerk himself upright, fighting to keep his eyes open, but after a few minutes he would slump forward again.

It felt as if they had been on the march for days without end, Andrew thought. It seemed so long since the day they had entered Derby. They had gone so far and their hopes were high, only to be dashed by the news that they must turn back for Scotland. What had been achieved? His weary mind had puzzled over this until it had become numb. A soldier obeyed orders, he did not question them, had been his Uncle Alasdair's reply but Andrew knew that Alasdair too, wondered at the futility of this march home.

In the bitter days of January they had come to the field of Bannockburn where Robert Bruce had defeated the forces of Edward of England and had secured Scotland's freedom. There they had awaited the attack of Hawley whom they assumed would march from Falkirk. He had not, so they had taken the initiative. It had been a victory for them, with Flanders veterans fleeing before the screaming Highland charge, but it was a battle without strategic importance. They had marched on into the Highlands in ever-decreasing numbers as men became disheartened and deserted to their homes to tend their lands. A voice whispered in his head how pleasant it would be to return to his home near Inverness, to the roaring peat fires, good food and a dry bed to sleep in, but he jerked himself back to reality as his uncle spoke to him.

"Is the boy alright?"

Andrew looked past Robert to the slumped figure of his youngest brother. "Aye, he's just exhausted, like us all! Where are we bound now?"

"Culloden House, the home of Duncan Forbes, just before Drummossie moor."

"There will be shelter and rest there?"

"For the prince, Murray and the others. We'll have to make shift as best we can."

"We've only some hard tack and cheese, and nothing dry!"

"Don't worry, lad, we'll find some sort of shelter—the plaids will dry before the fires, we'll manage."

"Cumberland's army is in these parts."

"I'll not deny it. This will be the last battle, the one which decides everything, our future, Scotland's future. Remember Andrew, why you are here. We are fighting not only for our freedom from the Union, but to avenge past injustices, the hardships and the cold-blooded murder of Clan Ian Abrach!"

"I don't forget!" came the muffled reply. "They say Argyll is with Cumberland?"

"He is, with almost his entire Clan."

Andrew looked around him at the men who rode and marched with heads bent as the sleet lashed them. "And so is Clan Donald."

Alasdair wondered what would become of them, these one hundred and thirty from the Glen of Dogs. Would Clan Ian Abrach pass into obscurity, drift quietly into history after this battle that he was certain now faced them, or would the old spirit be revived? Would they grow and prosper and become again the band of warriors they had once been, small though their sept of Clan Donald was?

Their ranks had been swelled a little by contingents of Grants, Frazers, Chisholms and MacCleods and men from Clan Chattan, and the Scots and Irish mercenaries from France, but still he estimated that they only numbered five thousand men in all, and before them lay Cumberland with all his divisions. Well-disciplined, well-clothed, better-fed, better-armed and with tents to sleep in at night and not the cold wet ground, wrapped in sodden tartans, like themselves. His own eyelids were drooping and he had to shake himself awake. Not much further now, he hoped. What did it matter if the ground were cold and wet and his clothes soaked? A small fire was all he asked and sleep, blissful sleep that would bring oblivion and erase for a few hours the pressing fears that haunted him.

Two hours were all they received before the rant of the pipes roused them. Stiff, numb and only half-awake they dragged themselves to their feet. For two days they had been marching to and fro, but Cumberland had been evasive. Word ran through the MacDonald ranks that they were to stand to the left of Clan Chattan and there were angry mutterings, for the MacDonalds had always stood to the right, the place they had traditionally occupied since Bannockburn.

Sleet was falling, driven by a merciless wind that seemed to prevail be it June or December. The ground was high and ideal for cavalry. Some of the prince's advisors had advocated the boggy moor beyond the Nairn water, but he was adamant. This, he knew, would be the decisive battle and he was determined that he alone should take full command. So with the sleet almost blinding them, their bellies empty, their frozen limbs enclosed in heavy sodden tartans, their bonnets pulled well down over their foreheads, the Highland Army waited in battle order, though there were nearly a thousand who had been so exhausted that not even the screaming of the pipes had roused them and they slumbered on.

To the far right in the front line were the Atholl men, then Locheil and his Camerons, the Appin Stewarts, the Frazers, in the centre Clan Chattan, flanked by the Farquharsons, then the mixed clans and Roy Stewart's Edinburgh battalion, and on the left men from every sept of Clan Donald. Behind them were the Irish mercenaries, the Scots Royals, the Duke of Perth and his men, Glenbucket, the divisions of Lord Lewis Gordon, the Ogilvys and to their right the men of Avochie. Behind them stood Kilmarnoch, Strathallan, Pitsligo, Balmerino and Elcho, these latter two surrounding the prince on his grey gelding, while in the prince's rear were Fitzjames' Life Guards.

There was a sunken road partly bordered by a stone wall which stretched down as far as the river Nairn and upwards enclosing a large area. At eleven o'clock some of Clan MacIntosh first saw the coming of the Government forces and heard the ominous drum-beat. Through the driving sleet marched three red columns, the scarlet and white of the standards seeming flamboyantly brilliant against the dreary sky. The small stone farmhouses of which Culwhiniac was the largest were within the stone-walled enclosure, and whoever took this enclosure would win the day, but the majority of the prince's forces did not even know of its existence.

An hour later, an eternity Alasdair thought, the two armies still stood facing each other. For half an hour the pipes had ranted on and the shouts of "Close up! Close up!" had been heard along the line of Highlanders. The pibroch of the Camerons was the first to sound, as it had been when the Royal Standard had been raised at Glenfinnon.

"You sons of dogs, of dogs of the breed,
O come, come here on flesh to feed!"

Strangely there was no sound on the moor from the Government army. To Alasdair, cold, hungry and exhausted, the silence seemed eerie and unnerving, then from the centre ranks there was an explosion and a cloud of smoke as the Royalist artillery opened up.

Craning his neck, young Andrew could see the ball pass harmlessly over the head of Lord Bury. It burst in the rear of the Government army. The broad Highlander who stood next to the boy spat on the ground, cursing the artillery for the fools they were. Then, borne on the wind, they heard the faint cry from the enemy ranks.

"Sponge! Powder . . . ram! Load . . . ram! Ready, FIRE!"

The air was suddenly rent with the continuous thundering roar of the Government artillery. It seemed to shake the very ground upon which they stood, and it was deadly accurate. All around him men were falling, screaming horribly as limbs were torn away. He heard the choking sobs of young Ewan and heard Robert tell the boy to look to the front, that they had nothing to fear as now most of the shot was going over their heads and blasting the rear ranks close to the prince himself. He could hear the roars of frustrated rage as the clansmen begged their chiefs for the sign to charge.

There seemed to be confusion amongst the prince and his advisors and most of the chiefs, knowing they could no longer hold back their men, called for the signal to charge. But there was no signal. The sleet still drove in their faces and now on their left flank they could hear the pibroch of the Campbells of Argyll's regiments. They were running in green tartan, their bonnets ornamented with sprigs of myrtle, the badge of Clan Dairmaid, and the yellow or red saltire to show their loyalty to the Hanoverian king. Behind them came the red-coated, white-gaitered soldiers of the infantry. To their rear the Government militia and horse had outflanked them but between them was the road, a deep ravine whose slopes were slimy and muddy and too treacherous for either side to charge down and engage the enemy. But the Clans had broken.

Clan Chattan at the centre broke first, screaming the battle cry, "Claymore! Claymore!" and the MacIntoshes, MacBeans and MacGillivary followed screaming "Lock Moy!" and "Drumglass!" The clouds of smoke from the Government artillery and the thundering of the guns still continued, the battle cries of the Clans and the screams of the wounded all mingled together into an inferno of confusion, blood, and destruction. Locheil and his Camerons, the Atholl men and the Stewarts of Appin followed Clan Chattan, only to run into the grapeshot that now came from the Government guns. Lead balls, nails and old pieces of iron tore into the ranks of charging Highlanders, ripping through bone, sinew and flesh, tearing open men's chests and bellies, mutilating arms and legs. Soldiers fell screaming and writhing in terrible agony on the ground and some of them, charging beside their fathers, were boys no older than fourteen. Over the deafening confusion of battle, the screaming rant of the pipes could still be heard.

Ewan's face was drained of all colour; even his lips were bloodless. Beside him sat Robert, his eyes red-rimmed from the smoke and tears of rage and frustration. Andrew felt he could stand no more. He dragged the dirk from his belt and threw down the pistol, for it would be of no use to him. Dismounting, he lifted his broadsword, almost in unison with Alasdair whose face was haggard, his eyes deep-set and burning with anger. Their cries of "Advance Donald!" were lost amidst the ear-splitting noise, but they ran forward over the wet slippery heather. Through the dense smoke that hung like a thick cloud over everything there came a blinding, blazing flash of musket fire. The Government infantry fired a continuous volley, dropping back as the next rank moved forward, then standing and firing again as the second rank dropped back to reload.

Alasdair could neither see nor hear his nephews. He stumbled over the bodies of the fallen, staggering onwards towards the flashes of light that spat death and mutilation. Through the smoke Andrew saw the red coats and with a flame of pure hatred racing through his veins he charged forward, the basket-hilted broadsword raised high. He broke through the first line of infantry, striking out to left and right with sword and dirk, thrusting and dragging as his weapons found their targets. He felt the blood warm and sticky on his hands and arms, but whether it was that of the soldiers or his own he did not know or care. Still swinging the broadsword he reached the third line and saw before him the glinting steel of the bayonets. The bright, hard glitter was the last sight that met his eyes as he went down beneath a circle of bayonets.

Robert had not got as far as his brother. His feet had carried him on over the bodies of his fallen companions on the wet ground: wet not only from the sleet but from blood. He had only run a few hundred yards when the grapeshot broke both his legs. He stumbled, still upright for a few seconds, then the fire and smoke dimmed as the second round of grape tore open his chest and the darkness of death closed his eyes forever. Standing like an animal at bay, Alasdair howled his frustration at the scarlet ranks. He could get no closer to them, for the steady murderous fire had almost stopped the advance; only a few clansmen, crazed with fear and pain, kept on running forward until they fell or were lost in the smoke. Never in his life had he felt such impotent consuming anger. They could get no closer, all they could do was stand and scream abuse and in desperation tear out the very stones at their feet and hurl the ineffective, puny missiles at the steady line of scarlet.

Keppoch's men broke and turned first. Back towards the rear they ran, throwing down their weapons. The saying "those who fight and run away, live to fight another day" was in their minds, as they thought of their glens and their families. At last Alasdair realised that there was nothing else to be done but to follow them.

Men still fell around him, but he ran on. He had never seen such carnage. The ground was covered with the dead and dying, with men whose entrails spilled out on the earth beside them, men whose limbs were twisted and shattered or severed, the arm or leg, the hand or foot or head lying several yards away. They had lost; this battle that was to have promised everything had turned into the worst slaughter the Clans had ever experienced. All Alasdair could think about now was getting back to Rannoch, to Andrea and Adeline, away from the battlefield. Behind him he could hear hooves drumming as Kingston's horse rode in pursuit. He stumbled again, this time down the slopes of the sunken road, thick with bushes and tangled clumps of heather and ling.

Beneath the fragile barrier of a gorse bush he lay, panting, his heart feeling as though it were about to burst and his lungs as though they would explode. He had minor wounds, grazes upon his arms and forehead where he had narrowly missed the grapeshot. He lay there, his head throbbing, not knowing whether it was the sound of battle that was still raging above him, or the hooves of the cavalry that were riding so close by him that he could have reached out and touched them. He lay curled beneath the low branches of the bush, almost completely hidden by the ling, his head resting on the cold steel of his claymore. Down his smoke-blackened face the tears ran, tracing clean rivulets down his cheeks and falling on the blade of the claymore that had never been used.

Chapter 17

Across the river Nairn on the brae of Cregan Glas a group of three women riders waited. Around the heads of two of them were plaid shawls but the third wore the blue bonnet with the eagle feathers and white cockade.

Jeannie had begged them not to go, but Andrea was adamant and Mairaid insisted on accompanying her mother. Seeing that nothing could dissuade Andrea, Adeline had left Mitchell in Jeannie's care in Inverness and had ridden out with them. They had sat there for five hours, the sleet stinging their faces and soaking into their shawls. It clung to Andrea's hair, to her cloak, but she ignored it. Her body was taut and tense as she sat motionless, her eyes fixed upon the two opposing armies on the moor across the river. Mairaid and Adeline shivered miserably and there were tears in Mairaid's eyes.

"Why don't they move?" Andrea cried impatiently, hearing the wail of the pipes, blown away from them by the wind. "What's holding them back? Is the prince a fool? Can't he see that if he does not take his advantage now, it will be a long and costly battle?"

"He must have his reasons," Mairaid replied.

Adeline tried to wrap the plaid more tightly around her. Why in the name of the Almighty had she come here, she wondered? She should have stayed at Inverness, but somewhere in the silent ranks of the Government forces was Phillip. She had been a fool to come for, whichever side gained the victory, she would be forced to bear the pain of grief, either for herself or for Andrea and Mairaid.

When the prince's artillery had started Andrea breathed a sigh of relief. "Thank God! It must be now! They must go now!" But only the sound of the pipes and guns drifted across the river. There were no fierce battle cries from the Clans, no surge of the tartan lines towards the enemy. Still they stood and then had come that deafening roar as the enemy artillery opened up. It was difficult to see through the smoke but of one thing she was certain: there was still no movement from the Clans. Occasionally a scream or cry was carried on the wind. As the noise continued the tears of rage poured down her cheeks. Such brave men to be led by such fools! They would have been better led by Gordon himself, alone, without the council of the others!

Mairaid saw her tears through the mists that swam before her own eyes. Somewhere in the smoke stood her three brothers and her father, and she loved them all! She heard the shout of approval as Clan Chattan broke and the MacIntosh battle cry, but Mairaid did not look up. Her brothers were with her Uncle Alasdair, she knew, not with the MacIntoshes, but how soon would she hear the cry of Clan Donald, as Keppochs, Glengarrys and the other MacDonalds broke and charged into that deadly smoke that hid the shot until it ripped men apart? Adeline was also silent, her hand over her mouth, the tears pouring down her cheeks. At last Mairaid could stand it no longer. She reached out and pulled her mother's arm. "Come away, Mother! Please, please come away?"

Andrea shook off her hand. "No! Your brothers are out there—everything depends upon this battle. I will not leave until it is all over!"

"My father is out there, too, and Phillip . . ." but Andrea did not hear her, she was lost in a world of her own. The noise and the smoke were carried towards them by the wind which had changed direction, and the sleet had at last stopped. Through the gaps in the smoke they could see the tartan ranks being decimated, see the stand, kneel, fire, drill of the Government infantry. There was nothing Mairaid could do and so she bent her head and began to cry, softly, desperately. She was certain that before the day was over all those she loved, except her mother, would be dead.

Dusk was falling as Andrea at last turned her horse towards the river bank.

"Where are you going?" Adeline asked woodenly. It was as though she had been drained of all feelings; never had she seen such appalling slaughter, so much horrible mutilation.

"To find my husband, my brother and my sons!"

"There are sentries on Drummossie moor." Mairaid's words came from a throat parched with silent sobbing, lips cracked with cold.

"They will not hinder us. The women come when all is over and take away their dead, it has always been so," came the tired reply.

The waters of the Nairn were icy cold as they rode across, but none of them seemed to notice. They rode up through the walled enclosure and then Mairaid abruptly pulled her horse to a standstill, her eyes widening with horror and disbelief, her stomach churning. "Mother! Oh, Mother! Do you see what they are doing?"

A strangled cry was Andrea's reply as she spurred her horse forward. Amongst the bodies of the soldiers, most of them clad in tartan, the sentries picked their way, methodically bayonetting to death the wounded.

They dismounted so as not to ride over the dead and dying. These were the men of Clan Chattan who lay around them, most of them dead, and Adeline and Mairaid could scarcely prevent themselves from vomiting at the sights they saw. Andrea was working her way over towards the right flank, where the MacDonalds had stood, when she was challenged by a sentry.

"I am looking for my sons—have you no pity? Who gave the order that the wounded were to be murdered?" Her voice was cold and tight with anger and grief.

"The duke himself!"

"Duke! The fat Hanoverian. . . ."

Mairaid grabbed her arm and pulled her away, seeing the soldier raise his musket.

"We have orders that no rebel, either dead or alive, is to be taken from the field!"

"Do you know where Captain Phillip Gowry is, of the garrison at Fort William?" Adeline cried.

"Why?"

"He's my husband!"

"A fine party! War makes strange bedfellows!" the soldier jeered.

The spirit of the old Adeline flashed briefly. "I asked you a question, answer me or you'll have your commanding officer to answer to, I swear it!"

The man gave her a stubborn, sullen glance. "I don't know and that's the truth!"

"Then do I have your permission to seek my husband, or does the duke's command to murder the wounded extend to his own troops as well?"

The soldier looked away, flinching at the biting sarcasm in Adeline's voice.

"There wasn't anything said about our own wounded, most of them have been taken off anyway."

She took a few paces forward, followed by Andrea and Mairaid.

"Not you two!" growled the sentry.

For a minute Mairaid thought her mother was going to leap at the soldier's throat, but a conspiratorial glance from Adeline checked her.

The soldier walked away and then halted a few yards away from them, near enough to be ready to stop them should they try to follow Adeline, yet far enough away to dissociate himself from them.

Slowly Adeline picked her way over the bodies, her vision so blurred by tears that she hardly saw them as men, though most of them bore little resemblance to the valliant fighters they had been a few hours earlier. They were shapeless bundles of bloodsoaked cloth with here and there the white flesh of an arm or leg, the bloody fingers still crooked around a dirk or sword.

She came at last to a figure in a red coat and she bent down like an automaton and looked into the man's face. It was not Phillip. She walked on towards the MacDonald lines. There were a few red coats, but most of the Government forces had been removed to field hospitals behind the lines. She bent down over a man and dashed away the tears with the back of her hand. It was Robert, his features contorted in rage and pain, both his legs shattered, his shirt and kilt stained with dark congealed blood. She reached out and touched his cheek, then she rose and walked on, not seeing the soldier who was approaching her.

"Adeline! What are you doing here?"

She raised her head and saw, through her tears, Phillip standing before her. His face was grimy with smoke, his uniform torn and dirty, the white gaiters that came to the thigh were covered with mud and splashes of blood. Relief made her sway dizzily. "Phillip! Phillip! Is it really you?"

He caught her around the waist and held her close to

him. "Yes, I was lucky! But why are you here?"

"We have been here since this morning, we... we saw it all and now... now... they are butchering the wounded! Is that truly the order you have?"

He nodded. "I'm afraid so!"

She looked up at him and there was such bitterness in her eyes that he felt as though he had been stung.

"Would you butcher Alasdair, Andrew and Ewan? Robert... Robert... is already dead, I saw him back there."

He didn't answer her. "Phillip, for my sake, please? Please help me find the others? Even if... if they are dead, at least I can spare Andrea the misery, the uncertainty... please, Phillip! For me?"

He took her hand and led her after him, while she dared not ask herself what he would do if they found them and they were alive.

It was Andrew they found first, his body half-covered by two other MacDonalds, recognisable only by their tartans. Red and Black of Glengarry. Again she knelt and touched the cold cheek. Poor Andrea! He helped her to her feet. "Phillip, what will you do if... if we find the others... alive?"

"I don't know. Let's find them first."

There seemed no end to the bodies, she thought, it was like walking through a sea of blood and death. She kept her eyes fixed upon the gold epaulettes on Phillip's shoulders until he stopped again.

"Who is it?"

"Ewan."

She was afraid to speak, the question stuck in her throat. "Is... is... he...."

"He's alive." He stood up and turned to face her. "I have my orders."

She stared at him for a long time, then looked down at the boy. There was a bloody gash on his temple and the blood had dried on his cheeks. "If you kill him, Phillip, then kill me too! I would rather be dead for I could never look at you again without remembering...."

"I can't carry him. You will have to, but you must wait until it is dark for if you are seen you will be shot!"

"What kind of a man have you sworn loyalty to, Phillip? What kind of man would order a woman shot bearing away the body of a wounded boy? He is no Christian, he is a murderer! Worse, he is a butcher!"

He turned away from her and began to walk back to the perimeter of the field while she gently raised Ewan in her arms. His left arm hung limply and was covered with blood, but there was nothing she could do about it. She laid him down again. He had felt the movement and opened his eyes, not seeming to know where he was.

"Ewan, it's me, Adeline! Don't you recognise me?"

"Adeline, where are Andrew, Robert, and Alasdair?"

"Andrew and Robert are . . . are dead and I don't know where Alasdair is . . . but your mother and Mairaid are here. As soon as it is dark I will take you to them. Can you walk?"

He lay there staring at her. "Then all is over, all is lost?"

She nodded. "We must get you away from here quickly, before anyone sees us or they . . . they will kill us both!"

"Who were you talking to?"

"Phillip. It was only because of him that you are alive now—had it been anyone else you would have been butchered where you lay."

He struggled to rise, but loss of blood and shock had made him weak and dizzy and he leaned heavily on her. She would never be able to carry him should he faint, she thought with rising panic, yet she had to get him away from this terrible field of carnage, back to Andrea and the horses.

"Please try to walk. I'm not strong enough to carry you!" she pleaded. The light was bad, dusk was rapidly falling but at least the darkness would hide them. He leaned on her shoulders and slowly and painfully they made their way back towards where she had left Andrea and Mairaid. She prayed that the other sentry would not be there.

He had gone and as she saw the two huddled forms,

she cried out. Andrea rushed forward, relieving her of her burden. She clung to her youngest son for a moment. "Where are you hurt?"

"My head and my arm!" he croaked. Suddenly all he had witnessed—the sights no boy of his age should ever see—all the feelings of terror, revulsion, anger and despair he had somehow managed to hide that day, rose like a bubble and burst. He was a child again, a child whose body was hurt and whose spirit was broken, and he clung to his mother and sobbed out every minute of that nightmare of a day.

She held him close to her. Her bairn, injured and afraid—her arms held him tightly as though to protect him from memories that would haunt his dreams forever and from which there was no protection. Her eyes were closed, her head bent over his, and from beneath the dark lashes the large, scalding tears dropped onto his head. She listened in silence as she heard of Andrew's maddened charge into the enemy lines and of the hail of murderous grapeshot that had torn Robert apart and so many of her own MacIntosh clansmen. She thought of all the mothers and wives who were waiting at home for men and boys who would never return.

"And Alasdair and . . . and your father?" she whispered, fearing the answer.

"I saw Alasdair running towards the road but there were horsemen after him. . . ." Fresh sobs overtook him and he was unable to speak for some minutes. Then he raised his head and fought down the choking lump in his throat. "I saw . . . I saw my father fall . . . to. . . ." Again the awful sobs racked him and Mairaid threw herself into Adeline's arms, crying brokenly.

"To what? To what, Ewan?"

"To Andrew's claymore!" Suddenly the anguish burst forth. "We were all fools! We were led by fools! It was a fool's errand, we were a rabble, we stood no chance against them! It was all wasted, Mother! Wasted! What of them now? All those men and boys, slaughtered for no reason. . . ."

"There was a reason!" Andrea was fighting back despair

herself. Everything had gone. In one short day her husband and two of her sons and probably her brother had been killed, but worst of all, far worse than the carnage that surrounded her, or the grief that was tearing her apart, was the knowledge that her husband had died by the hand of his own and eldest son. "There were old battles, old wounds to be avenged, the fight was for the Crown, for Scotland's freedom!"

"Are they reason enough that a son should kill his father? I . . . I remember when I was a bairn, they would ride together . . . they would practise with the wooden foil . . . he taught Andrew to kill. . . .!" Ewan's mouth was twisted with despair as he gazed up at her, his face streaked with mud, tears and blood. "Scotland will never be free! It was a dream—a blind and crazy dream! Will they never learn? George of Hanover is here to stay, the English will be our masters for ever!"

"No! No!" She almost screamed the words at him. "Never say that! Too much blood has been spilled, too many hopes dashed for that to be true!"

"But it is true, Mother! Open your eyes and look around you! The Clans are destroyed, the dream we fought for lies in the mud with the trampled standards and where is the prince for whom they all died? Is he dead too? They died in vain, they are still dying. . . ." His words were cut off by the scream of a man into whose chest an English bayonet had just been thrust. It was dark now and it was Adeline who reminded them of their own danger. Supporting her only surviving son Andrea led them away from Drummossie moor, away from the smell of death and despair that hung over the thousands of men who lay where they had been struck down. For as long as she lived Adeline would remember Culloden Field.

They were beyond the battlefield now and the darkness had swallowed them up. Andrea heard the impatient neigh of their horses which they had tethered to some low bushes and she gave a sigh of relief. Her heart felt like lead, her eyelids were almost too heavy to keep open and her eyes were sore, though she knew there were plenty more tears yet to come. Mairaid mounted; the plaid had fallen from her head, her face was like chalk, her eyes were half-closed and her whole body seemed to portray her misery and shock. With Adeline's help Andrea got Ewan up into the saddle, then mounted herself, holding him in front of her. She looked at Adeline. Adeline had come to Rannoch a spoiled, determined girl, but it was not that girl whose eyes met her own. Adeline was a woman now, a woman who had experienced almost as much sorrow as she herself, for this was not her country, this cause—lost now it seemed forever—was not hers, but she had committed herself for the love of her brother and her husband. And she had begged for Ewan's life as Gabrielle had once done for Andrea's father, and they were ties that would never be broken.

"There will be another battle," Adeline said softly, reaching up and squeezing Andrea's cold hand. "But it will not be fought with musket and sword, there will be no generals to command, no cannon—it will be fought in the heart of every mother, wife and sweetheart. We all shall grieve for the rest of our lives. You for your husband and your sons, Mairaid for her father and her brothers, Ewan for them also and me . . . I shall grieve for my brother and for my husband, for though he has been spared, I know that between us for ever will lie Alasdair's death!"

"Where shall we go now?" Mairaid asked pitifully. "There are soldiers everywhere."

"Home!" Andrea answered.

"To Glenmoy?"

"No, that was never home for me! Home to Rannoch, to the moorlands and the Glen of Dogs, to Rannoch Chase!"

"Someone must have seen the grey dogs of the Feinn last night! In the glen the women must have seen the grey, silent shapes running beside the waters of the Coe, they must have heard the sound of their feet, for few MacDonalds will return to Glencoe!"

"Tales, superstitions, Mairaid!" Adeline chided gently. "There is enough tragic reality today. No need for morbid tradition!"

For three days the dead of Culloden Field were left, the ground patrolled by English sentries. The carrion-crows found plenty to feast upon, and parties of soldiers crept out from Inverness at night, intent on plunder, despite Cumberland's order that there should be no looting of the dead. Each morning the shout, the roll of the drum and the sound of the lash were heard in the town as the offenders were punished, but this was no deterrent. The gibbets were set up in Inverness, Fort Augustus and in Edinburgh itself as the rebels were rounded up and hanged, then carried away, naked, to mass graves. The tolbooths, the kirks, every form of gaol was filled with prisoners, while the transports anchored in the firth and moored at Citadel Quay were packed, awaiting orders. Many men died of their wounds, fever, and gangrene before the floating hulks set sail for the Colonies with their human cargoes.

At the house, Glenmoy, the three women had stopped for the night. They had bathed and dressed Ewan's wounds, had eaten some gruel and poured the last of the brandy down his throat. Adeline and Mairaid had made up three bundles of food and for safety's sake they had dressed Ewan in Mairaid's clothes. Not daring to stay until dawn came, they set out, retracing their steps towards Loch Ness and the Great Glen and Fort Augustus. From there they would travel on through Keppoch's lands to Fort William and finally to Rannoch Moor. Behind them lay the dead, the dying, the prisoners and a futile dream, while ahead they faced scouting parties, rounding up the fleeing rebels, murdering women and children if a clansman were found beneath their roof.

It was a long journey, fraught with dangers. Adeline held Mitchell tightly in her arms. She had not seen or heard from Phillip since they had parted on Culloden Field but she knew he would come in search of her and his son when he was free to do so, and that he would know where to find her. She prayed that when he came he would bring no detachment of soldiers with him.

Chapter 18

He had lain there until darkness had fallen, then he had crept out from beneath the shelter of the bushes and bracken. He had lain and listened to the battle until the noise had gradually died away—or perhaps he had fallen asleep. Now there was no sound, except that of the wind that blew ceaselessly over Culloden Field. He had crawled up the steep sides of the ravine and made his way down to the Nairn water, where he lay on his stomach and drank deeply, then splashed the icy water over his face. The cuts and grazes began to smart but they were as nothing to him. He sat on the springy moss of the river bank, trying to formulate a plan in his mind. He could not go back. He did not know what had happened to his nephews, or his clansmen, maybe he would never know, but of one thing he was certain. The battle was over and the Clans would never march out again.

He wondered what had happened to the prince. This cause that he had made his own, from love and loyalty to his mother and his grandfather, now seemed so futile. Janet and Charleston belonged to another world, a world and a life he would probably never see again. The countryside and Inverness would be swarming with troops and the sight of the tartan was enough to bring him to the gallows, but he had no other clothes. Stiffly he rose. He would have to make his way back to Rannoch, skirting the main byways and towns and villages. He must get back to Andrea and Adeline and if he was fortunate enough to reach them, he must try to remove them from Scotland. He would take them all back to the haven of that other Rannoch that prospered peacefully beneath warm blue skies, where they could live in safety and comfort, and try to forget this nightmare they had endured.

He picked his way carefully and stealthily around the perimeter of the stone wall, making for the outskirts of Inverness. Hopefully he would, under cover of the darkness, be able to reach Glenmoy where he would find food and some other clothes. He was bent low and did not see the soldier until he was almost upon him. Instinctively, he lunged forward with his dirk, missing the man by inches.

"Would you kill me, Alasdair? Has there not been enough killing in this family for one day?"

Alasdair lowered the dirk, recognising the voice of Phillip Gowry.

"Why are you here?"

"As a sentry, to stop looting and to see that no bodies or wounded rebels are removed! My orders are to kill every rebel on sight, to finish off the wounded with the bayonet!"

"Then why do you not finish me?"

He could not see Phillip's face in the darkness.

"Because of Adeline. Because you are my brother-in-law, and to put you to death would be to drive her away from me. She pleaded with me, not half an hour since, for the life of Ewan MacIntosh."

"Adeline was here?"

"With Andrea and Mairaid: they saw it all! Andrew and Robert are dead, so is my father and Ian MacIntosh. We are both the losers today; the victory is an empty one for us." There was no mistaking the bitterness and grief in Phillip's tones.

"Where are they now?"

"I don't know, but I think that they will try to make for Rannoch, though Ewan was wounded and they are likely to be stopped, even . . . killed!"

"Then it is not over yet? They will kill the women?"

"It will not be over for many months, perhaps even years. The duke is determined to subdue the Highlands once and for all. This will be the last battle, the Clans will never rise again!"

"What of the prince?"

"The Pretender? He has eluded us so far, but he will be caught!"

"And then?"

"I don't know. Taken to the Tower and beheaded, most likely!"

None of it seemed to have sunk into his brain. Remorse and grief and anger would come later, but not now. There was too much for his tired mind to cope with.

"Get away from here, Alasdair, before you are seen! Never let it be known that you have seen me!"

Through the darkness Alasdair groped for the other man's hand. "Tonight we are not soldiers but kinsmen! God bless you, Phillip!"

Phillip's hand was as cold as his own as it gripped his numb fingers. "Go back to Charleston, Alasdair! Go back and take Andrea, Ewan and Mairaid with you—this land will not be fit for any man, woman or child when the duke has done with it!"

"What of Adeline?"

"I will find her, she will be safe with me. She is my wife, and we have Mitchell to think of now."

"Charleston is her home!"

"When we were wed, she knew what lay ahead of her—she knew she would have to follow the drum."

"Then take care of her, Phillip!"

"Of that I promise!"

He had gone, a shadow disappearing in the darkness, and Alasdair was alone. Now he knew his only chance lay in getting to Glenmoy and substituting other garments for the tartan he had worn with such pride.

He reached Glenmoy nearly two hours later and found it in darkness. He crept in, not daring to light a candle, and stumbled about until he found a chest in one of the bedrooms. He opened the lid and felt inside, then he breathed a sigh of relief. There were clothes of some description; he prayed they were those of Andrew or Ian who were much his size, or had been. By feeling and tracing the edges with his fingers he could discern that the first object was a jacket, a man's jacket. He quickly placed it on the floor and fumbled inside the trunk. His search was rewarded and soon the wet, torn, muddy tartan was thrust into the chest and he was dressed in the shirt, waistcoat, jacket and breeches of his dead nephew. All he needed now were boots.

The light that came in through the window was dim,

for dark clouds were scudding across the sky, almost obliterating the moon's light. He could see the bed in the centre of the room and dropped down beside it, his hand feeling beneath the heavy bedcover whose fringe reached the floor. His fingers closed over the soft leather of a pair of top boots and he drew them out. They were a little too large, but better that than to small, he thought as he pulled them on: he had many miles to walk.

His targe and broadsword he had laid in the trunk with his discarded tartan, but his dirk he kept, pushed down inside his boot. He had no money and no food, no horse and no time left now, for already the first streaks of light were beginning to steal across the leaden sky. Finally he picked up a heavy dark riding cloak and wrapped himself in it, made his way downstairs and out through the back door. He would not be so conspicuous now, but he would have to beg food where he could and sleep beneath the hedges in fields. It was a long way to Rannoch, down the Great Glen.

Midday found him south of the town of Inverness and seated beside the driver of a rough wooden cart, loaded with turnips and other early vegetables, bound for Fort Augustus at the southern end of Loch Ness. He was grateful for the ride, for he had walked many miles and his feet were sore, and he was so weary that he would have dropped before he had gone another mile. He dozed intermittently, having told the man that he was bound for the fort on business but that his horse had tripped and fallen, becoming lame and useless as a result.

"Aye, the track is nae good for fast riddin!" the driver had agreed as he had helped him up. They were passed on the road by detachments of soldiers. Sometimes they were stopped, sometimes they were asked if they had seen any of the rebels. They both replied, "No," and the driver added sotto voce, "an' if I had I wouldnae tell ye!"

"You sided with the prince?" Alasdair asked.

The man shot him a suspicious look. "You be a government man then?"

Alasdair shook his head. "No, I was just askin'. I take no part."

"Now that's a fine thing to say, indeed it is! And that's what I am thinkin' too, it dinna matter much t' me which o' them sits on the throne an wears the crown on his craig! German or Stuart, there's nae much to choose when a' is said an' done. We never prospered under any o' them!"

Alasdair had not replied. It seemed to him that there must be many folk, especially in the Lowlands and the towns, who held the same view. Now the feelings of grief and shock had had time to seep into his brain. Andrew, Robert, Ian MacIntosh and Robert Gowry all dead and so many others, too many even to count. The driver had informed him, "The rebels hae bin left there t' rot, and rumour hae it that there is worse yet t' come for a' those that hae supported them or gae them food and shelter." He had bent his head at the man's words, thinking of Andrea and Adeline and the wounded young lad. If he was fortunate enough when he reached Fort Augustus, he might be able to find something to eat, and from there he would have to walk. There would be no wagons travelling to Stratherrick, Ruthven, Garvamore and Rannoch. The country was wild and the going would be rough.

They said their farewells at the gates of the fortress town, the driver turning down one of the narrow side streets while Alasdair stood staring around him. He was feeling faint from lack of food and sleep, but he had no money. He stopped outside the only coffee shop and sniffed appreciatively. At least he could warm himself, he thought, and he might be able to beg a cup of something warm. He went inside, bending his head as he stepped through the low doorway. It was packed not only with townspeople but with soldiers from the garrison also. He edged himself into a corner, fairly close to the fire, and pulled an empty mug in front of him so as not to draw attention to himself. He looked around furtively. The customers were mainly soberly dressed men like himself; he counted only half a dozen red coats, but one would be enough. He raised the empty mug to his lips and pretended to drink.

"It's empty, sir, shall I refill it?"

He turned and looked up, startled by the voice. The young serving maid stood beside him, a fresh-faced girl of about eighteen with dark curling hair and bright blue eyes.

"Er... no, I think I'll just bide here a while longer."

Her eyes had travelled down to where his legs were crossed under the table, and as he followed her gaze he saw with horror the dirk protruding from the top of his boot. He looked up at her. It only needed one word and he would end up in the tolbooth and from there it would be a short step to the scaffold....

"Aye, sir, you bide here, I'll fill your mug and bring ye a bit t' eat!" She smiled down at him, but there was a warning look in the deep blue eyes.

He held his breath the whole of the time she was away, his eyes riveted to her form as she threaded her way between the customers. His heart missed a beat as she passed the small group of soldiers, but she did not stop and soon returned with a mug of steaming coffee, a portion of fowl and some wheaten bread on a wooden platter.

"Eat up, sir," she said, then bending lower over the dish she whispered, "Will ye make a show o' passin' me some siller, eat up an' then for Guid's sake, go! I dinna know who ye are, but hide yon dirk and Guid be with ye!"

He made a pretence of passing her some coins as she straightened up and turned to leave him. He blessed her as he drank the hot liquid and tried not to bolt the food. At least there were still some brave enough to help a fugitive. He was loath to leave, for the heat and the food had made him drowsy, but mindful of her warning he pushed the dirk further into his boot and dragged himself to his feet. He jostled his way through the throng with excuses for his boorishness to those men he caught with an elbow or a knee, until at last he was outside again. He turned down the street towards the gate. Half of his journey was over and so far his luck had held—now he could live only from day to day, hoping, praying that he would reach Fort William safely. From there it was only a day's journey to Rannoch.

Andrea's journey had been slow because of Ewan, and painful. They had eaten sparingly of the food they had brought with them, and they had been stopped many times on the road. Each time Adeline's blood had frozen in her veins and Andrea's heart had dropped like a stone. Ewan held the baby in the crook of his good arm and Mairaid held the reins, for they were mounted on the same horse. Andrea told each patrol that they were returning to their glen, that now, alas, they were all widows and that Mitchell and Mairaid were fatherless. Would the soldiers take pity on them, they had many miles to travel and the child's mother was hardly over childbed fever? Surely the good soldiers of his Majesty King George would not hamper or harm defenceless women?

It made her stomach churn to speak the words in a low, pleading whine and once she had choked and spluttered on the name of the Hanoverian King. But it had worked so far, though she had heard tales of women and young girls raped and then bayonetted to death, of babies swung by their feet, their heads smashed against the walls of their homes before their mothers' eyes. Those poor women, crazed by the sight of the butchery of their children, had then been raped and murdered. Old men and women had been locked in their homes and the thatch fired so that they burned to death. All rebels found were killed instantly or taken to the nearest town to be hanged. There was not one town in the Highlands without laden gibbets.

Once Andrea had heard Clan Ian Abrach referred to as "The Gallows Herd", and now she thought bitterly that it was a singularly inappropriate description, for of the 130 who had joined the prince, only a handful would ever get back to their glen. There was some comfort that they had died in battle and not become the fruit of the gallows tree.

When at last they came to the lands of the Keppoch MacDonalds they had received a little help from the women of that Clan, but it had been left to them to inform these wives and mothers of the slaughter at Culloden: slaughter which still continued. Grief was something they all shared now; hunger, illness and death would come later.

They had been with the Keppoch MacDonalds for almost a week when in the distance they heard the thin wailing of the pipes. They all rushed out excitedly, for it was a sound they had never thought to hear again. It was the MacGregors. Outlawed since before the Massacre of Glencoe, they had gone out for the prince, proud to be able once more to use their own Clan name. They were from Glentrae, Glengyle and Glenlyon, and their motto was "S Roigmal no dhream"—"Royal is my race." As they approached Andrea could see that they were still armed, for they marched with claymores drawn, and the pine-sprig badge of their Clan in their bonnets. Their ranks were decimated but they refused to disband until they had reached their homes. There were about three hundred of them, and those who had found their homes burnt lived in the corries and continued to harry the patrols sent out from the garrison. But they halted as the women came from their homes, bringing food and drink.

"Where are you bound?" Andrea asked their tall sandy-haired chieftain.

"Home, mistress. Why, when we passed Finlarig Castle yon' Campbells durst nae move than their cats!" He looked more closely at her, after a burst of sardonic laughter. "Mistress have I nae see ye before?"

"You may have. I am Andrea Charlotte Stuart, and I am bound with my only surviving son and my daughter for Rannoch. Will MacGregor help me?"

He took off his bonnet. "You're the daughter of Alizon Stuart, the child of King Charles?"

"I am, and I have lost nearly all my family, and all my mother's wealth on Culloden Field!"

"Then we will offer ye our protection until ye reach your home, mistress. But if we meet with those bastard redcoats ye must fend for yourselves, though we will fight to protect ye!"

She thanked him and he replaced his bonnet as she turned away. Outlaws, broken men they might be, but they still had their loyalties and their respect.

Andrea's little group rode on two hours later at the back of the column protected by a rank four deep of MacGregor clansmen, and the column was led by their piper. Despite everything, Andrea felt her spirits rise again. Though they were beaten these men refused to admit it, but were marching home, still armed, with heads held high, to the sound of the MacGregor pibroch. They had had years of experience where hardship, treachery and stealth were concerned and she admired them. They were tough fighting men, for in the conditions in which they lived only the hardiest survived, and she wished that all the Highlanders had been moulded like them. But it was too late now. She had wanted to reach Rannoch with some remnants of her pride and dignity intact, and with the help of these men that was exactly what she was going to do.

Even Ewan had discarded his disguise and now wore his tartan and bonnet with pride. The wounds he had sustained had not been serious and were almost healed, but she still feared for him. In the months to come the patrols from the fort would come looking for any man who had managed to get back to his glen, but she knew the hiding-place in the attic where her father had hidden from the soldiers all those years ago. It would be simple enough task to conceal her son.

At last, nearly four days later, they drew rein and stared at the moorland that stretched before them. The weather was warmer and the new green shoots were beginning to thrust up through the brown earth. The buds on the trees were unfurling and away in the distance a waup called plaintively, as if welcoming them home, yet not forgetting the sorrow they brought with them.

Andrea turned her horse out from the ranks and rode to the front of the column. "We will leave you here, MacGregor. Our thanks and may God go with you!"

"The honour has been mine, Mistress Stuart. Ye can see the house, a few more miles and ye will be home!"

She held out her hand for him to grasp in farewell but to her astonishment he took his bonnet from his head and kneeling, lifted her hand to his lips and kissed it. "That's in remembrance of your grandsire!" he said quietly before he rose. Mounting, he wheeled his horse to the right and the column followed.

They watched them go until they were a long way off in the distance and only the wailing notes of the pipes could be heard, mere echoes on the wind. They turned away and Andrea shaded her eyes with her hand. MacGregor was right; she could see Rannoch Chase, its dark outline against the sky, the chimneys twisted and tall. Home! They had come home at last! Andrea dug her heels into the flanks of the highland pony and it broke into a trot, then a canter. Behind her she could hear the steady hoof-beats as the others followed her. The house was becoming nearer and nearer, its stark outlines so dearly familiar. Here she had ridden at the end of the day in childhood, home to Alizon who always greeted her with a smile and a laugh at her tangled hair and untidy clothes. Rannoch Chase: the home from which she had gone as a bride nearly twenty years ago, and now . . . now she was returning a widow in her middle years.

Her husband and two of her children were dead and unburied. Never would Andrew and Robert lie with Alizon and her father on Eilean Munde; she would never know where they lay, nor Ian either.

They had reached the wall that bounded the small overgrown garden. The house was empty: no welcoming light in the window, no wisps of curling smoke rising from the chimneys into the bluish-grey sky where the evening star hung like a huge candle. They rode around to the courtyard at the back and dismounted. There was no sign of life anywhere. Andrea led the horses to the drinking-trough and then crossed the yard to the door, noticing the weeds growing between the cobbles. She pushed against the door and as it opened she stepped cautiously inside. The place was as silent as a churchyard on the Eve of All Hallows and she shuddered, running her hand over the range, her fingers coming away covered in dust and leaving three clean streaks upon the heavy iron top. She went on through the kitchen and into the rooms beyond. Everything was as it had been the day that Adeline had left. She heard their feet echoing on the flagged floor of the kitchen. The house was as cold as the kirk in winter.

"No one has been here since we left." Adeline sounded puzzled.

"For which we may be thankful!"

"But I asked the women of the glen to watch the house. . . ."

"Maybe they were too afraid, or maybe they have already heard. . . ."

Andrea stared around her. "The first thing we must do is get the fires going. There are some logs and some peat in one of the barns. Ewan and Mairaid, bring some in, it is as cold as Christmas in here. Then we must look for something to eat and put warming-pans in the beds, and air all the linen, but most important of all we must have warmth!" She turned and smiled at Adeline when Ewan and Mairaid had gone. It was a tired smile, as if there were too many burdens for her shoulders to carry.

"Do you think they will know, that someone will already have told them?" Adeline asked.

"I don't know, but first thing tomorrow I must go to the glen and find out. Perhaps when they notice smoke and lights from the house, someone will come. We will wait and see."

Chapter 19

Next morning there was still the same eerie silence over the house and the moor and, looking towards the entrance of the glen, Andea could discern no figures making their way towards Rannoch Chase. It was a beautiful April morning, a morning that should have filled her with joy, the kind of day that made the blood sing with joy just to be alive, but her heart was as heavy as lead, her eyes were dull, no spark of laughter in them. The beauty of the Highlands was a mockery. The birdsong was mockery, like salt in a wound. This same sun, same blue sky, same awakening of the earth was surrounding them where they lay rotting.

Her heart would never be light again and sorrow would be with her as close as her shadow, and it would follow her to the end of her days. She walked back into the house and called to Adeline that she would ride to the hamlets along the floor of the glen. This was another burden she must undertake: she must tell wives and mothers that their men were not coming back, that they had been slaughtered without ever having come within ten feet of the enemy, died ignominiously and terribly.

"There will be no need, they know already." Jeannie emerged from the kitchen, wiping her hands on her apron.

"How?"

"Young Morag came early this morning, bringing eggs. Her mother had seen our lights last night. Two of the men are home, but not MacIan."

At least she would be spared her errand. She put down her cloak again. "Has the girl gone?"

"No, her mother told her to stay on and see if there were any tasks she could help with, and there are many!"

Andrea managed a brief smile of affection. Jeannie had been with her from her infant days, and now she was growing old and her joints ached in the damp weather. "I'll speak to her, would you send her in to me?"

Jeannie nodded and returned to the kitchen, while Andrea sat down in a chair with its back to the window through which the sunlight streamed. She had no wish to see the beauty of the April morning.

Morag MacDonald entered quietly and bobbed what she hoped was a curtsey. She had been brought up to respect and look up to Alizon Stuart, and now that she was dead her mother had told her that Mistress Andrea must be afforded the same respect, even though she had married a MacIntosh. Morag was a true Celt with almost black hair and dark brown eyes, and she was small of frame and tiny of hands and feet. She saw seated before her a woman in her middle years, though handsome still. Sorrow had etched deep lines in her brow but her eyes were wide and appraising, her mouth sensitive.

"You sent for me, mistress . . . ?"

"My husband is dead, Morag, so you may call me Mistress Stuart, as my mother was called."

Morag bobbed again.

"It was kind of your mother to send you. Are there many of you at home?"

"Not now, my father and my brother were killed at Culloden,"—there was a catch in the girl's voice—"so there is only my mother, Fiona and me."

"How old is your sister?"

"She's nigh on eleven, mistress."

"Then she will be able to help your mother?"

The girl nodded.

"Then Morag, will you stay here and help Jeannie? She's not as young as she used to be. The great fortune my mother brought with her from the Colonies has almost gone, but I shall be able to pay you, and no doubt your mother will be glad of the money."

"That she will, mistress, we don't know how we are going to manage now, mistress, not with Father. . . ."

"We'll all manage, Morag. I shall do as my mother did—you must all look to me for help, it is my duty."

Morag thanked her and then turned towards the door. Just as she reached it she said hesitantly. "Mistress Stuart?"

"Yes, what is it? Don't be afraid."

"Did you really ride out yourself and raise Clan MacIntosh and did you pin on the white ribbons with your own hands and did they really call you 'Colonel Charlotte'?" It all came out in a rush, the words tumbling over each other.

Andrea's smile was bitter. "Yes, it is all true, though much good it did us. It would have been better had I left them alone, most of them would be alive today!" Her eyes had become misty and there was a faraway look in them as Morag quietly let herself out of the room.

She pulled herself back from the reverie, the bitter memories of the past. There was so much to be done. She must check the outbuildings for implements and seed, for wool and flax, stray animals must be caught. She would have to make plans. The seeds must be sown if they were to eat this winter. If all those who remained in the glen were not to starve she must organise them so that they could help each other. The rebellion was over and they had lost, but life must go on, no matter how bitter it was. She had Ewan and Mairaid and for this she must thank God.

She, Adeline and Mairaid made a thorough search of the house and outbuildings. They found linen, peat, logs, a few chickens roosting in one barn, some sacks of oats and barley, the ploughshares and harrows. The other barn revealed in its loft bundles of raw wool and flax waiting to be washed, combed and spun, then woven into cloth and coloured with dyes made from the heather and lichen. Ewan had taken Andrea's horse and had gone to search the moor for straying sheep and cattle, and she did not expect him back before evening. Jeannie and Morag, their hair tied up in dust-caps, were pulling out furniture and throwing rugs and bed-linen over the sills of the windows, and the air seemed thick with dust.

Mairaid had care of Mitchell while Andrea and Adeline pored over the lists they had made. Andrea had remembered the secret panel in the attic and had climbed up to the roof, pulled away the accumulation of junk and pressed the spring. She had knelt down and felt inside the dark dusty space and her fingers had closed on a small box. She had taken it out and placed it on the top of another old chest. It contained a bag of gold coins, a gold targe brooch, a miniature of Alizon, and another bag, very much smaller and older than the bag in which the coins had reposed.

She opened the thong that held it closed and tipped out the contents. In the palm of her hand nestled two diamonds, at least two carats each, she guessed. They were the last of the stones that Alizon had taken from the secret drawer in Bradley Kirkbride's desk. Just two stones she had kept back against such a day as they were now facing. Even in the dim light that came from the one tiny attic window they flashed with fire. All the colours of the rainbow sparkled through them as she turned them in her hand before putting them back in the bag. She replaced the box and its contents behind the panel and closed it.

The sight of the stones made her feel more secure. At least she had money enough to see them through this winter and next. She would buy more stock and Rannoch would prosper again, as would the glen.

She was tired and it was almost dusk as she descended the stairs, hearing voices in the kitchen as she came into the hallway. Ewan was back, she heard him talking to Morag and smiled. She was a pretty girl and a MacDonald . . . she stopped and quickly turned her head. That was not Ewan's voice! It was a man's voice but not that of her son! She ran forward and pushed open the kitchen door and then with a wild cry she flung herself into Alasdair's arms.

"Oh! Alasdair! Alasdair! I thought you dead!" She was crying and laughing at the same time. "How? When? How long has it taken you?"

"One question at a time and not until I've eaten!" he said, holding her at arms' length, though there were tears on his own lashes. "I was lucky, I got a ride as far as Fort Augustus, but the rest of the way I walked!"

She could not take her eyes off him as Jeannie bustled about preparing him a meal. He was so thin, Andrea thought, and there was an air of dejection about him, but she knew that feeling only too well herself. Later when he had eaten and rested she would tell him of her plans, of the money and the diamonds. Later when he was himself again.

It was next morning before she had a chance to talk to him, for after his meal he had been so exhausted that he had fallen asleep, his head on his arms on the scrubbed deal table. With Ewan's help she had put him to bed. She tried to sound enthusiastic as she told him of the gold, the diamonds, the seed and the stock and her plans for the future. But her voice faltered as she saw the look of bitterness and sorrow return to his eyes, and finally she could not go on. "What is it that you have not told me?"

"Andrea, it is not over yet! Even now detachments of Cumberland's troops are marching out from Inverness and Fort Augustus and probably Fort William. They will take the stock, the seed, and anything else they can get hold of. Any man found will be taken prisoner and sent to the gallows or if he is lucky, transported."

"But it is all over!" she cried in disbelief.

"No, Andrea, it is only just beginning! Cumberland is determined to crush the Clans forever, and he will do it by starvation and transportation! There is only one thing we can do, we must leave Rannoch and take ship for Charleston. All of us, you, me, Ewan and Mairaid, Jeannie and that young girl, if she wishes to go!"

She shook her head again. She had heard him but she still did not fully understand. "What . . . what of Adeline and Mitchell?" she stammered stupidly.

"Phillip will come for them, they will be safe, but we must not be here when he comes. Already he has disobeyed orders, he would be taken before a Court Martial if it were found out. He let you take Ewan from the battlefield, and he let me go when he could have killed me or sent me prisoner to Inverness. We cannot ask any more of him. Adeline will be safe, though I wish I could take her too. Charleston is her home, but she has made her choice. But we must be gone before the troops arrive. Do you understand me, Andrea? We MUST all leave, and leave now!"

She stared at him steadily, then she dropped her eyes. "You must go, and Ewan and Mairaid, Jeannie and Morag too, but I must stay!"

"No! I won't leave without you!"

"I . . . this is my home, I would sooner die here, besides I have sworn to do what I can for the people of the glen and I am a Stuart—I will not go back on my word!"

For almost an hour he tried to reason with her. He cajoled, he threatened, he coaxed, but it was no good, she refused to agree to go with them. At last he rose. "Then there is no more to be said."

"No. Except that you must take the money for your passages."

"We shall not need all of it, you cannot live on fresh air."

"I will try to hide the rest, but if we don't have seed,

or oats or wheat for bread how will we live through the winter?"

Now he must tell her, he must warn her. "Andrea, they may not leave you in peace."

Again she stared at him stupidly. She had thought it all over, that they would now be free to live their own lives, to think and plan for the years ahead, but it was not to be so. "Why?"

He reached out and took her hand between his own. He had seen them both, she and Adeline, spirited, headstrong, stubborn, and now both seemed so dejected. "Because of 'Colonel Charlotte'! Don't you remember? Cumberland remembers. They say he is like an elephant, he forgets nothing!"

"He resembles one too in his bulk!" she spat with some of the old spirit.

He managed a wry smile. "Now, will you come with us?"

"No! They gave me that name and I was proud of it, I still am. I am proud of Clan MacIntosh and . . . and I miss Ian so!" It was the first time he had seen her break down and cry and it unnerved him. He took her in his arms, feeling the sobs tearing through her. She had loved her husband dearly and they had lived happily together for nineteen years. All that could not be forgotten because he had remained loyal to King George, a fact she had known from the very beginning. She had loved him and now she missed him terribly, and she wept also for her sons. "They died together, Alasdair! Ian was killed by Andrew, his own son! That is why I weep, not only for Robert but for the terrible tragedy of Andrew and Ian!"

He swore bitterly. War like this was worse than anything that man could devise. War against the Cherokees, the Spaniards, the French he could understand and that was bad enough, but war that set father against son, brother against brother, where sons killed their fathers! It was as if Satan had been let loose and all the fiends of hell with him. "Will you come, Andrea?"

"No, Alasdair, I cannot! This is my mother's house,

mine now, and in the glen are my people. I must stay, for here, too, are my memories, but Ewan and Mairaid must go, they have their lives before them: mine is half-over. I know you will guide and protect them as your own and I know, too, that Janet will be a mother to them. I will be happy so long as I know they are safe and have a future!"

There was nothing else to be said. He promised her he would always protect them, that he would treat them as his own children.

The arrangements had not been easy to make. There were parties of soldiers roaming the glens and hills, and communications were non-existent, but at last Alasdair had managed to secure a passage for them all. They would sail from Loch Linnhe around the coast to Glasgow, from where they could take ship to Charleston. Ewan had flatly refused to go when Alasdair had first told him and Mairaid, too, had sworn that she would not leave her mother alone to face whatever lay ahead. But Andrea had been firm with them both until finally, reluctantly, they had been forced to agree. Jeannie was going too and Morag had the permission of her mother to accompany them. Alasdair had agreed to take her younger sister, Fiona, as well. "For there's not much left here for her now, sir, and I'll manage. I've had my life, I dinna want to spoil that of ma bairns!" the woman stated.

They were all ready to leave. They would travel up the glen to the ferryman at Ballachulish. He would take them down the loch to where the ship lay at anchor in the deeper water. Andrea and Adeline stood in the doorway at the front of the house, Adeline with Mitchell in her arms. In turn Andrea had kissed them all, even down to the eleven-year-old Fiona MacDonald. Into Mairaid's hand she had pressed the two diamonds. "Take them, I will have no need of them and it will be something. . . something to remember me by. Have them made into a brooch or a necklace. They are going back to where they belong!" She had turned quickly away lest Mairaid see the tears in her eyes, but Mairaid was blinded by her own tears. Adeline came and slipped her arm around Andrea's waist as they prepared to move off. "It is hard. . . ."

"But it is best for them. They will at least have a future! I do not!"

"You don't know that!"

"They will come for me soon, Adeline, and I pray God that it isn't Phillip they send!"

They came two days later. She saw their red coats in the distance, red specks moving across the moor. She stood in the long gallery, watching them growing closer. She had prayed it would not be Phillip, for Adeline's sake. She stood, her hands resting on the stone sill of the tall mullioned windows, the sunlight streaming down on her head. There was a small party of them, eight or ten, she counted as they came into full view of the house. So many for one woman, she thought. But perhaps they had heard that Alasdair and Ewan were here also. She silently offered up a prayer that they were by now sailing for Glasgow and would soon be on the high seas towards freedom.

Adeline came running up the staircase. "Andrea! Andrea! Soldiers! There are soldiers almost at the door! If you hurry you can hide in the attic! Then they will find only me and they won't harm me, even if I have to go back to Fort William with them!"

Andrea shook her head. "No, I've known they would come soon and I will not put you and Mitchell in danger—they may not believe you, and I've heard the tales of what they do to babies . . . already too many have died because of me!"

Adeline threw her arms about her. "Andrea! Andrea! They will kill you?"

"No, but they will take me as a prisoner."

"I can't stay here alone!"

"You must, it won't be long now before Phillip comes for you, they will not harm you. Go down now to Mitchell, I will follow you. I, myself, will open the door to them."

With a backward, scared glance Adeline fled down the staircase to her baby son. Andrea looked down. They were dismounting, she could hear the jingling of bits and stirrup irons and the clank of spurs upon the stone steps. Slowly, with her head held high, she went to meet them.

They had found the door open and pushed into the hall, crowding into the small space. She stood halfway down the staircase and surveyed them with an icy contempt that concealed her fear.

"You are Andrea Charlotte Stuart, known as 'Colonel Charlotte' by the men of Clan MacIntosh, whom you did incite to rebel against their lawful sovereign, King George II?" the lieutenant barked.

"I am, though I had no need to incite them and George of Hanover I do not regard as my lawful sovereign!" She had fully committed herself now with those words, which would be considered treason. "I bear the name of Stuart: my grandfather was King Charles II, King of England and Scotland. I supported my kinsman in his lawful claim: he is the grandson of my grandfather's brother, King James II." The words were spoken slowly as though she were speaking to a child or an idiot and her icy tones grated on the lieutenant's ears, turning his cheeks red with anger.

"Be that as it may, I arrest you, Andrea Charlotte Stuart, on the charges I have stated and for the charge of treason! You will be taken to Inverness and then to Edinburgh to stand trial!"

She inclined her head stiffly. "I offer no resistance—I feel sure you would not stoop to butchering a lone woman!" Still the same frigid tones, heavy with contempt. Her words found their intended target: the Duke of Cumberland was now being endowed with a new title, "Butcher Cumberland."

Slowly she walked down the remaining stairs and held out her hands. "I assume that I am to be manacled?"

"No—I have no such orders. You have residing with you one Mistress Adeline Gowry and her child, the wife of Brevet-Major Phillip Gowry?"

"Yes, she is here—she will be pleased to hear of her husband's promotion!"

He stared at her in some confusion. She was an avowed rebel who had claimed allegiance to the Pretender, she was herself a Stuart, a grand-daughter of Charles II, yet she was on intimate terms with the wife of a Brevet-Major in the king's army. . . .

"Adeline! Phillip has sent for you!" she called, her voice carrying clearly.

The door to the parlour opened and Adeline stood there with Mitchell in her arms.

The lieutenant turned to her. "You are Mistress Gowry?" His tone was respectful.

"I am. My husband has sent for me?"

"Yes, I am to escort you to Inverness."

Adeline turned to Andrea and smiled. "Then we shall travel together for the last time." Her voice was light, showing no sign of the fear and sorrow that was burning in her.

The lieutenant gazed from one to the other in amazement while a few of his men sniggered behind him.

"May I have a little time to pack some things for myself and my child?"

"You may, but the prisoner comes as she is. Take her out!" Aware of the ill-concealed mirth of his men he barked out the order sharply and Andrea walked between them into the driveway.

"Am I to walk?"

"No. If you have a horse you may ride."

"You will find what animals we have in the stables."

The Lieutenant turned to his sergeant. "Saddle up two, one for the major's wife and the other for the prisoner!"

As she stood in the driveway, she looked up at the walls of Rannoch and wondered if she would ever see them again. She doubted it. The sergeant led two sturdy horses out from the stables as Adeline appeared in the doorway carrying Mitchell and two bundles, one of which she passed to Andrea. "A change of clothes, Lieutenant, that is all."

"I have no orders. . . ."

"You have my orders, verified by my husband when we reach Inverness! She is a lady, not a common drab!"

"She is a traitor!"

"She is my friend and my brother's sister!"

The lieutenant shrugged, then assisted Adeline to mount, signalling a man to help Andrea. She brushed aside his hand—she did not need the help of any soldier! She sat stiff and upright in the saddle, her eyes wandering over the house for the last time. With a slight jerk they started forward, the reins of her horse tied to a leather thong which was tied in turn to the saddle of the dragoon in front of her. As they passed through the gateway both she and Adeline turned and looked back, then Adeline smiled at her, bolstering her courage. She must leave Adeline at Inverness but at least, until then, they were together and she knew she would be tolerably well treated. But beyond that she could see nothing.

Chapter 20

When they reached Inverness, Andrea was taken straight to the garrison and placed in a small room outside which a sentry stood guard. Adeline had kissed her goodbye and had held her close for a brief minute before the lieutenant reminded her that her husband was waiting. So now she sat alone upon the wooden bench in the tiny room with stone walls and one small barred window high up near the roof. She was afraid. At last she admitted it to herself. While Adeline had been with her she had managed to keep her fears at bay, but now they descended on her in full force and try as she might, they would not be beaten back. The old aches, the grief and bitterness were still there: she was alone . . . facing certain interrogation and either imprisonment or death; there seemed to be no compassion now where women were concerned.

The minutes dragged by, turning slowly into hours. She became cold and the room grew darker. She covered her face with her shaking hands: her whole body was quivering but it was only with cold, she told herself. She thought of Alizon. She, too, had known what it was like to be imprisoned and in far worse conditions than this, but did she have yet to face the horrors of the Edinburgh tolbooth or the filthy, fever-ridden holds of the transports? That last thought offered a ray of hope. If she were transported and survived the journey, she would make her way to Charleston, to Alasdair and her children.

She raised her head as she heard the rasping, grating sound of the key in the lock, and the door was pushed open. She remained seated, for she was afraid that if she tried to rise her cramped legs would not support her. She looked up into the dim circle of light. It was Phillip Gowry.

"Phillip?"

"I came because Adeline insisted I should."

"All is well with her?"

He nodded curtly. "I'm sorry to see you brought to this, Andrea, but . . . you knew what you were doing and you knew the penalty!"

"The English call the Highlanders barbarians, yet they have never slaughtered women and children. Twice within sixty years have the English cut us down, not caring, without a shred of humanity."

He looked away from her, unable to meet her eyes. "Twice?"

"The first time it was done in such a way as to make even the most black-hearted villains shudder. Murder under trust! Have you forgotten Glencoe? You have a short memory, Phillip!"

"It is not for me to defend my orders. You are to be taken on to Edinburgh and tried for treason."

"And then hanged, no doubt! I don't fear death, Phillip—what is there left for me to live for now? What I fear is the uncertainty. Shall I see Adeline again before . . .?"

"No, you are to be allowed no visitors."

"And when am I to leave?"

"Tomorrow, at noon."

"Phillip, is there a chance that I will be transported?"

Understanding flashed into his eyes and was then replaced by what she took to be pity. "No, it is unlikely."

Hope died. "Then it will be either prison or death. I hope it is the latter!"

He turned to leave.

"Phillip, thank you for coming . . . give my love to Adeline and Mitchell, he's a fine boy. Don't let him grow up to be a soldier, Phillip! He's too dear to be struck down as were my sons!"

He looked at her, then nodded sadly. "I'll give orders to the turnkey to allow you as many privileges as possible. Bedding, and some water for washing. . . . That's as much as I can do, Andrea. . . ."

"I know, Phillip, and thank you. . . ."

He gave her no word of farewell but opened the door and left. It was dark again, and the key turned in the lock. With the light gone it seemed as hope had gone with it. She drew her knees up to her chin and clasping her arms around them, she let her head fall on to them. She hoped it was death that faced her, for if she had to endure years of being shut up like this she would go mad! Shut in some dark, damp, foul room away from the sunlight, away from the moors and mountains—death was infinitely preferable to that. She had spoken the truth to Phillip. She did not fear death, only the uncertainty that lay between here and Edinburgh and the verdict.

Adeline gazed out over the barrack square where the evening watch drilled in the fading light. She felt miserable and alone and although she had been greeted with open arms by Phillip, a great deal had changed between them. They did not speak of it, only of the trivialities of the journey, of Mitchell's health, of their happiness at being together again as a family, but there was something missing and she did not know what it was.

When she had asked him to go and see Andrea he had refused, and she had been shocked. She had begged and pleaded with him to go, or to let her go, reminding him of the days long ago when they had all been children together. At last he had agreed and now she was awaiting his return. She could see across the square to where the door to the guard room was closed. The light was fading, but she saw the red coat clearly when the door at last opened. After what seemed an agonisingly long time, he stood by her side.

"How is she?"

"Well enough."

"What did she say, did she ask of me and if I would visit her?"

"Yes, and I told her visitors are forbidden her."

"What will they do with her?"

"She is to be taken to Edinburgh for trial. She will leave under escort tomorrow at noon." The words were spoken in a flat, matter-of-fact tone.

"And then?"

"I don't know. Please try not to concern yourself unduly, Adeline, you have been through enough!"

She stared at him. She did not recognise this stranger who seemed not to understand how she felt about the woman she now loved as sister. "Phillip, what has happened to you? Once you would not have spoken like that."

"I can do no more for her," he snapped, misery making him angry. "I spared her son and her brother at the risk of my own neck! She knew what she was doing and she knew the consequences!"

This could not be her husband, she thought in panic. She ran to him and clutched at his jacket, staring up into his face, searching it for some sign of compassion. There was none.

"All I care about is you and Mitchell! We are a family again, that's all that matters!"

She broke away from him. "No! No! It is not all that matters! Andrea matters to me! It was she who nursed me after Mitchell was born. You at least owe her that much, or did you not care if I died, as long as your son lived?"

She saw the pain in his eyes and he took her in his arms. "Adeline, you know that's not true! I love you! This damned rebellion has changed everyone, it has turned the world upside-down and when it rights itself none of us will ever be the same!"

"What will they do to her in Edinburgh?" she whispered into his shoulder.

"I won't hide anything from you, Adeline. They will find her guilty and she will face either imprisonment or . . . or death!"

She dragged herself from his embrace. "No! No!" she

screamed at him. "They can't murder her, too! You have to stop it, Phillip, you must find a way! You must let her escape, you must do something!"

"Adeline, there is nothing I can do," he pleaded. "I will endanger you and Mitchell if I try. I myself would help but I have you to think of!"

She held her hands over her ears, unable to bear to hear any more. Was there no end to their cruelty? Compared to Cumberland, Attakullakulla was civilised! She wanted to go home, away from this hideous place with its distorted loyalties, its hostile barren crags. Its glens, were now as silent as graves as the men were taken from them and hanged, leaving their women and children to starve. She wanted to feel the hot sun on her face, the salty breeze from the ocean on her cheeks, and smell the sweet perfumes of the flowers. She hated this place, she hated these barbaric people! And now he had become one of them! If he loved her as he claimed he did he would have helped Andrea. He would have found some way, but still she heard him repeating those words, "There is nothing I can do!"

"I want to go home! I want to go home, Phillip!" Her voice rose hysterically higher.

"You are home!" He held out his arms to her but she backed away.

"Culloden has changed you. This land is no longer my home, I want to go back to Charleston! I *will* go! I won't stay here and watch Andrea die or lie rotting in prison until disease finally frees her from a living death! I'm going home, Phillip, do you hear me! You cannot stop me, I hate this land and I hate you!"

He got up and stood staring at her. His arms had dropped to his sides and his face was white. "Adeline . . . you don't know what you're saying . . . you must rest now. I'll ask one of the surgeons to mix you a draught. You will feel better when you have slept, the journey and now this. . . ."

Anger shook her small frame. "Stop treating me as a simpleton! I'm no child! I crossed the world to find you and marry you. It would have been better to have stayed at home! I want no sleeping-potion, I need no rest! I am going home! This land is too much for me to bear and I do not know you any more! You are a soldier, obeying orders like a man who has no mind of his own, ruthless and senseless! I want no part of you or your country, Phillip Gowry! I am going home to Charleston, home to Alasdair and Janet, and I'm taking Mitchell with me. I never want him to grow up to be a soldier!"

"Adeline! For God's sake. . . ." He tried to take hold of her hands.

"Don't touch me! I would sooner take my chances with the Yemassees and Tuscaroras than with Butcher Cumberland!"

He turned abruptly away from her, his pride and love bitterly hurt. "Go, if you wish! I will arrange for you to travel tomorrow with the prisoner." Now he would not on principle call Andrea by her name. "From Edinburgh you can take ship from Leith. I'll not stop you, Adeline, but if you should reconsider, I'll be here . . . waiting!"

"I'll leave tomorrow with Andrea! Make the arrangements!"

She was still shaking with anger after he had gone. She looked around the sparsely furnished room. There was the bed, a table and four chairs, a chest on which stood a basin and jug and a skin rug on the floor. So this was where it all ended. She might as well have been widowed. She could have borne that, she would at least have had happy memories.

She picked up the sleeping child. A few more days with Andrea before they would part forever, a few more hours with Phillip . . . she wondered if he would come back. No, he was too proud for that and she did not want him now, he was not the man she had married, he had changed, the army had brutalised him. The same self-indulgence that had carried her across the Atlantic to find him, now made her refuse to see what misery he suffered. She could spare no thoughts for how he must be feeling. She only knew he had refused to help Andrea.

There seemed to be nothing of Gabrielle in him now, she thought, he was his father's son. He was a Gowry.

Slowly and wearily she repacked the few belongings she had brought from Rannoch. Then she crept between the coarse blankets, where Mitchell lay sleeping soundly. She had had nothing to eat since noon but she was not hungry. She was tired, with an exhaustion of spirit as well as body. It was all over. The time she had spent here was as nothing to her now. Tomorrow she would start the long journey home, but at the end of it waited that other Rannoch, her family, her friends, her own people. She would make a new life for herself and for her son there.

It was the sound of marching feet and the shouted orders on the barrack square that woke her. She must have slept soundly, she thought dully. Reveille had not wakened her and no nightmares had come to disturb her rest. She rubbed the sleep from her eyes and reached out for Mitchell. Her hand came into contact with the coarse linen sheet. He had gone! She shot upright and peered around the room. Her dress and the bundle were there on the chair, but there was no sign of the child. She almost fell out of bed and dragged her dress over her head, her fingers fumbling with the buttons in her haste. She scraped her hair back into a knot as she rushed out of the room.

She ran down the steps and into the barrack square, her feet skimming over the cobbles until she reached the guard room.

"Brevet-Major Gowry? Has anyone seen my husband this morning?"

The group of soldiers looked at each other then shrugged. "Saw him just after reveille, mistress, but don't know where he is now. Try the adjutant!"

She retraced her steps and at last came to the adjutant's office. She was breathless and her hair had fallen around her shoulders, her face was ashen and her eyes like those of a terrified doe. He was there.

"Phillip, where is Mitchell?" she gasped.

The adjutant looked uneasy and with a jerk of his head Phillip dismissed him.

"Where is my baby? What have you done to him?" she

screamed, not caring if the whole garrison heard her.

"I thought you were going home?" His voice was controlled, steady and without any emotion.

She ran to him and began to beat on his chest with her small fists. "Where is my baby?"

He caught her hands. "Stop behaving like someone demented, Mitchell is safe and well!"

She went limp with relief, for all manner of terrifying thoughts had possessed her since she had found him gone. "Where is he? Why did you take him?"

He still held her wrists and although his grip was hurting her she did not flinch or cry out. "He is on his way to my sister—she will see he is well cared for, then when he is old enough. . . ."

She tried to lash out at him but he held her firmly. She began to scream and kick out like a fury. He had snatched her baby from her as she slept! He was a devil incarnate and she wanted to tear out his eyes with her nails, she wanted to kill him! Desperately she looked around for a weapon—there was none. "I'll go and take him back! I'll have my child even if I have to kill her and you, too!"

"He's my son and he'll be brought up a Gowry, with his loyalty to his king, not nurtured as a traitor in some barbaric society!" A nerve twitched in his cheek but the rest of his face was rigid.

"You're no fit person to be a mother, Adeline . . . . You're . . . You're unstable, and you're utterly selfish, you don't care about anyone except yourself. You've never once thought of how . . . all this could have affected me. My son stays with me!"

"Then you had better kill me now, for if I live, I swear I will find him, and I will take him home! He'll be a planter, a civilised gentleman, not cannon fodder or a beast without a soul like you!" In terms of sheer brute strength she knew there was nothing she could do against him at this time, but some day . . . Oh! It would have been better to have stayed in Charleston. Her eyes narrowed; she was Darnley's daughter and she had inherited his vindictiveness. Phillip turned his back towards her and stared out of the window.

"You will ride at noon with the prisoner, you will ride at bayonet-point if necessary, and at gunpoint you will board the ship at Leith. He is my son, Adeline, and he stays with me. You could have stayed too if you wished. You made your own choice...."

She threw herself in utter fury against him, sinking her teeth into the back of his hand. He flinched but he did not release her. She bit again, this time drawing blood, almost with fury. He drew back his free arm and hit her squarely across the face. The blow sent her reeling to the floor, and she felt the sharp pain as her head hit the stone hearth, then everything was lost in the darkness.

When she came to her head throbbed so much that she could barely lift it. Through half-closed eyes she looked around her. She was in the room where she had spent the night. She raised herself on her elbow and groaned, holding her head, then she remembered. She got to her feet and for a second the room danced sickeningly about her. She stumbled to the door and found it locked. She looked towards the window: it must be nearly noon she thought. She splashed some of the cold water from the jug into the basin and washed her face, drying it on the rough towel. By now Mitchell would be on his way to Margaret in Ruthven and she... she would never see him again! She sank down on the bed, swaying dizzily. Now she knew how Alizon had felt all those years ago when Darnley had taken Alasdair away. Would she be forced to wait as long as Alizon had waited... but she was luckier than Alizon, for she knew that her son was alive and would be well cared for, and she would come back for him!

There was nothing she could do now, she fretted, for she was to be escorted under guard to Leith. But she would come back and she would bring men with her, her own people, and she would kill Phillip Gowry! All she had was that hatred to sustain her now, it would have to carry her through the interminable days and nights that were to come, but it would suffice.

She heard the door open and a sergeant stood there. "It is time to leave, mistress. You are fit to travel?"

"So he would not come himself? A coward as well! Yes, I'm ready to travel!" She rose and put on her cloak and picked up the bundle, while the soldier stared past her, embarrassed.

She followed him out into the courtyard where a detachment of dragoons were waiting with Andrea. When the sergeant had helped her mount, she turned to him. "Tell Brevet-Major Gowry that I shall come back for my son, and when I do I shall not be alone! And when I find him I shall kill him!"

There was a sharp cry from Andrea and an embarrassed cough from one of the dragoons. The sergeant stared up at her, some of the florid colour draining from his face.

"Mistress, I dare not take that message! I know nothing except that you are to be escorted with the prisoner to Edinburgh and then put aboard ship at Leith, and I have orders to manacle you if you should try to run off. Those are my orders, mistress!"

"Ah, we all have our orders, don't we, Sergeant? Go and tell him what I have just told you, for if you don't, when I return I shall kill you, too!"

The man quailed visibly at her words, spoken so quietly that most of the other dragoons had not heard them, but it was the look of pure, burning hatred in her eyes that had unnerved him. "I . . . I'll tell him, mistress, but now . . . now we must be on our way."

They had left the fortress town behind them before Adeline spoke again. "I am going home, Andrea!"

"What has happened, Adeline? Is it because of me, for if that is so then I wish you would go back! I don't want to be the cause of hatred between you and Phillip. . . ."

"There is no going back! He is no longer my husband—I hate him and I meant what I said! He's taken Mitchell from me, snatched him from my side as I slept and has sent him to his sister in Ruthven. So we are both prisoners now. You heard what the sergeant said, if I try to run I will be manacled and those are Phillip's instructions! I'm going home, but only long enough to gain strength and support from my own people, then I shall return and God help Phillip Gowry!"

"But why did he take Mitchell?"

"Because I said I was going to take him home. I hate this land now—he told me what would happen to you and swore that there was nothing he could do to help you!"

"Adeline, he's right! He would only endanger himself and you. I don't fear what lies ahead of me—what is there left for me now? Ian is dead and Andrew and Robert. Ewan and Mairaid are safe... I'll be happy to give up now!"

Adeline stared at her and the tears sprang to her eyes. "Oh, Andrea, what has happened to us all? Why could there not be peace between us, we could have been a family united if only...."

"There are too many 'ifs,' Adeline! Life promises nothing, it is what we make of it. I could have married a MacDonald and still have become a widow and have lost all my children, you could have married a planter's son and lived peacefully on your plantation...."

"Or have also been widowed and murdered in my bed by Indians or Spaniards...."

"Go home, Adeline. Alasdair will welcome you and I entrust Ewan and Mairaid to you, tell them you were with me and gave me great comfort."

How could Andrea face death so calmly, Adeline wondered. She reached out and took Andrea's hand in her own, squeezing it gently.

"Mistress, I must warn you that no contact must be made with the prisoner!" She heard the sergeant's voice behind her.

She turned around. "Sergeant, go to hell!"

Chapter 21

Three days later they had ridden into Edinburgh, through the same gate that Adeline had entered with

Anne, it seemed to her a century ago. The city had not changed much. It was still packed with people and the buildings still rose four and five stories high into the sky. They halted outside the tolbooth and a small crowd gathered to see if there was any entertainment to be had. Andrea dismounted as did the sergeant and two of his men.

"Stay here and watch Mistress Gowry! I'll deliver this one and then we'll go on to Leith."

Andrea turned to the sergeant. "Sergeant, she is my brother's half-sister, but she is dearer to me than any sister I could have had. I beg you a few minutes?"

He looked around at the small crowd and nodded. He had no wish for any trouble, and the Edinburgh mob were notorious for rioting upon the spur of the moment for any cause that appealed to them at the time.

Andrea took Adeline's hand again. "Tell them I love them and that I am always thinking of them. As . . . as long as they are safe. . . ." she swallowed hard, fighting back the tears, "then everything is not lost!"

The tears welled up in Adeline's eyes as she bent to kiss Andrea. "If only I could stay with you until . . . oh, Andrea! God be with you, may He protect you!"

"Adeline, do you remember that old saying of my mother's?"

"You mean 'Cha Till, Cha Till'. . . ."

"Promise me that you will not return with hatred? Time will heal, but for Ewan and Mairaid, 'Cha till no mi Tuille' . . . Adeline! They will return no more!"

The crowd was increasing and the sergeant was growing edgy. "Enough! Inside with you . . . Mistress Stuart!" It was the first time he had ever addressed her by name.

She smiled up at Adeline. "God be with you! Don't weep for me for I shall be happy!"

The last sight Adeline had of her was a glint of silvery hair between the red coats, as she passed into the tolbooth.

She had been in this room for days, she thought. She had traced and counted every brick in an effort to keep at bay the hysterical fear that would rise up in her. She would tell herself she was not afraid, that this was the worst part of it all, the waiting, after this agony of mind nothing could harm her. She had suffered far too much, she told herself, there was little they could do to her now. Each night she prayed for her children and that the judgement on her would be death, for that would be quick and merciful. The verdict was a foregone conclusion, but the punishment . . . the punishment was as yet unknown, and it tormented her day and night.

She had no money, so she could not buy food or fuel or blankets as some of the prisoners did. The room was small, damp and freezing at night and the food, a slice of black bread and a cup of water in the morning, another cup and a bowl of watery porridge at night, was barely enough to keep her alive. She had refused it at first but hunger had at last got the better of her. Each time the warder brought it she asked him when she was to stand trial, and each time he either shook his head or shrugged. He never spoke to her. Her clothes were dirty now, her hair tangled and unkempt. When she finally went to trial she would look like a beggar and not the grandaughter of a king. She thought of Adeline and of Alasdair and her own two surviving children. It was better this way—if they were free then she would be happy to die.

They came for her next morning, the warder accompanied by the Governor and a coarse overblown woman who proved to be his wife.

"You will go before the Lord Advocate today and the Justices. My wife will help you to tidy yourself."

She looked down at the bowl of hot water and the greyish towel the woman held, and then spread the folds of her dress between her hands. "Is there nothing I can do about this?"

"Lord, mistress, ye be lucky t' get soap an' water, dinna ask fer more! It's only 'cos it's the Advocate himself that ye are t' hae these!"

All three of them stood and watched her while she scrubbed the grime from her hands and face and dried herself on the musty-smelling towel.

"May I have a comb?"

The Governor's wife passed her one and she began to straighten the tangles. The woman sucked in her breath as Andrea combed out the long tresses, which even though badly in need of washing still remained beautiful.

"Why, hen! I hae never seen hair o' that colour afore! How is it a lady sic as ye has come t' this pass?"

"For what I believed in, what I still believe in. My cousin's rights!"

The warder laughed: it was a harsh, ugly sound. "Would ye listen t' her! Ma cousin!" he mocked.

Andrea turned her large brown eyes upon him, their depths sparking with tiny flames of anger. "My grandfather was King Charles II, look at me, man! Have you not seen pictures of him, have you not seen the statue in Parliament Close?"

He dropped his gaze.

"She is who she says she is, but she was born wrong side o' blanket! She's a Stuart alright, but a bastard! Are you ready?" the Governor barked.

She had only a piece of plaited straw with which to tie back her hair, but she felt cleaner and tidier and it gave her a little strength to face them.

She was escorted to the court by the Governor and the warden. As she entered the room she looked at the rows of black-gowned justices and bailies, and then up at the dais where sat the Lord Advocate, the Duke of Argyll. Her heart sank; there would be no mercy from him. He knew her well enough.

"Andrea Charlotte MacIntosh, née Stuart, you are charged with treason against his Sovereign Majesty, King George, in that you incited the men of Clan MacIntosh to rise in rebellion and that upon your arrest you did declare that you do not recognise our Sovereign Lord as your rightful king. Is this true? How plead you?"

"It is true. I offer no defence. I would do the same thing again and I do again declare that George Hanover is not my rightful sovereign. I owe allegiance only to my blood kinsman, Charles Edward Stuart!" Her voice seemed to echo around the high hammer-beamed room and there was a hushed, shocked pause, before a babble of voices cried out against her.

"Silence!" The voice of Argyll brought the court to order again.

"Then there is nothing more left for us to do, Mistress Stuart! I am a merciful man, the Duke of Cumberland is also merciful, as is the king you spurn. Your loyalty is misplaced, but your blood is respected. You will be taken from this court-room and escorted to the gate of the city. There you will be turned loose, banished to your house in the Highlands, though you will forfeit all the lands and titles to those lands to the Crown! And thank God that your king is a just man, for it were left to me you would rot in prison for the rest of your days!"

His words had come like a bolt of lightning. She had expected death, even longed for it, but banishment had never occurred to her. She was to be allowed to go home to Rannoch! She stared unseeingly ahead of her, discerning only the black outline of Argyll. Was there some hidden menace in her sentence, she wondered, or had Cumberland wearied of his title "Butcher" and the indignation his atrocities had caused in England?

The warder had to take her by the arm and lead her away, and it was not until she felt the sun on her face that she fully realised what her sentence meant. She would have no land, no money, but she would have a roof over her head and the freedom of the glens.

"I don't believe it! It must be a mistake!"

"No mistake, though I'm bound t' say I am fair mystified mysel'. I thought they'd hae hanged ye!"

"I can go home!"

"Ye'll no' be allowed t' leave it! Ye'll have to stay there."

She kicked out at the rubbish that lay rotting and stinking in the gutter. "Am I to go now?"

"Aye, I'm t' tak ye t' town gate an' see ye on your way!"

She turned her face upwards towards the sun. Still she did not trust Argyll, there must be some trap in it somewhere. Maybe he thought that life at Rannoch would be too painful to bear, that she would go out of her mind with sorrow and loneliness. But she would have the women of the glen, and in time her memories would become dear to her. She would manage somehow; she would stay sane and happy even if only to spite Argyll.

Her elation disappeared as she realised how far she had to go, on foot and with no food or money. If folk knew her name she would be as much shunned as the prince himself by all save a handful of loyal supporters. She did not even have the money to pay the ferryman at the Queensferry, so she would have to take the long route by Stirling, then head northwards to Perth. Here she would turn westwards, using the peaks of Schiehallion, Carn Mairg and Meall Buidhe as her guides, until she reached home. A journey of nearly one hundred and twenty miles, on foot and over rough country, begging what food and shelter she could. She sat down by the side of the road and stared across the waters of the Forth. It was June; it would be August before she would reach Rannoch, if she were lucky. This, then, was Argyll's mercy! She rose to her feet and started down the road that skirted the river bank, making for Linlithgow.

By the time she reached Stirling the soles of her shoes had worn completely through and her feet were cut and bleeding. She had found food and shelter sometimes, but most often she had slept under hedges and walls, and only spring water had filled her empty belly. Her clothes were hanging on her and she knew she looked like a scarecrow, but she trudged ever northwards towards Perth. It was when she was not far from the town that she began to notice that the tickle in her throat had become an irritating cough and once or twice she had had to sit down to catch her breath. It came from sleeping out, she thought, she had never been used to it like many folk.

Hunger was her constant companion now and it slowed her down, for she tired easily. The hot July sun beating down on her head did not help, it made her sick and dizzy. Day drifted into night and into day again and she neither knew nor cared whether it was July or August. Only one thought drove her on, in her spinning mind the word "Perth" swirled round and round; she knew if she reached the town she would have to stay there, for she was in no condition to travel further.

By the time she got to Perth she was almost in a state of collapse. The sun had turned her skin red-raw, then it had peeled and was becoming as brown as a nut. It had been painful, but no more so than her feet, tied up in strips torn from her petticoat, or the constant throbbing of her head, the aches in her limbs and the pains of hunger in her belly. Her lips were cracked and swollen with the sun, but she doggedly trudged on, stopping frequently to rest, and the cough grew worse, and often at night she would wake sweating.

As she reached the town gate she stopped, leaning against the portals, wondering where to go, who would help her. She must find someone before nightfall or she would be turned out as a beggar, and the gates closed against her. Her eyes travelled to the spire of the kirk. She would go to the minister. In the kirk yard oak and yew trees spread their branches and she dropped down in their shade, leaning her back and throbbing head against a gnarled trunk.

She was so tired all she wanted to do was sleep. The sun was sinking slowly, a huge ball of red fire in a sky that seemed to burst with red-gold light. She closed her eyes against its glare, the beauty of the sunset lost upon her. It was here that the minister's wife found her and shook her awake.

"Be off with you, woman! You know that no beggars or vagrants are allowed to sleep in the kirk yard! Be off with you!"

She tried to rise. "Mistress, I am no beggar. I am returning to my home, I have come a long way . . . from Edinburgh . . . and I have much further to go . . . help me, for the love of God, mistress. Let me rest for a while longer?"

The woman bent down. "How do I know that it is not a pack of lies you are telling me?"

"You don't, but trust me, mistress. I came to the kirk because I had nowhere else to go and I need help—I know no one here, I trusted in the Lord to help me. . . ."

The woman relented. "Come back with me to my house. I am the minister's wife, your trust has not gone unfounded." She helped Andrea to her feet and almost dragged her to the house where she called out for her maid to come and help her. It was as though a taut line had been cut, a line that she had clung to for her very survival, and she sank slowly into oblivion as the two women placed her in the bed.

How long she slept she did not know, time had no meaning. She could remember being lifted up and fed from a spoon, then sleep would claim her again. She remembered the racking cough that dragged her from slumber and the warm flannel and poultices on her chest, the foul-tasting liquid that was poured down her throat. She did not know that in her sleep she raved, calling for Ian, Andrew and Robert and for Alizon, her mother. She was a child again, running to the safety of Alizon's arms, she was a mother who sat watching two armies meet on Culloden Field, she cried out for her sons and for Ewan and Mairaid. At last the day came when she awoke and her mind was clear, and she remembered everything. She tried to get up but she fell back; she had not realised she was so weak.

"It's no good thinking you can just jump up out of that bed! Lie still!"

She turned and saw the minister's wife sitting beside the bed, and she was smiling. "You have been very ill, there were times when we feared for you."

"How long have I been here?"

"Two weeks."

"So long! I did not mean to inconvenience you, mistress, all I wanted to do was rest. . . ."

"Nonsense, do you think I could have turned you out?"

"God bless you!"

"If all you said in your fever is true then you have suffered much. . . ."

Suddenly she was afraid, wondering what she had cried out in her delirium. "What . . . what did I say?"

"Many things: you are a widow, that I know, and you have lost all your children. You have been imprisoned but were freed and your home is on Rannoch moor."

"I was banished by the Lord Advocate for treason, for supporting the rebellion and the prince." She felt that she could keep nothing from this woman who had been so good to her, who had dragged her from the very brink of death.

"Sometimes we stray a little from the path, but the Lord is our Shepherd. You will stay with us until you are well enough to go on."

She struggled to rise again. "No, I have already caused you much trouble. I must go on, I must get home before winter comes, what month is it?"

"August—there is one more week of the month left but you will not leave here until you are well. I've not nursed you only to have you go out and undo all my work by dying by the roadside or on some lonely highland track!"

Andrea sank back on the pillows, thanking God that there were still such people in the world as the minister's wife of the kirk in Perth.

It was the third week in September when she walked out through the gates of the minister's house and turned and waved to them both. She felt strong and well, her clothes had been replaced by warmer ones, not new but decent, and there were shoes on her feet and thick stockings. She wore a heavy cloak and in her hand were a few shillings the minister had given her. She had nothing to give them in return but her prayers, and these she offered with brimming eyes.

"My dear, if I cannot help a soul in need then it is time I gave up my calling!" the minister told her.

"I will always remember you both, not a day shall pass that I will not thank God for meeting you!"

"Go now and God go with you, you've many miles yet to cover."

And so she had walked away, turning at the end of the street to wave again.

At Ballinluig she turned from the road and onto the moorland track that would take her to the hamlet of Coshieville where she would turn and make her way down Glen Lyon, Campbell country. At Invermedran she would see Ben Dorian and the Black Mount, then she would be home. What money she had she would use to pay for food and a roof over her head at night, no matter how poor, for the nights were cold now and her cough was troubling her again.

At Coshieville she bought as much food as she could. She knew there would be no one in Glen Lyon who would help her and she still had almost another week of journeying. She had thought she would never reach Rannoch, that it had been Argyll's intention that she should die a slow lingering death upon the road, a worse death than that of hanging. It would be October before she reached home, she thought as she trudged down the glen, looking neither left nor right as women and bairns came to their doors to stare. But at least she would be in a warm bed at night when the first frost came and not beneath some hedge or in an open-sided draughty barn.

At last the Black Mount rose before her eyes. It was a clear, sharp autumn day and the leaves were already thick upon the ground, forming a carpet of russet, brown, gold and yellow. She could see the small huts of the sheilings on the lower slopes and the heather blazed purple, lilac and blue across the whole stretch of the moor.

She sat down on a boulder and looked around her. She had never thought to see any of this wild beauty again, and her heart felt lighter than it had for nearly eight months. She ate the last of the goat cheese and the flat rye bread and then rose. Just beyond Loch Ba lay the house in a hollow of land. Less than an hour now! Her steps quickened until she was almost running, but she had to stop for a terrible bout of coughing racked her. When it was over she felt weak and dizzy and passed the kerchief the minister's wife had given her across her lips. She looked at it in horror, for where it had touched her mouth there was a dark brownish-red stain.

Lung fever! She had been spared to reach home only to die of lung fever, coughing her life's blood up until it choked her! Argyll had done his work well! Mercy! She laughed aloud at the word—the Campbells of Argyll did not know its meaning.

At last she rose and walked slowly across the spongy mossy ground. There was no need to hurry now. Rannoch would be waiting and would still be standing when she died, and that would be before spring came again to the moor. She walked with her head bent, her feet dragging, determined not to look at Rannoch Chase until she was there, standing right before it.

She came at last to the remains of the garden wall. The grass and flower-beds were overgrown, choked with weeds, as was the herb garden, where the herbs had run wild. She sighed deeply and then looked up.

She was not prepared for what she saw and she stood, shaking her head in disbelief, her features drawn and haggard, her eyes sunken. Her gaze travelled upwards to the one remaining chimney, for the others had crashed to the ground with the roof. Only the outer shell of the house remained, its walls blackened with soot, the roof timbers charred and lying in piles. It had been fired. . . . She felt the tears on her cheeks but no sound of sobbing came from her throat; the tears were being squeezed from her heart.

Banished to her house, he had said! He had known all the time that Rannoch had been put to the torch. He had sent her out to walk the long, agonising miles, driven on by the thought of home, knowing that if she ever reached it, this was what she would see. This sight was to her more terrible than anything she had ever witnessed and he had known it! In the charred embers of Rannoch Chase ended the dreams of the Stuarts, bastard though the line was. All the suffering, the heartbreak had been but a prelude to this, the end of everything she loved.

She was overtaken again by the racking cough and again there was blood on the kerchief when she drew it away from her mouth. She was dying. Soon the winter would come and the snow would cover the burned-out shell of the house, obliterating with a white blanket the remains of the holocaust in which it seemed they had all perished. It would cover her too, for she knew that soon she would lie beneath the frozen ground. They would bury her here, not on Eilean Munde, but here at Rannoch where once she had been so happy.

She walked into the front yard and sat down on the blackened step of the empty doorway, closing her eyes and leaning her head against the fragments of the lintel that still smelled of smoke. The moor was as silent as the Glen of Dogs had been when the first of the MacDonalds had returned after the Massacre. For them, for her, for the Highlands it was the end, she knew that now. Argyll and Clan Diarmaid had triumphed at last and for the last time.

THE END